CHRISTOPHER FLORY

Bloodlust

a Detective Renquest thriller

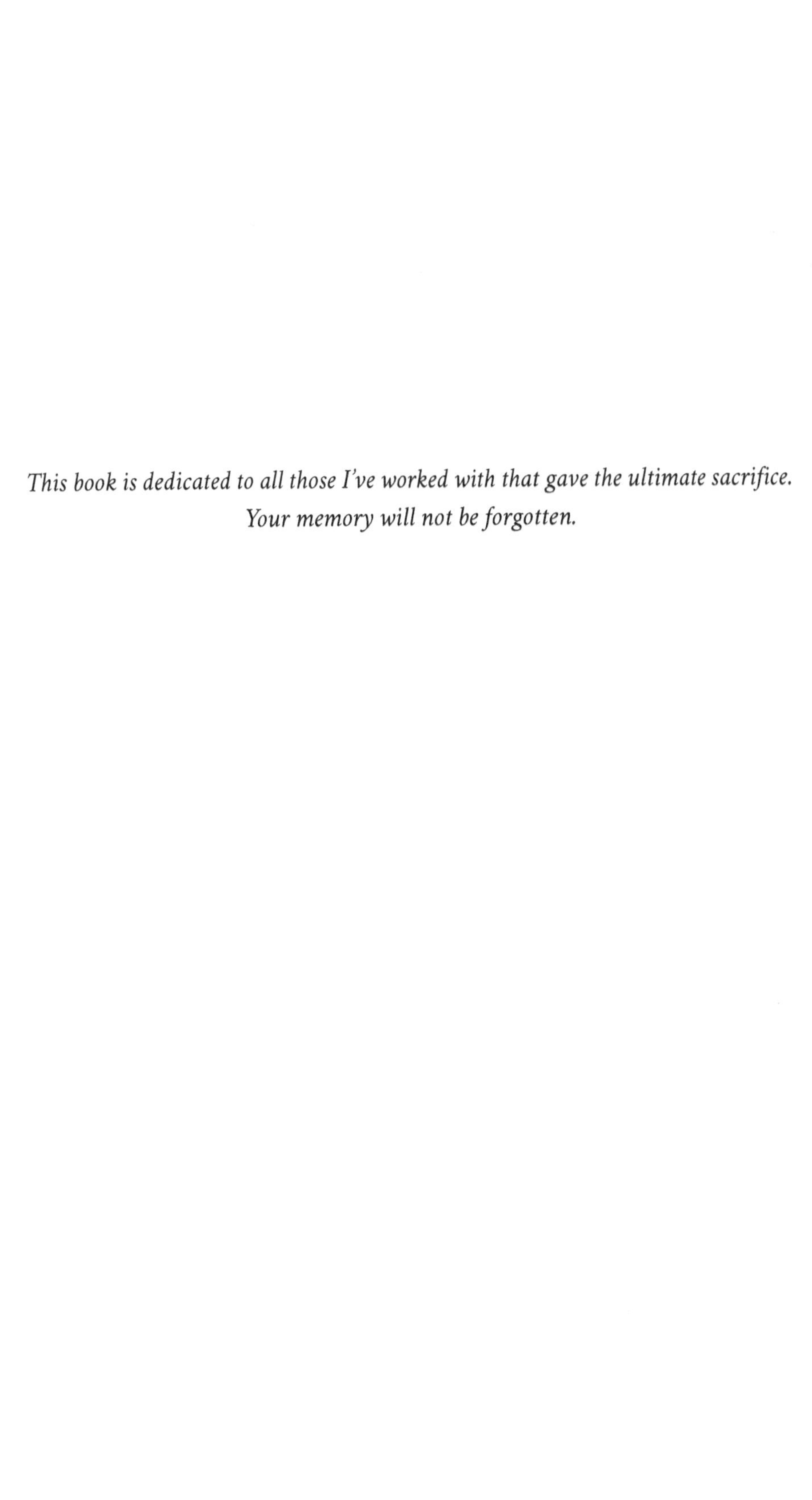

This book is dedicated to all those I've worked with that gave the ultimate sacrifice.
Your memory will not be forgotten.

Contents

Chapter 1

The cold steel of the table felt surprisingly good against his back. He'd been lying on the makeshift medical slab for three straight hours. Staring at the ceiling. Imagining how it felt to be embalmed. A small incision on the side of his neck. The large-gauge needle pushed into the slit, then forced into the jugular vein. All the blood slowly siphoned from his body. A machine clicked in the corner. Tubes moved the precious liquid from his body through the cleanser, then back into his body again. He couldn't help thinking about the life-saving fluid. A liter bag was as precious as a barrel of oil. More precious to him. No one ever died directly from lack of access to a barrel of oil. But blood—that was necessary. He tried his best to make sure every drop he captured got stored properly. The equipment had cost him tens of thousands of dollars. A new industrial refrigerator. A top-of-the-line generator to ensure power if the grid fails. He had everything he needed. To avoid issues, he scrutinized every detail. He wouldn't lose an ounce of the red gold. He couldn't. It was too important.

The entire cleansing procedure took a little over an hour and a half. He added thirty minutes of recuperating time before venturing out. The process of removing excess iron from his bloodstream left him weak and vulnerable. It was the exact reason he fashioned the room with only one door. A simple handle and a deadbolt. Some security measures were better the old-fashioned way. To get inside, one had to pull the door open with the key inserted into the tumbler mechanism. As a child, he once watched a show about the Cold War on television. During one segment, they focused on the secret bunker built for members of congress at Greenbriar Estate, about a two-hour helicopter ride from DC. The main blast door, manufactured to withstand a near direct hit from a Russian nuclear warhead, weighed several tons and required special equipment to install. Yet, it was so well-balanced, one person could open and close it. With a mere push of the hand and the solid steel door would swing in either direction. He always found engineering involving that much weight and balance amazing.

He dedicated hours to studying engineering after work and on the weekends. He did little else besides eating and sleeping. Even those necessities took a backseat to his obsession. One day, when finishing the installation of the table, he looked at the door to the room. It was solid wood. Oak, he thought, though he was not an arborist. In fact, he knew little about trees and products made after harvesting. Oak seemed like a good guess. He knew people had been using it to build everything from tables to boats for centuries.

He climbed into his rust-covered 1999 Ford Ranger pickup and made the twenty-minute drive to the local home supply box store. Once inside, he found the aisle packed with doors. Floor to ceiling. Interior doors. Exterior doors. Even sliding doors with enclosed screens that closed to keep insects out if someone wanted to let in the outdoor air. Solid doors and hollow doors. And Garage doors. But what he was interested in was steel fireproof doors. No pre-drilled holes for door handles. He wouldn't need those. After a little back and forth with the dumbass kid, who the company thought would be good to interact with paying customers, he located the exact door he came for.

He paid in cash, as he always did. No reason to leave a paper trail. The risk was already there. Every store had security cameras. Some aisles, the ones stocked with expensive tools, had cameras that randomly took pictures of shoppers as they casually passed by. Those areas were no-go zones for him. He loathed the fact that people were dishonest, forcing companies to take such drastic measures. For this reason, he bought most of his tools on the internet. Not Amazon. That company had too many eyes in the sky. Too many ties to big brother. Luckily, there were other social media marketplaces that didn't track your purchases and search history. Anonymity and cash were the backbone of the business. These sites were his bread and butter. He used garage and estate sales to find what he couldn't get on the internet. It was a great way to gain the items he wanted without drawing attention to himself. No one ever questioned you when you purchased a spade and a half-full bag of zip ties at a yard sale. The sellers just want the things to be gone, not giving a thought to how the new owner might choose to use them. Purchasing items from people was even better than using the internet. After he bought something, there was no trace he had ever been there once he left. A perfect scenario.

Once back in the room, he threw the supplies onto the metal table. He stepped back. Staring at the pile of wood, fastener screws and brackets. He had everything he needed now and would soon be able to truly begin his work. And maybe get this terrible sickness out of him.

* * *

It was a new day in a new city for Detective Renquest. He recently accepted a position with the Arlington Police Department as lead homicide detective. It was a three-hour move to the north, but a necessary one. After a serial killer murdered several hookers and shot his partner, Parole Agent Paul Dodge, the department disbanded the sex crimes task force he had led for over five years. The incident brought too much attention following the stabbing death of a State Police Captain who'd used a local prostitute as bait to trap the killer. Everyone wanted the case to vanish. When the whole thing went tits up, the department needed a fall guy, and he was the sacrificial lamb.

They gave him a couple of months to find a new position. The chief even wrote a glowing recommendation detailing his years of selfless service and dedication to the job and the community. Reading the letter made his stomach churn. First, they basically fired him, and then, because they didn't want adverse publicity, gave him a hero's send-off. Fuck them and that city. Less than five years from retirement. Forced to start over. In a new town, with new people and a new bureaucracy. There was a part of him that wanted to just quit and take his reduced pension. Move to Central America, maybe Belize, and live out his days drinking tequila and banging hookers in a shack on the beach. The American dream. How the other half lives.

In the end, it was coaxing from his ex-partner that convinced him to accept the new job.

"Don't give the bastards the satisfaction," he had said.

And Dodge was right. This old dog still had some fight in him. No one was going to tell him when to quit. Besides, he wasn't sure he could rest until they apprehended the self-proclaimed savior, the escaped serial killer who shot Dodge. Dead or alive. He owed it to his partner and all the victims. Those were the two things he put above his own happiness. Well, that and his dog, Custus. It was simply him and an old dog after his partner packed up and moved back to the Midwest after being shot. Renquest wasn't a sentimental guy, but he felt some sadness the day Dodge left. He knew he'd be back one day, but it wouldn't be the same. He would miss his partner of over five years. It was hard to find someone who would have your back the way Dodge did. But it was his friendship he'd miss most of all.

The summer sun sank a little earlier, taking with it some of the humidity of the day. The nights cooled, and the dew lay heavy on the grass in the mornings. Sometimes, when the wind blew from the east, bringing with it the salty smell of the ocean and the bay, it brought the smell of home. He missed that, too.

It was a new day and, despite the turn of events in his life, he made a conscious decision to make a real go of it in his new town. The job was a promotion and gave him the role he had always coveted — chief detective. The only role higher in the department was the police chief. But with that role came a political one, answering to the mayor, county council, and a civilian oversight board. Nothing but red tape in that role. As chief of detectives, Renquest could mold the minds of junior detectives, most probably a decade or two younger than him, and share his years of knowledge with them. Turning them all into first-class criminal investigators before he retired his shingle. He wasn't sure if he really believed any of that, but positivity was a conscious decision he'd made with the new job. Like turning over a new leaf.

After showering, he made some toast with jam and had a piece of leftover bacon from the day before. The move had upended his life, and he hadn't quite regained his appetite. He would need to find a coffee shop he liked close to his condo or work, as the coffee maker he brought with him broke when the moving van almost got into an accident. The driver had to swerve to avoid another car on the road with a flat tire, forcing the trailer to lean heavily to one side, and the box containing the machine got crushed between the wall and the rest of the load. He loved that purveyor of black gold. Funny how it was the only thing ruined in the move.

He put on his tie, adjusting it in the mirror before slipping on his jacket. One last look at his ensemble, then a quick run through his thinning gray hair with his fingers, and he was out the door.

His condo was on the third floor and had a view of Fairfax Drive, one of the major thoroughfares dissecting the city of Arlington. This dissection went from east to west and ran from US 66 to the Clarendon neighborhood, where the street name changed to Clarendon Boulevard. It then finished its trip to the Potomac River and the DC border. His office was in the county courthouse, about a five-to-ten-minute drive, depending on traffic. Or he could take the Metro train from Ballston station to Courthouse station, which was three stops. But he didn't enjoy taking the train. You had to adhere to a schedule. The train decided when you left and when you arrived. And the whole thing was underground. He had never been a fan of subterranean transportation. Especially with hundreds of people packed into an eighty-five-foot tube traveling at sixty miles an hour. Way too many things could go wrong. A collapse from above. Or worse, an active shooter. A modern-day Bernhard Goetz. Only instead of having a six-shot revolver in a jacket pocket, it would be a short-barreled semi-auto rifle. Fifty rounds in fifteen seconds. Targets packed in like sardines with nowhere to go. A literal shooting gallery. A cop's worst nightmare.

He hit the button labeled G1. The elevator hissed and began moving down, eventually stopping at the first level of the garage area. With the push of a button, the headlights blinked twice, and he opened the door and slid into the driver's seat. The engine came to life after pushing the start button on the dash. The Dodge Charger's wheels broke loose as he turned onto North Taylor Street and right onto Fairfax Drive. He passed the local law school as he approached the five-point intersection where Fairfax Drive switched names to Clarendon Boulevard. Its courtyard filled with bright-eyed, optimistic students gathered at the tables in the courtyard outside the front entrance. He watched as young men and women stood, waving their arms as they talked to captive audiences seated around them. No doubt practicing for a future time when the knowledge garnered in the building behind them would be used to persuade juries and judges to side with them on different civil and criminal issues. He imagined some sitting across the aisle on the defense side of the courtroom. Doing everything to break *his* case into pieces to get their client off. The light turned green, forcing his focus back to the road.

It took two laps around the block to find a parking spot on the street near the courthouse. The secretary in human resources gave him a sign to place on his dash, which had printed in bold black letters: OFFICIAL POLICE BUSINESS, and would allow him to leave his car on the street, free from the worry of parking enforcement or the city's tow trucks.

A line stretched outside the courthouse. He didn't have a key fob for the officer's entrance yet, forcing him to maneuver the security checkpoint along with the rest of the masses showing up for court or county-related matters that day. A call ahead to the sheriff's department probably would have allowed him to bypass the line, but he was in no hurry today. He waited his turn like everyone else.

As he approached the metal detector, the deputy glared uneasily at him as Renquest pulled his temporary ID badge from his jacket pocket. The young deputy gazed at the piece of laminated plastic.

"The name's Renquest," he said, placing the ID back into his jacket pocket. "I'm the new chief of detectives."

The deputy said nothing, instead dismissing him and waving him past. The machine beeped as he passed through the archway, but the deputy didn't give him a second glance. He felt a hint of hesitation and wondered if he had made the right choice. This was a big move. Did he belong in such a large metro area? Would he be successful or fail miserably? He shook his head and used the side of his pants to wipe the nervous moisture from his hands. Within a few minutes, he stood in the front lobby of the Arlington County Police Department.

An older woman seated on the other side of a thick plexiglass window noticed him and smiled.

"Can I help you, sir?" she asked.

Her voice was high-pitched and a little irritating to him. It reminded him of the actress in the nineties who played a maid for a rich family. Nails on a chalkboard. He hoped she wouldn't notice him shiver.

"Good morning. My name is Renquest, and I am here to see Chief McNally."

"Well, hello, Detective! The chief is expecting you." Her hand reached below the counter, and the door to his left buzzed. "Just step inside and I'll be around in a sec to take you back to see the chief."

Renquest smiled and nodded before reaching out, pulling the door open and stepping immediately into a hallway. The door closed, locking behind him.

Chapter 2

The hall was about 25 feet long. Wooden pigeonholes designed to hold individual mail lined the left wall as he entered. The right side contained various posters concerning federal and state work requirements, along with other general employment law mandated to be posted in a way accessible by employees. Renquest peered over his shoulder and noticed a sign above the door. Black letters read; *The first line of defense is a respectful attitude.* It suited him.

By the time he had turned back around, the receptionist was standing in front of him. A smile on her face.

"It was the chief's idea when he took over a couple of years ago. He wanted to effect some change, and the first thing he did was to have that sign made and hung up above the main door."

"I couldn't agree more," Renquest said.

The woman turned and cantered her head toward the end of the hall. "The chief is waiting."

As the two approached the last door on the right, the woman stopped and gestured for him to enter the office. As he turned the corner and stepped through the doorway, a man behind a solid wood desk, stained dark and covered with stacks of files, stood to greet him. The man was tall, around six-foot-three and two hundred pounds. He was lean, and his physique resembled that of someone whose feet pounded out a lot of miles of road running. His hair was short and blondish, cut in a military style. High and tight. He was a handsome man and smiled big enough to reveal a front row of perfectly white teeth.

"Bill, come on in! Chief Jon McNally. I'm glad we could finally meet."

Renquest had never met the chief in person, only talking to him on the phone during the interview process. The flu pandemic over the past year had changed the way a lot of things were done. During the height of the outbreak, most companies and government agencies switched to phone interviews to keep personal contact to a minimum and help slow the spread of the virus. With his department fully vaccinated, things slowly returned to normal.

"Glad to be here," Renquest said.

The men bumped fists. The handshake was another casualty of the times. And while the fist bump seemed more like a college fraternity secret handshake than a formal greeting, it was going to be around for a while.

"Have a seat, Bill," the chief said, pointing toward two chairs on the other side of the room.

Renquest wondered which one he was supposed to sit in and decided on the one facing the window with the early morning sun shining on its brown vinyl seat. Chief McNally slid into the chair across from him.

"How was your trip up?"

"Not bad. The movers got here a day late, but almost everything was intact."

The woman who had met him at the reception desk poked her head through the doorway. "Excuse me, but I wondered if Detective Renquest would like anything to drink?"

Chief McNally glanced at his new detective.

"I would love a coffee. Two sugars, please."

The woman disappeared back into the hall and returned with a steaming mug within a minute.

"Thank you," Renquest said. He took the mug and shot the woman a smile.

"That'll be all, Molly," McNally told the woman as she disappeared into the hall, closing the door behind her.

"So, Bill." The chief paused. "I'm sorry. That was presumptuous. Do you like being called Bill, William, or Renquest?"

"You're the boss, and I couldn't care less to be honest with you. But most people call me Renquest." It was a lie. He hated being called either version of his first name.

"Renquest it is. As I was about to say, let's get down to brass tacks."

Renquest nodded.

"I hate to throw you to the wolves on the first day but, as you can see by the mess on my desk, we have a problem in my," he paused. "I mean, our town."

The new detective leaned forward in his chair. "What kinda trouble are we talking about?"

"The worst kind."

"Is there any other?"

Chief McNally shook his head and turned his attention to the pile of files spread across his desk. He stood, walked over, and took one from the top. He held it out for Renquest to examine.

The old detective let out a small groan as he rose from his chair. Then he reached out, taking the file in one hand and reaching for his jacket pocket to retrieve his readers with the other. After placing the glasses low on his nose, he sat back down and began leafing through the inch-thick stack of papers in the manila folder.

"That was the first one," McNally said as he leaned back against the edge of the desk.

The detective peered over the rim of his glasses. "Is he still alive?"

"Yes."

"It says here the victim had several liters of blood drained from his body."

"That's correct."

"Why?"

"We don't have the answer to that yet. That's why you are here."

Looking past the chief at the other files on the desk, he parsed his eyebrows. "The others?"

"Yes," McNally answered.

"Are they all like this one?"

McNally nodded. "The first four."

"How many are there in total?" Renquest asked, turning his attention back to the file propped on his lap.

The room was silent. Renquest looked up at his new boss, who was staring out the window. "Chief, how many?"

"Seven, that we know of."

The chair groaned as the veteran detective eased out. He walked to the desk and tossed the file on top of the others, and blew out a breath before addressing his boss again.

"A moment ago, I asked about the other victims. You mentioned four. Now you say you have seven. What's with the last three?"

"The other three are dead."

"So, you have four vics alive. Three dead?"

"That about sums it up," McNally said.

"Should we believe the dead ones are unrelated to the others?"

McNally rose from his seat to meet the gaze of his new detective. "Other than they all live in Arlington, you mean?"

"I was hoping for something a little more specific," Renquest said sharply. Realizing immediately that taking a tone with your boss on your first day probably wasn't the best idea.

If the remark bothered McNally, he didn't show it. "There are some elements of the crimes that overlap."

"Were the dead ones drained like the others?"

The chief nodded again. His weight shifted from one foot to the other.

"What are you not telling me?" Renquest said.

His new boss turned away. The smile faded from his face. Replaced with a sullen look. "The last three had *all* their blood drained."

"All their blood!" Renquest exclaimed. "How? Did the killer slit their throats and let the blood drain slowly? The crime scenes must've been a mess."

"That's the strange part. Each victim had the same puncture mark on his or her arms. The blood didn't spill out. Someone removed it. Medically. Like when they take blood at the hospital."

"More like at the morgue," Renquest said.

"Not a drop to be found at the crime scene or on the body. Clean as a surgical room."

Renquest had leaned completely back, his haunches resting on the edge of the chief's desk, before he realized his mistake. Embarrassed by his lack of candor, he pushed off and stepped away, stopping halfway across the room before turning back around and facing Chief McNally. His new boss let out a chuckle. "If you stop this madman, you can come and sit on my desk anytime you want."

The detective nodded. "Sorry about that."

Chief McNally smiled and quickly diverted back to the case. "So, what are you thinking?"

Renquest worked on hundreds of murders during his career. His hand moved to the edge of his receding hairline as he pondered the small amount of information provided to him in such a short time. Some assailants included jilted lovers or spouses unwilling to continue without their partners' full commitment. Others were mentally unstable. Their minds naturally warped through no fault of their own. God's lack of attention to detail when making them or a drug-addicted mother unable to give up her fix while pregnant. Then there were the clear psychopaths and sociopaths. Most often white males ranging from thirty to fifty years of age, suffering from illusions of grandeur or narcissists incapable of empathy. Children raised in a one-parent household, consisting of an alcoholic mother or an abusive father. No siblings, or a sibling's death in childhood.

This subgroup of predators learned to kill early, experimenting on captured or wounded animals, like squirrels and stray cats. Torturing the animals. Killing them slowly. Watching and learning about death. Making mental notes on techniques and reactions to pain. These were the future serial killers of the world. The same type who would find amusement in draining the blood from a live victim and watching them die a slow death.

"I'm thinking I need to review the files. All of them," he said, gesturing toward the chief's desk. "Is there a place where I can work?"

Chief McNally stood straight, reached out and shook Renquest's hand, placed an arm on his shoulder and pointed him toward the door. "Let's show you your office."

The two men entered the same hallway that led him to the chief's office and turned back toward the reception area. The chief stopped two doors down from his own, on the opposite side of the hall.

"We'll have maintenance hang a placard later today," he said, handing Renquest a keyring containing one metal key for the door to his office and a fob for the police entrance to the courthouse. "That fob will get you into every area in the department. You'll have the same access as I do. Records, equipment, garage access, and the weapons room."

Renquest nodded, turned, and opened the door to his office. He gawked at the amount of space allotted to him. Light poured in from the large window that ran from wall to wall along the back of the room, culminating on the biggest hardwood desk he'd seen. The left side of the room contained a conference table with eight black office chairs. Four to a side. A high-backed tan chair sat perched at the head of the table. There was a smartboard that covered a large part of the left wall, with several dry-erase markers stored upright on a plastic shelf to the left of the board. A sign hung below them that read: ***No permanent markers***!

The two men shook hands one more time. "I'll have Molly bring the files to your office. Let me know if you need anything else."

"Thank you, Chief."

"I'm glad you're here, Bill," Chief McNally said as he turned, but stopped before making it three steps. "I almost forgot. Your detective badge is in the top drawer of your desk, and you can go down and check out a weapon from the firearms vault. The sergeant at the desk will fix you up with ammo and whatever other gear you need. Which reminds me, you will need a pool car."

"I prefer to just use my vehicle. I have emergency lights installed with a siren if I need to use them."

"Your call. The county won't reimburse you for mileage, but you can fill your tank at the county station. Just use the key fob to access the pumps."

"Thanks again."

Renquest watched as his new boss turned and walked down the hall. He disappeared into his office, closing the door behind him.

He returned to his office, making his way to the large desk in front of the window. Opening the center drawer, he found the gold badge shaped like the crest of the County of Arlington, with an eagle perched on top and the title Chief of Detectives emboldened across the bottom. With the badge firmly gripped in his right hand, he clipped it onto his belt, then pulled his jacket over it to hide it from public view. He never enjoyed advertising his job to the world. Too many people don't like cops these days. Next, he reached back and grabbed the chair, then eased into it before pulling himself up to the desk. The top of his desk was void of anything except for a landline phone. No computer. No stapler or pens. Not even one of those large paper calendars. A barren, wooden landscape. He was staring blankly at his desk when a knock interrupted him.

"Excuse me, Detective."

He looked up and saw a young woman standing in the doorway. "Come in," he said.

The woman stepped in. It wasn't Molly. She had a stack of folders in her arms. "Where would you like these, sir?"

Renquest stood, walked around his desk, meeting her before she made it halfway across the room. He reached out and motioned for the young woman to hand him the stack of files. "I'll take 'em."

As she slid the files into his awaiting arms, she asked, "Can I get you anything else?"

He turned and dropped the files onto his desk. "Could use a computer."

"The county IT guy will be up this morning to set it up and provide you with your access to the department systems. I'll let you know when he arrives."

"Thank you." He paused. "I'm sorry. What's your name?"

"Margaret," the young woman said in a soft voice. "Margaret Reinert."

"Thank you, Margaret. I'll holler if I need anything else."

With that, the young woman left. He eased back behind his desk, removed a file from the top of the pile, and then began reading. It was going to be a long day.

Chapter 3

Renquest spent most of the day reviewing files from the abductions and the three murders, though he was a little perturbed. The reports contained few details about the victims and the crime scene, which confirmed his own belief about why they had hired him. The lack of any profile for the suspect didn't sit right with him, either. It was standard practice to have a psychologist or FBI profiler produce a psychological profile of a subject suspected in the deaths of three or more people. Here, the victim list was up to seven. The murder of the last three clearly signaled a rapid escalation in the suspect's behavior and timeline. He was becoming more confident. More calculated. But that also meant an increase in risk. Risk leads to mistakes. Mistakes lead to capture. Therefore, the lack of action in getting a solid profile concerned him more than the lack of detail in the crimes themselves. But he wasn't ready to question the policy choices of his new boss just yet. *Not a good way to start your first day*, he thought.

The time had crept close to three in the afternoon. His stomach made a noise that sounded like a trash compactor crushing a bin of gravel, and he noticed he was getting lightheaded. He had gotten so wrapped up in the case files that he forgot to eat lunch. A terrible choice for someone with a tendency toward hypoglycemia. Normally, he would have a candy bar stored in his desk. Maybe some nuts in a baggie in his jacket pocket. But today, he decided not to worry about in-between-meal snacks on his first day. A decision he now regretted.

The woozy detective stood and made his way down the hall to the receptionist's area. Molly was at the receptionist's window talking to a citizen who seemed not to like the parking ticket left under his wiper blade. The young woman named Margaret, who had brought the case files to his office, was sitting behind a desk. Her fingers moved fast as they tapped out words and sentences on the keyboard. She didn't notice him enter the office.

"Excuse me."

The woman looked surprised.

"I didn't mean to startle you."

She let out a breath. "It's okay. Sometimes I get so caught up in my work, I forget others even work here. I swear, a truck could drive through the front doors and I wouldn't hear it."

"I'm guessing that might get your attention," Renquest said.

"Sometimes I wonder."

Renquest smiled. "Where is a good place to get a bite to eat around here?"

"It's a little expensive for me around here, so I pack my lunch," Margaret said.

"It's my first day. Thought I'd try the flavor of Arlington."

Margaret tilted her head and pursed her brow. A moment passed before she spoke.

"I think some officers get menus from the local places. Where do they put them?" She stood from her chair and walked across the room to a table littered with newspapers and magazines. She pushed some periodicals to one side and uncovered a pile of takeout menus buried underneath. Clearly, no one had needed to use them for some time. "Ah, here they are. Most of these are from places across the street, by the movie theater."

She handed him the stack of menus containing no fewer than ten options.

"Thanks," he replied.

"Can I get you anything else, Detective?"

"That'll do," he said, leafing through the choices.

"Something you're looking for in particular?"

He stepped to the table covered in magazines and tossed the pile of menus on top of a stack of newspapers. "Where can I get a good cheeseburger?"

The young woman looked down and back up at him and smiled before answering. "There is a diner close to here. Go out the main entrance of the courthouse and cross the street to the metro station. Take the train one stop to Clarendon and get off. Once on the street, you will see the silver train car-shaped diner one block to the southeast. If you see the memorial statue, you'll see it."

He nodded and said, "Thanks. Want me to bring you anything back?"

"No thank you, Detective. I'm leaving in an hour."

With that, he stopped by Chief McNally's office and informed him he was going to get a sandwich for lunch, who reminded him he could leave at his leisure and didn't need to report in unless it was case related. Renquest apologized for the interruption and made for the front entrance of the courthouse.

Once on the street, he decided against taking the train and found his car parked on the street. He slid in, removing the sign from the dash, and headed for the diner Margaret had told him about. He remembered passing the Metro stop she had mentioned on his way to work and figured it would be easy enough to find. And it was. Within twenty minutes of leaving the station, he was taking a sip from his diet soda and eating a rather tasty cheeseburger.

He wiped his mouth with the napkin and laid a twenty on the table for the check. Full of carbs and protein, he headed back to the office. When he arrived, he found Chief McNally waiting for him by the officer's entrance.

"Just wanted to come and see if my fob worked," Renquest said.

"I'm glad you showed up. I need you inside."

"Something wrong?"

"They found another body." The chief motioned toward the door. "Get in here. Everyone's set up in your office."

Renquest followed McNally through the halls and into his office. Once inside, he noticed several people he had not met yet surrounding the conference table, which now had a coffee pot perched on one end and a stack of files from his desk spread across the glossy wooden top.

The people in the room looked up at him as he entered with the chief.

"Listen up, everyone," the chief's voice boomed over the chatter in the room. "This is Bill Renquest. The new chief detective. He will run point on this investigation from now on."

All the eyes in the room were on him. An uneasy feeling washed over him. He didn't like the attention. Or was it because he imagined more than one set of eyes staring back at him, piercing him with judgment? Wondering why this guy got the job over them. It's how he would have felt. It's how he had felt. He would just have to show them why he was there.

Chief McNally continued, "I want to make it clear to everyone in this room. My decision is not a reflection of the work you all have done so far. We have made a lot of headway in this case. But I think it's time for a fresh set of eyes. An outside perspective, or an inside perspective now, can be a good thing. Especially in a murder investigation. Bring Detective Renquest up to speed and then get out there and catch this guy."

There was a resounding "Yes, sir" from the group at the table. Renquest said nothing and felt even more out of place since he hadn't taken part in the group cadence. The chief gestured toward Renquest before leaving the room, and all eyes turned to him. It was a deafening silence.

The discomfort of the silent room and everyone staring at him forced Renquest to break the silence. "So, why don't you tell me your names and positions?"

A rather lanky, thin man was the first to speak. He looked to be about thirty-five years of age, with a balding head. He wore a button-up shirt with no tie and carried his weapon in a holster positioned in the small of his back. The man reached across the table and offered his hand.

"I'm Detective Ryan Flaherty. Good to meet you."

The second handshake came from a woman. She was short, about five feet-five inches tall in shoes, but had an athletic build. Her hair pulled into a ponytail, which draped halfway down her back. She wore a uniform, but her posturing screamed command staff.

"I'm Captain Rachel Brooks," she said, shaking his hand.

"Nice to meet you, Captain."

The third and last person at the table to introduce himself was a uniformed lieutenant named Marco Sanchez. He didn't offer to shake hands or interact, other than to say his name. His eyes were full of distrust of the new guy.

Renquest had seen that look many times. Hell, he had even felt it himself a time or two. This was someone he could work with.

Once they finished the introductions, Renquest poured a cup of coffee, then pulled out the chair closest to him and sat down. The others followed suit.

"Well, let's get at it. I've read the files, and I have some concerns."

"Concerns?" Detective Flaherty asked. His brow furrowed, his eyes carrying a stare full of contempt.

"Simmer down. I'm not suggesting the work y'all have put into this so far is not up to snuff. In fact, what I saw was the exact opposite. The interviews were timely and accurate. You asked all the right questions and communicated your findings in coherent and concise reports."

The accolades seemed to relax the group a bit. Flaherty leaned back in his chair and uncrossed his arms. So did Brooks and Sanchez.

Renquest continued, "My concerns lay more with the decision-making process concerning investigative tools."

Captain Brooks glanced at the others, making Renquest feel she might have some of the same concerns as him.

"Speak up, Captain. This is a safe space. Anything said in these meetings stays in this room." His pointed finger bounced from each member of his new team. "No idea is too dumb, and no criticism is off-limits. And that goes for me as well. If you don't like the way I am doing something, you can let me know during our daily meeting. Or you can come to my office anytime. Understood?"

The three nodded.

"Good. Now, Brooks, say what you were thinking."

This time, she didn't look at her fellow officers. She focused on Renquest as she leaned forward in her chair. "Sir, I was wondering something."

"Spit it out."

"Well, I was wondering why no one had placed a call to get the FBI in on this yet. No offense to you, but I would have called the Bureau before hiring a new chief of detectives."

"No offense taken, Captain. Your sentiments echoed my own. While most local agencies don't like to get federal law enforcement involved in their cases, the profiling unit of the FBI doesn't take jurisdiction. They simply come and review the case material and provide a psychological profile we can use to help narrow down a suspect pool."

His response seemed to put the other two at ease. Sanchez Spoke next.

"Do you think we are dealing with a serial killer here, sir?"

"That is a tough determination to make. There are specific criteria that need to be met before labeling someone a serial killer. Victimology being one. Are there any similarities in the vics? Is there a pattern the killer follows for each attack? Does he use the same weapon or different methods to do the deed? Everything we need to know is in those files." His hand swept across the table, grabbing the nearest file and tossing it to Sanchez. "Did you all read all the files?"

The collective group all said, "Yes."

"What I mean is, did you read each other's work?"

Flaherty and Sanchez said nothing.

Brooks looked around the table, then smiled. "Yes."

Renquest nodded. "Good work, Brooks. Now, I need to get down to the scene before the coroner bags and takes the body." He stared at the two men in the room. "You two get to reading the rest of the reports. We will meet back here at eight tomorrow morning." His attention turned to his new captain. "Brooks, you're coming with me. Get your keys. You can drive."

A passing bicyclist found the latest body just inside the county line near the W&OD Trailhead. The W&OD was a long-abandoned railroad easement that the county had transformed into a paved biking and walking path that wound through Northern Virginia from Arlington to Purcellville. Nearly forty-five miles in total. Brooks told him that a person could walk or ride trails like this from Washington, DC, to Pittsburgh, Pennsylvania. Renquest had no intention of finding out the truth of that nugget of information. His idea of exercise was tossing a tennis ball to Custus in a fenced-in yard. A low-impact workout. No sweating involved.

The two officers pulled up, and a patrol cop waved them through the perimeter checkpoint. Once parked, Renquest and Brooks walked about fifty feet up the trail and found the coroner and a paramedic placing the body on a gurney. The victim received a toe tag, and a pull of the zipper sealed the body inside the thick black plastic bag.

"Hang on, Doc," Brooks said. Holding her hand out as if she were stopping traffic at a busy intersection. "This is Chief Detective Renquest. He'll need to get a look at the body before you take it back to the slab."

The woman, annoyed by the interference in her duties, let out an exasperated sigh and stepped back from the gurney. "Hurry, will you? I've got to get it back before the rest of the staff go home, or I'll have to unload this thing by myself."

Brooks shot the woman a glare, resulting in the woman returning to the back of her van.

"Sorry about that. She doesn't play well with others," Brooks said.

"Neither do I sometimes," Renquest said. "Now, let's unzip and see what we've got here."

Brooks grabbed the metal tab and pulled. The zipper receded with the growl of a feral cat. Renquest pulled the sides of the plastic bag back, exposing the face and torso of the young man inside. He had dark skin. Most likely of Asian descent. Appeared to be in his mid-forties. Black hair and brown eyes. He was very thin. His arms were smaller than Renquest's wrists, and his cheeks sucked in, forming large dimples on both sides of his face.

"What's wrong with his cheeks?" Brooks asked. Her nose snarled and upper lip parsed.

"It's from dehydration. The skin loses its elasticity and draws tight. The neck area and face are the first places to show the effects."

About that time, the coroner appeared from behind the van. "That's right, Detective. Not your first body, I suppose."

"Unfortunately, no."

The woman stepped closer and handed him a pair of surgical gloves. "Doctor Johansen."

The detective donned the gloves, reached into the body bag, and gently lifted the victim's left arm.

"You won't find what you're looking for there," Johansen said. "Check the inside of the left leg."

Renquest looked back. Johansen smiled at him. Then he folded more of the bag back until he could see the thigh of the left leg. A piece of fabric was missing from the inside of the pant leg, exposing the skin underneath. He saw a small, discolored patch of skin.

"Puncture wound?"

Johansen nodded.

"Looks like he used a pretty big needle," Renquest said.

"At least a fifteen-gauge."

"He would have felt that for sure."

"If he were alive, it would have been immensely painful," Johansen said.

Brooks stepped next to Renquest and peered into the bag. "Doc, do you think he was dead when they drained him?"

"I won't know for sure until I get him on the table, but my best guess is he died before or shortly after it started."

"How can you tell?" Brooks asked.

Johansen looked at Renquest.

"The bruise on his leg," the detective said.

"What about it?" Brooks asked.

"It's very light. If he'd been alive for too long after the jab, the bruise would be darker."

"I don't understand," Brooks said.

"Doc, do you want this one?"

Johansen moved closer to the gurney and pointed to the exposed thigh. "You see that discoloration?"

"Yes," Brooks said.

Johansen handed Brooks a plastic bag containing a wallet with no driver's license and a set of keys.

"If the victim had lived long after the insertion of the needle into his arm, the bruise you're looking at would be more prominent. As blood flows to the wound area to flush the affected skin with oxygen and antibodies, it pools. Here, the color is light, meaning the heart stopped pumping shortly after the needle entered the vein and less blood made its way to the wound site."

Brooks scratched her head. "So, if the heart stopped pumping, how did he drain the body?"

"That's why we need to let the doc take the body and do the autopsy."

Renquest reached down and pulled the zipper back up, closing the bag, and waved at the coroner, signaling she could load the body into the van. He then turned and faced the area next to the trail marked by yellow crime scene tape.

"Go back to the car and get some booties and two pairs of gloves."

Brooks hustled back to the cruiser and returned with a box of blue shoe booties and fresh gloves for her and Renquest. The pair slid the shoe covers on, then Renquest bagged his old gloves before pulling the fresh pair over his sweaty hands.

The two ducked under the crime scene tape. Once inside the cordoned-off area, the veteran detective's eyes scanned the entire crime scene. Almost immediately, something caught his eye. The glare from the late afternoon sun glinted off a piece of metal partially covered by weeds along the side of the path. He knelt to pick it up, then rubbed the object between his fingers.

Chapter 4

The light from the refrigerator shone through each glass container, giving the blood a dark red appearance. Almost a burgundy hue. Gelatinous and heavy. But he could still see them. The artificial cold of the refrigerator forces the microorganisms to hibernate. Some samples had more swimmers than others. It depended on the person the blood, until recently, had been in. If they lived a clean life, the tiny invaders would have less of a chance to take hold and corrupt the person. A person of lesser morals provided the perfect breeding ground for parasites. The rot inside them fed the invaders. Helping them grow. There was nothing anyone could do once that happened. A life of pain awaited them. Every day. The same fate. Immeasurable. Eternal.

Unfortunately, there was no way to differentiate between the infected and uninfected without examining their blood. When he first started looking at cures for the disease, the same one that took his mother, he only took small amounts of blood from test subjects. But this method proved ineffective. The organisms caught on. They hid deeper in the body. It was as if they could sense the light after he pierced the skin, choosing instead to retreat far into organ and muscle tissue to avoid being captured. This made it hard to get a quality sample. There would need to be more blood if he wanted to continue his work.

But more blood meant more problems. If he took too much, the person would die. His intention was never to harm or kill anyone, but he needed to continue his research. You see, he had a theory about the organisms and how they manifested. It was genetic. A trait passed down from parent to child. All the donors he'd gained a sample from had come from a troubled past. Many samples came from seemingly innocent individuals, yet the acute infection he found revealed a tainted ancestry. They never stood a chance. It didn't matter if they crossed paths with him or not.

The label on the jar in the refrigerator looked different from the others. Oversized writing in black permanent marker spelled out the words: *TEST BATCH: CLEANSED*. Carefully and methodically, he twisted the lid off the jar. The blood was warm when it entered the jar, forcing a natural vacuum process as the liquid cooled and sucked the center of the lid down. The top made a popping sound as the seal lost its grip on the jar's rim. He poured the *clean blood* into the hopper of the machine he had spent so many hours designing and building. One pint exactly. Then, he inserted the needle into his arm. He let the blood from his arm flow back into the hopper until the pressure equalized. His skin felt icy against the stainless-steel table. He lay back, his head resting on a foam cushion, which provided more support than a standard pillow. His fingers moved, finally locating the switch he had installed to provide power to the pump. He flipped it, and the room filled with a low hum, followed by a click every few seconds. The cold blood flowing into his arm forced his fists to clench. He closed his eyes and let the machine do the rest.

* * *

Renquest peered at the tubular-shaped object he plucked from the ground. It was hollow. Its ends frayed as if a sudden shearing had occurred. The entire piece was only a few inches long and the same diameter as the graphite center of a pencil. Brooks knelt beside him, and he handed her the plastic baggie containing the evidence.

"What do you think it is?" she asked.

"Looks like it could be an old hype needle."

"It's still shiny. Couldn't have been here long."

"The material is medical-grade stainless steel. Years in the sun wouldn't have tarnished it much."

"What about DNA?" Brooks asked as she stood. "Do you think we can recover anything?"

Renquest took one last look around before standing. He let out a small groan as his knees straightened, pushing his body upward. "Maybe. There might be some blood residue inside the shaft. If they can extract it, if it's there, we might get a DNA profile."

"That's a good sign," Brooks said with a smile.

"But even then, we need a profile to compare it to. We'll run it through the database and see if we get a hit." His voice trailed off.

"You don't sound too positive, sir."

Renquest ignored the comment. "I want you to take that to the lab as soon as we get back. Tell them I said to move it to the top of the list."

Brooks stared at him; her mouth half open as if she had something to say, but didn't know if she should.

Renquest noticed. It was the same look he'd seen on her face back in the office. "What is it, Brooks?"

"We don't have a lab, sir. We use the State Police lab out in Manassas for DNA and other evidence that needs to be tested."

He shook his head. "Ok. Have Flaherty run over there first thing in the morning. I want this to be a priority. Tell him to say whatever he needs to get it done. Understood?"

"Yes, sir. What do you want me to do?"

"Tomorrow, I want you to pull the files on any drug-related busts in this park. Then expand that to an area four blocks outside this location."

"Ah, that'll help us discover if the needle was from a user or if it's related to the case?"

"Exactly. All convicted drug users have a DNA sample taken at sentencing or at the local probation office when convicted. If we have some profiles on file, the lab can run a comparison and maybe rule out the needle as being part of the crime."

"Or rule it in."

"Maybe. But we won't know anything until the lab can tell us if they're able to get a viable sample from that," he said, pointing to the object in the plastic bag. "Let's head back to the station and get it logged into evidence."

The two made their way back to the police cruiser. Each one's eyes scanned the ground and path in front of them for signs like tire tracks or drag marks. Neither saw anything. As they approached the car, Dodge noticed a trash bin at the trailhead. Garbage had overflowed and was now littering the area around the base of the can.

"Brooks," he said, nodding toward the waste receptacle. "When does the city collect the trash?"

"I'm not sure."

He walked over to the container and pulled the sides of the trash bag up. He used a piece of cardboard to compact the garbage before he closed the bag over the top, tying it shut with a simple knot. After pulling the waste from the metal container, he noticed Brooks was staring at him with a bewildered look on her face.

"Pop the trunk."

"You're going to put trash in the trunk of my cruiser?"

"Technically, it's the county's cruiser," he said.

"Well, I'm the one that has to get the smell of garbage out of the car, so it's my cruiser when people want to throw rotting garbage into the trunk."

"You're confused, Brooks. This isn't garbage."

"Sure smells like trash to me."

"Oh, that? That's the smell of evidence." A chuckle escaped his lips.

Brooks looked at the plastic bag in her hand, which contained the small shard of metal. "This doesn't smell like evidence."

Renquest tossed the refuse bag into the now-open trunk and closed the lid. He made his way to the passenger door and slid in, closing the door behind him. Brooks followed and piled into the driver's seat and started the engine. The two looked at each other.

"Maybe we should roll down the windows," Renquest said.

"Yeah," Brooks said, as she hit the window-down button on the door panel and a blast of fresh air washed through the car's cabin.

As Brooks eased into traffic from the parking lot, Renquest could see his decision to take the garbage with them annoyed her, forcing a smile on his face. He liked Brooks, and her reaction helped him decide something he'd been wondering about. Who would be his principal partner? For now, it was Brooks.

Once back at the station, Renquest pulled the bag from the trunk. Even the short ride back to the station filled the trunk space with the odor of rotten food and stale beer. He quickly closed the lid before Brooks rounded the corner and took the full brunt of the offensive smell.

"I'll take care of this. You log the needle piece into evidence. Then go upstairs and tell Flaherty about what we found today and make sure he knows I want a rush on the DNA testing at the lab. We need those results back as soon as possible."

Brooks nodded.

"Oh, and send Sanchez down. I'm going to need some help to sort through all of this."

He held the bag up and turned it upside down. Its contents spilled across the parking garage floor. Cans clanked against the concrete, and flies escaped their once-black prison.

"Sanchez will not like that," Brooks said.

"Then he can get a squad car and go on patrol."

A smile spread across his new partner's face. "Yes, sir."

He watched as Brooks turned the corner and walked out of sight. Then he walked over to the cruiser and popped the trunk to let it air out a bit. He felt a little bad about how bad the inside of the cruiser smelled. He really hadn't thought the intensity would increase that much on such a quick ride. As he stood over the open compartment, he saw an orange and white fiberglass rod. It was about two feet long and appeared to be a piece from one of the poles the city places around the curbs in the winter to help the snowplow drivers locate the edges of the road as they clear the lots.

He took the rod and made his way back to the trash pile, which was now beginning to draw attention from passers-by. He smiled and nodded at a couple of patrol officers who stopped to see why there was a putrid pile of trash scattered across the garage floor.

"Afternoon, fellas," Renquest said.

The two officers shook their heads in unison and left him there. A fiberglass rod and a heap of trash. He knelt and began poking around the pile. Using its dull end to move cans and used paper plates to one side, wadded-up bags and other items to the opposite side. About halfway through the sorting process, Sanchez appeared from around the corner and stopped short of where Renquest was working. A look of bemusement on his face.

"What the hell are you doing?"

"Grab the other half of this rod from the trunk of the cruiser and get down here with me," the kneeling detective said.

Sanchez's look of bewilderment changed to one of disgust. "I'm not rooting through garbage like some common street beggar."

The statement stunned the veteran detective. He placed his trash tool on the ground and rose to his feet. He had a good six inches over his new lieutenant, and he used every bit to his advantage.

"Look, Sanchez. I don't know what was going on before I got here. Maybe you think you deserved the job. Maybe someone else deserved the job, and the chief didn't even look in your direction. In the end, I don't give a shit. I'm here now. If you have a problem with that, take it up the chain of command. But since I report directly to Chief McNally, and he hired me instead of you, I don't think that's going to get you very far. Do you?"

Sanchez said nothing.

"Now, you can pout about it, get mad and whine to the chief or whoever the hell listens to your complaints. Or you can get down here with me and sort through this pile of potential evidence. But I promise you, only one of those is going to help your career. The other will kill it."

The two men stood face to face. Neither said anything. Renquest had been in this position before, and he knew he would win. It was only a matter of when his opponent gave up. It turned out to be only a few minutes before Sanchez broke eye contact. He then retrieved the rod from the trunk of the cruiser and knelt by the trash pile. The two men sorted the items into piles. Common trash to one side and things that needed more examination to the other.

When the pair finished and had found nothing of importance, Renquest and Sanchez began stuffing the garbage back into the bag. Once the two men finished picking up all the garbage, Sanchez took the bag to a dumpster near the far wall of the garage and tossed it in. He walked back and, as he passed Renquest, he mumbled something far too quiet for the detective to make out.

"What'd you say?"

Sanchez stopped and turned to face his boss. "I said this was a waste of fucking time." Then he spun back around and headed inside the building.

As he watched his insubordinate lieutenant disappear into the hallway, he shook his head.

"Prick," he said to no one before heading inside the building. He passed his office and the now empty receptionist area, where he went through the front doors and out onto the street. It was a block and a half walk to his car. Sanchez was going to be a problem. But one he would have to deal with. He saw no need to elevate the issue to the chief. These types of disputes needed to be handled by him. That's what McNally hired him to do as chief of detectives.

Once in the driver's seat, his extended finger jabbed at the ignition button, and the engine came to life. A quick trip home to see Custus and a cold beer is what he needed to wash away the literal stench of the day. His first day had been both good and bad. But he learned a lot about his team. He now had some idea of the attitudes and proficiencies each member brought to the table. Information that would serve him well in the coming months. He drove straight to his condo and didn't even stop for food. Tonight, he'd make the delivery guy work for a living.

Chapter 5

Custus waited at the door when he arrived home. He was an old dog, but still enjoyed a few minutes of playtime when his master returned from a long day away. The two went outside. The old dog sniffed out a good place to relieve himself. Then, the old detective let his best friend wander the grounds and smell what he wanted. When he finished, the brown and partially graying hound mix turned and looked at its master, letting him know he was done and ready to go back inside. With a clip of the leash, the two headed back to the building and made the quick elevator ride up to their floor.

While he was waiting for his friend to take care of his business on the lawn in the courtyard, Renquest had filled the time by searching for nearby food options on his phone. The five-block radius surrounding his new place had every kind of cuisine one could imagine. And they all delivered. After what seemed like endless scrolling through Asian, Latin, Italian and even Russian options, he decided it seemed like a pizza kind of night. With a quick phone call, he placed the order.

By the time he returned to the room and unleashed Custus, the buzzer rang at his front door. He tipped the delivery kid five dollars and thanked him. Then he sat on the couch with the pizza box perched on his lap. He turned on the television and opened a beer. Custus curled up at his feet, looking over his body at the box.

"Don't worry, boy. You can have the crust."

As he watched the local news, he quickly gobbled down two slices and dropped the crusts to the floor, where the old dog devoured each in two bites.

When half the pie was gone, he placed the remaining half in the refrigerator and filled the dog's water bowl. After brushing his teeth, he was asleep five minutes after his head hit the pillow. Custus sprawled out next to him.

The alarm on his phone buzzed at exactly six in the morning. He showered and was out the door twenty minutes later. Normally, he wouldn't arrive at work before seven, but he wanted to be there when Detective Flaherty showed up to make sure he took the evidence to the lab first thing in the morning. They needed the results as soon as possible, and he didn't want any delays in the processing. A sample that is delivered first thing in the morning is theoretically at the top of the pile. The chance of a quick turnaround is greater. This was all based on his experience in his old department where they operated a lab. He had no way of knowing how many departments in the Northern Virginia area used the one in Manassas. More departments meant more cases. More cases meant longer wait times. That was something he'd have to learn to deal with.

As he opened the door and stepped into the hallway leading to his office, the aroma of freshly brewed coffee filled the air. The place was buzzing. Patrol officers were gearing up for the shift change. Some coming and others going. Officers filled the training room for roll call. Roll call is where the officers and command staff prepare for the day's activities, providing information on anything that may happen in the county that day. Including any lookouts or special crime areas that need more attention. Once it was over, the uniforms filed out to start their shift, and the station became eerily quiet again.

After listening to part of the sergeant's speech, he continued to his office, tossed his jacket over the back of his chair, and then sat down. A brand-new laptop sat centered on the desk. When he opened the device, a piece of paper, folded in half, rested on the keyboard. Picking it up, he saw it was from the IT department. Detailed instructions on how to log into the system and set his password for the various databases he would be using. He entered the username and password and waited for the machine to boot up.

Brooks stopped as she walked by his open door.

"Detective. I didn't plan on seeing you here so early."

He looked up from his computer. "I wanted to get here first thing and make sure Flaherty didn't have any issues with the lab yesterday."

"Traffic was hell last night. The drive would've taken him over two hours, and the place would've been closed by the time he got there. So, he came in at five this morning and headed over. The drive will be against traffic on the way there, but he may hit the tail end of the meat grinder on 66 on the way back."

US Highway 66 is the primary thoroughfare from east to west across northern Virginia. It stretches from US 81 along the Appalachian Mountains to the DC-Virginia line—it's well known for its congested traffic and constant construction projects.

"That's a good initiative. I'll make sure I let him know when he gets back." Brooks nodded.

"Come in and have a seat," he said, pointing at the chair across from him. "I have a meeting with the chief later. He wants an update about yesterday." Renquest leaned back, pushing his chair away from his desk. "Is there anything I need to know about going into this meeting? Not about the case, but about him that'll help prepare me?"

Brooks stared at him for a moment, then said, "Yeah, I don't think your meeting is really about the case at all. I believe it's about you. He'll want to know how things went the first day with all of us."

Renquest leaned back and crossed his arms over his chest. "Hmm... How do you think it went?"

Brooks smiled, then she pushed the chair back and stood.

"I guess you'll just have to ask the chief."

Renquest chuckled under his breath as she walked away. He liked her. And he thought McNally did as well. Information that might come in handy in the future.

The case files he had handed out the day before still cluttered the conference table's top. He grabbed two files, taking them back to his more comfortable chair and desk, where he reviewed the autopsy reports.

He wasn't half-way through the first report before a knock at his door pulled his attention from the coroner's report. Reading medical examiner's reports was something he hated. The writing style resembled that of technical manuals, making them very boring to read. He welcomed the reprieve. Looking up, he saw Chief McNally standing in his doorway. He dropped the file on the desk and rose from his chair.

"Sir?"

"Have a seat. You don't have to stand when I come into the room. Especially if it's your office. Though I might get used to it."

Renquest remained standing. "Come in, sir," he said. "Can I get you a coffee?"

McNally stepped into the room, stopped, and leaned back against the wall beside the door.

Renquest said nothing. Choosing to wait and see what his new boss had to say. He guessed a meeting took place between McNally and Brooks and wanted to make his boss press the conversation forward. It was one of those times when two people were trying to feel each other out. First to blink loses.

After a moment, his boss pushed himself off the wall, and three strides later he was standing opposite Renquest. The desk separated the two men.

"So, how was yesterday?"

The savvy detective immediately recognized this as a trap question, meant to see if his answers jibed with what the Chief had just been told by his confidant, Brooks. Renquest could have ended the game right then and there by mentioning Brooks' name. But he still thought their relationship might be something he could exploit if he found himself in a pinch down the road. For now, he would dance to the music selected for him.

"It was good. We found some evidence at the crime scene, and I had Flaherty run it over to the lab first thing this morning. We might get some DNA. If the sample is viable, we can compare it with some profiles. If we're lucky, we'll get a hit from someone in the system."

"That's good work. Sounds like you had a good first day." Chief McNally picked up a file from the desk. He opened it and scanned its pages before tossing it back down. "Any other updates or issues I need to know about?"

Now Renquest knew where this was going. Apparently, Sanchez made a complaint about their little trash-sifting incident yesterday in the garage. He'd now identified the roles of two out of his three team members. His first inclination was to out the lieutenant. But he guessed McNally already knew all about Sanchez.

"Nothing I can't handle, sir."

Renquest watched as McNally stared at him. His eyes strained, trying to get a read on his new detective. After a moment, he relaxed his posture and looked away.

"I just want you to know you can come to me with any issues. Case-related or personal, I'm here to help you in any way I can. If something or someone isn't working out, we can change it up. I want this case closed and a suspect in custody as soon as humanly possible, and that means supporting my chief of detectives with whatever he needs."

"I appreciate that, sir."

As McNally turned to walk away, he paused and looked back over his shoulder. "So, what are your plans for today?"

"I am going to take Brooks to the coroner and watch the cut on yesterday's victim."

"Sounds good. I'm glad to see you taking an interest in Rachel. I think she is a hell of a cop and a sharp investigator. She will learn a lot from a grizzled old veteran like you."

"I agree. She seems to have the makings of a good detective. Her instincts are on point, and she has an eye for detail. All she needs is a little coaxing in the right direction."

"Not bad on the eyes, either."

The statement made Renquest uncomfortable. He had no problem keeping his work relationships professional. It came from years of working sex crimes. Seeing woman after woman being treated as objects left a foul taste in his mouth. He vowed never to turn into *that guy*. The man who noticed a female's looks before she even spoke. A chauvinist. A misogynist. He blew the comment off as he wasn't sure if the chief was testing him.

"Hadn't noticed, sir."

The chief nodded and left, leaving Renquest to continue reading the autopsy files on his desk. But he couldn't stop thinking about the comment Chief McNally made about Brooks. The whole thing gave him an icky feeling he couldn't shake.

He'd made it through two of the files before another knock on his door jerked him from his thought-induced trance. It was Brooks this time.

"Hey, Detective."

"Got time to come in?" Renquest said, waving her inside.

"I'm all yours," she said, walking toward his desk, pulling back the chair and sitting, her legs crossed.

"I'd like to watch the cut today on our vic."

"Do you want me to put in a call to the coroner and find out what time she has the autopsy scheduled for?

"Do it."

His captain stood up to leave.

"Oh, and Brooks, I want you to be there today."

She stared back at him with a vacant look on her face. "You want me to witness the autopsy?"

Renquest stood to be on equal footing with his new partner. "Yes. In fact, I want you to be by my side from now on. If I go somewhere, you go. If I have a meeting with the chief, you have a meeting with the chief."

"So, you want me to be your shadow? Get your coffee and retrieve the files." Her face deflated.

"That's not what I am saying. I don't want you to be my shadow. You're my partner. We decide things together. Fifty-fifty. But that also means we rise and sink together. Partners must have each other's backs. It's almost like marriage. There is trust. A bond. We don't rat each other out to further our own ambitions. We work together as a team. Understand?"

"Understood."

"Good. Now go set up that appointment with the coroner and report back here as soon as you're done."

"Yes, Detective."

"Oh, and Brooks. Good job yesterday."

"Thank you, sir," she said.

She then turned around and walked out of the office. Renquest considered what had just transpired. By bringing her into his circle, he hoped she would be less likely to report back to the chief about the daily comings and goings of the investigation. His intention being to gain a partner he felt he could trust to have his back. She had good instincts and a keen eye.

But more than that, he could control Chief McNally's major source of information. Allowing him to catch and deal with things before they reached his boss's desk and freeing him to work his way. At his pace. He liked it that way. The detective had a healthy respect for the chain of command; however, everything had its limits.

Brooks returned within a few minutes, twirling the keys to the detective's pool car in her hand.

"Doc said she was getting ready to start the cut when I called. I got her to hold off for twenty minutes, but we need to go. Traffic will be horrible this time of the morning."

Renquest grabbed the folder he had started for the latest victim, put on his jacket, and the pair headed for the parking garage.

Chapter 6

The county offices were at the corner of Arlington Boulevard and South Washington Boulevard, about half a mile from the police station. It might as well have been five miles away, and Renquest was sure the two of them could have covered the distance quicker if they had ditched the car and walked. Traffic was at a near standstill from cars backed up from the massive number of commuters exiting for the Pentagon from US 50, a quarter mile ahead of them.

"Is it always like this?" he asked.

"Pretty much. The federal government employs most of the people in this area. It brings in a ton of revenue for the local businesses."

"It seems like they could use some of that money to make improvements and ease this mess a bit."

Brooks laughed at his comment.

"What's so funny?"

"This is an improvement! You should have seen it five years ago."

"I don't know if I will get used to this. It's such a time suck." His hand waved toward the line of cars in front of the pair.

"It is what it is. You must learn to deal with congestion and road construction, or you'll give yourself a heart attack worrying about it every day. If you're going to live in the DMV," the DMV being a local term for the DC-Maryland-Virginia metro area, "you accept the drive that comes with it." She looked over at her partner and nodded towards the building on the right. "Besides, we're here."

Brooks found a spot in the parking garage reserved for police, and the two made it to the coroner's office just as the medical examiner made the first incision.

"Thought you two wouldn't make it, so I got started."

Renquest had paid little attention to Dr. Johansen at the crime scene the other night. But she was an attractive woman. In her late forties, with short brown hair and deep blue eyes. She was short. In fact, she was so short she needed a small stepstool to help her reach the body on the table. Renquest would have guessed her to be five foot three inches tall, at most. But her height didn't take away from her command presence. Once you were in the cut room, you knew who was in charge. He respected that.

"Both of you get a gown on and some gloves with a face shield. And hurry. I've got a long list of bodies after this one to get to today."

Renquest and Brooks stepped out of the room and donned a gown and face shield, then returned to the table. Johansen pulled an overhead light directly over the torso, making the skin appear lighter than it was. It also enhanced every flaw. Each mole. Every sunspot and scar. The needle mark on the inner thigh Renquest saw at the scene now looked like a wound from a hammer blow. The light reflecting off the discoloration on the skin made the wound appear larger than it was.

Johansen made her first incision, starting at the top of the sternum and continuing down through the abdomen. The second and third cuts were along the bottom of the rib line on each side, allowing access to the internal organs. As the circular saw ripped through the bone and cartilage holding the rib cage together, the smell of burning flesh and bone filled the air. Renquest turned to check on Brooks. She didn't appear to be fazed by the foul odor. It was the opposite, in fact. She had a look of curiosity on her face and leaned closer to get a better view.

Once the saw finished tearing its way through the rib cage, the doc used a pair of bolt cutters to snap the remaining bone the saw couldn't penetrate. Then, with a healthy pull, the chest cavity opened like a double-hung garage door, exposing the heart and lungs.

"The muscular tissue of the heart appears to be in good shape," Johansen said into the microphone attached to her apron. "The lungs show no effects from smoking or respiratory disease."

She removed the organs one at a time and weighed each one before placing them in a pan next to the table. Next, she stuck her hands inside the cavity and felt around for anything unusual, like a tumor or unnatural tissue growth. She found nothing.

Renquest had seen many autopsies over his long career, and Johansen was as thorough as any he'd known. But he didn't need to know any of the information she had provided thus far. He was only interested in the puncture wound on the leg and the results from the toxicology report, which he knew wouldn't be back for a few days.

"Hey, Doc. If you examine the spot on his leg, we will get out of your hair."

The short Johansen peered over at him from under her protective face shield. "Don't want to hang around for the skull dissection?"

Renquest smirked. "Nope. I just need to know what you think about the leg wound. The rest is all medical geek stuff."

The short woman hopped down from her step stool and slid it a foot down the base of the table. Once positioned across in front of the victim's thigh, Johansen stepped back up and leaned over the body. She pulled a pair of high-powered microscope goggles from her pocket. She slid them over her head, pulling the lenses down in front of her eyes. At first, she was silent. Observing as she touched and stretched the surrounding tissue. Then she leaned back, stepped off the stool, and using her foot, slid it a few feet back from the table.

Renquest and Brooks waited for Johansen to remove her facemask, then followed suit.

"What is it, Doc?" Renquest asked. He tossed his face shield onto a table beside him, which had medical equipment strewn across its surface.

Johansen took a breath and held it for a moment, releasing it as she spoke. "The wound is a puncture wound, as we thought. A good-sized needle, too. I'd say eighteen gauge."

"Okay?" Renquest said, hesitation in his voice.

"But it's the condition of the vein itself that concerns me. It's collapsed."

"I'm no medical professional, but I have given blood before. I don't think it's uncommon for veins to collapse in on themselves during the donation process."

"That's correct, Detective. But I am a medical professional. One that's practiced for over twenty years, and I've not seen anything like this kind of damage before outside of a mortician's table."

"I'm not following."

"What I mean is, the structure of the vein didn't just fail. Something pulled it apart. Likely during the draining process."

Brooks stepped up beside her partner. "What could have done that type of damage?"

Johansen stared at the body on her table. "I mentioned the mortuary because funeral prep requires a pump to remove the blood from the body and fill the corpse's veins with a preserving mixture to slow decay. With a little too much pressure during the procedure, vein shredding can happen."

"What you're telling me is, our guy used some kind of pumping machine to drain the blood out of this poor guy?" Renquest asked, a surprised look on his face.

"That's exactly what I am saying. And from the bruising around the wound, the victim was alive when he started."

"Wouldn't that have been painful?" Brooks asked.

"Unbearable. He would have passed out from the pain long before the loss of blood killed him."

"Jesus Christ," Renquest grumbled.

"Oh, and one more thing, Detective. It wouldn't surprise me if we found a paralyzing agent present when the toxicology report comes back."

"What makes you say that?"

"If he were awake during the process, the only way to keep him from flopping all over the place in pain and ripping the needle from his leg would be to incapacitate him. And I see no signs of bondage on the ankles or wrists. And no one would have let this happen to them willingly."

"It appears we have a real psycho on our hands here," Brooks said.

"Appears so," Renquest replied.

Renquest thanked Johansen, then he and Brooks stepped back into the washroom. As they removed the protective gear and placed it into brown paper bags for storage until the case was closed, Brooks winced at the sound of the bone saw eating into the skull.

"Are you okay?"

"Yeah. It just sounds like fingernails on a chalkboard. I always hated that sound."

Renquest smiled and nodded. "Let's see what we can find out about the victim." He opened the door and held it as Brooks exited. "But first, I need a cup of coffee."

Brooks pulled out of the parking garage and made a left turn onto Walter Reed Drive. After a few blocks, she turned right onto South Courthouse Road.

"I know a good place for coffee not too far from here on Columbia Pike," Brooks said as she made another turn and headed west.

"As long as it's hot."

Traffic had let up some, as it was nearly ten in the morning. Most of the daily commuters were at work by that hour, and the only ones left on the roads were locals taking care of their daily errands. Grocery shopping and dropping off things at the dry cleaners usually happened after the morning rush, Brooks told him.

And Brooks was right about the coffee. It was both hot and full-flavored. Renquest tipped his cup toward her before taking another sip. She raised her eyebrow in a way that said; *I told you so.*

"Not too bad," he said. "Well, Captain. What do you think we should do next?"

"I could use a donut," Brooks said without looking away from her coffee.

"Okay. But I meant regarding the case."

"I know," Brooks said.

Steam lofted from the steaming liquid hovering just below the cup's rim. The vapors pushed over the edge as he blew softly to cool the drink so he could take larger swallows, forcing the caffeine-infused water into his bloodstream faster. He took another sip. Still too hot.

"I want to visit the crime scenes of the other victims. And I want to talk to the first four. The ones still walking around."

"We already interviewed them. They remembered little about their attack. Those transcripts should be in the files back at the office."

Renquest glanced over at Brooks, who was now chewing the remnants of a granola bar. He hadn't remembered her buying one at the counter and assumed Brooks had the snack stashed in a pocket of her fatigue-style pants. She looked back at him, covering her mouth with her hand before she spoke.

"What? I told you I was hungry."

He shook his head and made a snorting sound from his nose. "Good, that should hold you over for a few hours. I want to get back to the office and gather the names and addresses of those four, along with the locations of the other three murder victims. There is one piece of advice I can give you. If you want not just to make detective, but to be a detective, it is this: always do the work yourself. Don't trust the other guy did everything right. Make sure of it yourself by talking to the witnesses and taking your own notes. Use that information to compare against what you already know. People's stories change with the passing of time. They remember things. They forget things. We can never have too much information."

"Wouldn't people, victims of crime that is, come forward if they remembered something that could help us catch the person who hurt them?"

"Wouldn't that be a wonderful world to live in? In the real world, many victims just want to put the nightmare behind them. They have a false belief that if they simply forget about it and move on, everything will be okay. When, in fact, that never happens when people suffer a traumatic event. Trauma is a demon that chases you forever. It is relentless and powerful. It's neither forgiving nor vengeful. And with time, it becomes a toxic cloud that shrouds a person. Hiding them from the truth. Keeping them from the one thing that will help set them free."

Brooks looked out beyond the street in front of them. Past the cars and people. "That's depressing."

"Doesn't make it any less true," Renquest said. "So, what do you say we exorcise some demons?"

The young captain bit down on the corner of her bottom lip before taking the last sip of her coffee. She then tossed the empty cup into the nearest recycling bin. "Let's get the bastard."

Renquest gave his partner a nod as the pair climbed into the cruiser and started the short drive back to the station.

When Renquest arrived at his office, he noticed two large envelopes perched on the corner of his desk. After placing his coffee down next to the phone, he circled the desk, grabbing the two items as he passed and plopped down into his chair. He leaned back while grabbing his reading glasses out of his front jacket pocket and opened the first packet. As he pulled the contents from the sleeve, red lettering appeared that read *Coroner's Report*. He glanced at his wristwatch, wondering how he could have received the results so quickly. They had just been with Doc Johansen a few hours before. While he knew she could've finished the cut; he didn't think she'd had time to finish the preliminary results.

He flipped past the cover sheet and noticed the first page contained only basic information about the victim. Approximate age, weight, race, sex, and other physical descriptions gathered from a cursory examination. The second page comprised a description of the organs along with their conditions and weights. He knew all the information, as he and Brooks had attended the autopsy the previous day. His fingers flipped to the third page. That is where things got a little more interesting.

Listed at the top of the page was a photograph of a fingerprint card. The coroner attached the card to the report for identification confirmation. When they found the victim, he hadn't been dead for long. Eight or nine hours at most. Almost all those hours at night and out of the sun. Something that helped keep the body in good condition. He pulled the sheet of paper closer to his face, examining the fingerprints. Right away, he noticed pronounced ridges, meaning the victim likely didn't have a job requiring a lot of manual labor. Ridges wear down and smooth out on fingers used by bricklayers, construction workers, and in other fields requiring the person to handle rough or abrasive surfaces. He could even make out some whorls and arches that make each fingerprint unique to an individual. No scars or other abnormalities provided reassurance that he was correct in his guess about the victim's career field.

He saw nothing else in the fingerprints to be helpful, so his focus turned to the next section of the report. The identity section. The name in the box was Steven Pratt. A thirty-two-year-old Caucasian male. Seventy inches tall with blonde hair and blue eyes. Johansen noted no tattoos or body marks and no signs of intravenous drug use. There was also no mention of any major scars or signs of prior trauma. People who die violently often have signs on their bodies that show a hard life. Murders are rarely random in real life, and many murder victims grew up in violent households or now find themselves in violent relationships. There is a direct correlation between murder and prior violence. This man showed no signs of either.

He'd been focusing so hard on the details of the report that he'd failed to notice Dr. Johansen had stepped into his office and was watching him as he scoured her report for more information. She gained his attention with a slight clearing of her throat.

"Hey, Doc," he said as he looked up. "Sorry, I didn't see you there. You want to come in and have a cup of coffee?"

"Thanks, but I should get back to the office."

"What brings you here today?" he asked.

"I needed to talk to Chief McNally about something and wanted to make sure you got my preliminary findings," she said.

"That was about as fast a turnaround as I have ever seen."

"I have a couple of interns who listen in another room as I perform the autopsy and write the reports in almost real time. It was one program I instituted once appointed medical examiner."

"It seems to work out well," Renquest said.

"The quicker I can get the police information, the quicker you all can solve the case. We really do function as a team here."

"I'm seeing that."

"It was all part of Jon's," she paused at the slip of informality. "I mean Chief McNally's promise to the community when he became chief of police."

Renquest noticed, but remained silent. But it was the second time it had caught his attention in the last two days. He shrugged it off to overactive instincts and the natural curiosity of being a cop.

"I see you pinned down an ID from the prints."

"Apparently, our vic had an arrest for something in the past and was already in the system."

"Do you have any idea what it was about?"

"Nope. I just ID the body. The rest is for the detectives," she said.

"Well, I appreciate the heads-up. It should help a lot."

"I'll let you know when I have more to share."

Renquest pushed back from his desk and stood before she could leave. "Hey, Doc."

"Yeah."

"Do you think you could do me one more favor?"

"Well, I haven't done one for you yet. What I've done is called my job," she said.

The veteran detective chuckled. "Good point. Anyway, I was wondering if you could give the lab over in Manassas a call. They have the evidence I submitted, and a DNA profile would be helpful."

"Those tests usually take about two weeks to get back. The new governor's budgetary restraints are causing a backlog at the lab." Her face grimaced as she spoke the word governor. It was clear to Renquest she was no fan. He would be sure to keep his voting habits to himself.

"That's okay. I thought it might be worth a shot."

She smiled. "I'll see what I can do."

She said goodbye and disappeared into the hall.

He stood at his desk, thinking about the woman who had just left and the file on his desk. With a shake of his head, he sat back down and picked up the phone.

"Brooks. I need you to come to my office. I have a task for you."

The handset clicked as he placed it back on the cradle. A moment later, Brooks stepped through his office door.

Chapter 7

Brooks was wearing running pants and a t-shirt under a tank top. The fabric covering her shoulders was wet from the water dripping off her hair, and she appeared out of breath.

"What can I do for you, Detective?" she asked as she wiped sweat from her forehead with a towel.

"AC broke in your office?"

"Funny. No, I went for a quick run during my lunch break. Three miles! Got to keep meeting these physical standards."

"Sounds awful. I don't think I could run from here to the coffeepot if my life depended on it."

"Well, that's why we young guns are here. To make sure all the Johnny Knuckleheads don't get away from the old timers."

They both laughed, though Renquest forced most of his. Age was a sore spot for him, as his old partner, Paul Dodge, used to razz him about it all the time. But he didn't hold it against Brooks. In fact, he was glad she was comfortable enough to joke with him so quickly. Partnerships take time to develop. It's a long period of feeling someone out. Learning their habits. Testing limits. If she was already at this stage, he felt some trust had already seeped in between the two of them. He wasn't sure he'd ever find a replacement for Dodge, but she might fill some of the void left by his best friend's departure.

"Once you get cleaned up, I need you to run an NCIC on Steven Pratt. DOB of April fourth, nineteen-ninety."

NCIC stands for the National Criminal Information Center. It's the home of CJIS, which maintains the criminal records database for the FBI. Arrests, driving records, and vehicle information are all available in its cloud system. The system allows for updates to prosecutorial and sentencing information as the defendant's case progresses. The system assigns a unique identifying number to every person arrested, and it keeps the associated data indefinitely. A simple name and date of birth search will pull up people associated with those identifiers. Then, the requester can search the database for criminal histories by utilizing the unique number attached to each person. As good as it was, Renquest was aware of the system's limitations. Participation by individual departments was voluntary. Not everyone reported every arrest. Some reported only serious felonies. Outside of the federal government, states maintained access for their departments. Each state had its own system that tied to NCIC, and state officials provided training for its users. Mistakes happened, and innocent people's information got added to the database. No system is perfect. But overall, it helped officers do their jobs more safely every day.

Brooks said she would run the name as soon as she showered and changed, then slipped out as quickly as she'd entered.

Renquest sat back at his desk and continued reviewing the coroner's report. He saw nothing else that piqued his interest and tossed the file onto his desk. The package landed hard and slid across the desktop, stopping after hitting the second envelope that'd waited patiently for his return. He'd been so focused on the coroner's report that the other file slipped his mind.

His chair squeaked as he leaned forward over his desk. He took the second file, then leaned back in his chair. The blade of his pocketknife ran down the edge of the envelope, its contents spilling out into his lap. Over twenty photos. He stared at the collage of pictures. Afraid that if he moved, the whole mess would end up on the floor. After a minute, he reached down and grabbed the first picture from the top of the pile. One hand raised it to eye level while his other hand slipped the reading glasses over the bridge of his nose. The first thing he noticed was that there were two individuals in the photo. One man and one woman. The man, who looked an average height, was wearing an all-black skintight suit. He couldn't tell if the suit was leather or some sort of polyurethane material. The resolution was poor because of the zooming effect used by the person who developed the photo. He stood at the end of the bed, a leather whip in his right hand. The woman sat perched at the foot of the bed, stripped naked. The person taking the picture was outside, positioned about three feet from the window through blinds, which were open but not raised. Between the quality of the photo and the half-open blinds, he couldn't get a clear look at either person's face in the photo.

His eyes turned to the remaining pictures resting in his lap. He examined them one by one. While the women in the shots seemed to change each time, it was clear the man in the photos remained the same. The same dark, tight outfit. Same height. Same complexion. Same scene. A brooding man standing over a subservient woman. One man and twenty-two different women.

He put the photos face down on his desk. The envelope they came in cantered on his right leg, close to falling to the floor if he moved too quickly. He picked it up and brought the rigid envelope to eye level, then tilted it slightly to reduce the glare from the overhead lights. There was no identifying information on the front. With a flip of his wrist, the envelope turned over. The back was also blank. No names or unique markers to hint at where the package came from. It showed nothing about who sent it. Leaving him to wonder why this mess landed on his desk.

Someone wanted him to see them. But only him, so it would seem.

He dumped the pictures back into the envelope. Then he opened the only drawer in his desk that had a lock, and he tossed the package in. Pushing it shut and turning the key that was already inserted in the lock. He then placed the key in his pants pocket. He felt it was best to keep the folder and its contents to himself until he figured out exactly what the whole thing meant. With that matter set aside until later, his attention returned to the murders. But he couldn't put the pictures out of his mind completely and found his attention wandering back. He needed to get out of the office for a while. Get his mind right.

As he rose from his seat, Detective Flaherty poked his head around the corner of the doorway.

"Detective," he said.

"Morning."

"I dropped off the evidence at the lab this morning. I told the tech we needed it ASAP."

"Good. What did he say?"

"What I expected. They are behind and will get to it as soon as they can."

"I had the coroner call over and see if she could light a fire under their asses," Renquest said. "I hope that will help move this along quicker."

"Good idea. The doc can be very persuasive when she wants to be," Flaherty said.

"So I gathered."

"Anything else you need from me?"

"As a matter of fact, there is," Renquest said.

Flaherty took one step from the doorway and into the room.

"Have you eaten lunch?" Renquest asked.

"What?"

"Did you eat lunch yet?" Renquest repeated.

The junior detective stood with a look of perplexity on his face. "I was going to go grab something right after I spoke to you. Why?"

"Where?"

"A little sushi place across the street."

Renquest reached around behind and grabbed his jacket off the back of his chair. "Sounds good. Want some company?"

The younger detective seemed to be thrown off by his boss's invitation to join him for a meal. He stood silently, waiting for Renquest's next move.

"Come on, I want to stop by and see if Brooks wants us to bring anything back for her."

Renquest held out his hand, gesturing to his detective to lead the way. The two men walked down the hall and stopped at the NCIC terminal room, where Brooks sat parked at a computer. She turned when she heard the two men approach.

"Oh, hey, boss. I'm running that search on Pratt. I should have a printout in a minute or two." She looked at the two of them. Renquest saw Flaherty shrug his shoulders.

"I'm gonna take Flaherty here out for lunch. You want us to bring you back anything from the sushi place?"

"No thanks. I prefer my fish cooked and with a big baked potato on the side." She turned back to the computer terminal and began typing again.

"Suit yourself," the older detective said.

The two men turned, and Flaherty led the way through some back halls until the pair ended up at a side exit used by courthouse employees to avoid the mass of people waiting at the security checkpoint near the public entrance.

Lunch was good, but not great. Renquest had the Dragon Roll and understood why Brooks was not excited about the menu options at *The Golden Teacup*. The owners put a lot of energy into the ambiance, which apparently left little attention for the food. Flaherty seemed to enjoy his meal, though he ended up getting General Tso's Chicken, which Renquest now felt was probably the better choice of the two meals. The two detectives ate in almost complete silence, only stopping to speak to the waiter when he came around to offer more water or soft drinks. The plan to get to know his junior detective better had been a bust. He paid the check, and the pair walked back to the station without saying a word.

Once back in his office, disappointed that his plan to glean information from Flaherty had bombed so miserably, he found Brooks and Sanchez waiting at the conference table. The two were discussing something and abruptly went quiet as their new boss entered the room. He pretended not to notice the change.

"Have a pleasant lunch?" Brooks asked.

Sanchez sat quietly. Not making eye contact with Renquest.

"It was a little disappointing, to be honest," Renquest said as he pulled out a chair across the table from his two officers. "Is that the criminal history report of our last vic?"

Before Brooks could answer, Sanchez cut her off, opting to break the news she had discovered.

"So, the latest vic, Samuel Pratt, a thirty-two-year-old male from here in Arlington County. One misdemeanor arrest for marijuana possession back in 2010."

"That would have put him around twenty-two at the time of the arrest?" Renquest looked directly at Brooks, avoiding Sanchez completely.

"Yes, Detective," Brooks barked out before her partner could interject again. "Pratt received deferred prosecution after he completed a substance abuse treatment program in six months."

Sanchez jumped in. "Six months seems quick for a drug addict to get clean."

Renquest eyed his lieutenant, who now appeared to wish he hadn't made the comment.

"Just because someone smokes weed doesn't make them a drug addict, Marco," Brooks said, looking at her new boss for reassurance.

The veteran detective said nothing, choosing to wait and see if his underlings finished jockeying for position at his side. Both officers remained silent, staring at him. Waiting for his response.

When he spoke again, his voice was calm and his tone reassuring. "Brooks is right. Smoking a blunt every now and again doesn't mean a person is an addict. It's been my experience that some of these treatment programs the courts and probation use are money farms for the counselors and psychologists who own the companies."

"What do you mean?" Brooks asked.

"Well, they have a contract with the county for services the court deems necessary. However, the treatment providers get paid based on numbers. Many of the folks referred to them by the courts do not need services and are simply recreational users. The providers make a small sum from the evaluation, but the real money is in prolonged treatment and counseling. The longer a person stays, the more the company can bill the government."

"I'm sure they aren't all that way," Brooks said.

"Probably not, but it's worth checking out. We may get some more information about the victim from the intake forms. We also need to run a check with the Bureau of Motor Vehicles and see if we can nail down an address. I would like to talk to friends and family about Pratt's daily routines."

Sanchez stood. "I'll do the BMV check."

"Good," Renquest said. "Brooks, which means you get to talk to the counseling people and see if they can give us anything that might be useful. And don't let them give you any of that HIPPA shit! The medical privacy act doesn't apply in a criminal investigation."

"They are going to say it does," Brooks said.

"Be stern and make them understand. I will get Johansen to get the records for us if they don't feel the cooperative desire to do their civic duty."

"Do you think the doc will go along with it?" Sanchez asked.

"Doesn't hurt to ask."

"That's not been my experience," Brooks said with a roll of her eyes.

"You let me worry about that. Both of you see what you can find out about Pratt." Renquest stood and turned, then paused and faced the two officers again. "One more thing. You report to me on this. No one else; and that includes the chief. If he wants to know how the investigation is going, he can come and ask me. Understood?"

Brooks nodded. Sanchez raised his hand and scratched his forehead, just below his dark black hairline. "Chief McNally won't like that."

Renquest ignored the comment and turned away. The pair left. He had set the wheels in motion to see who would break the rule. He hoped neither of them would go behind his back, but he needed to know whom he could trust. His money was on Sanchez. There wasn't enough time to play nice. Especially after Renquest knew the prick had talked to the chief after the trash incident. But he had chummed the water, and now all he had to do was wait for the sharks.

Chapter 8

The sun was beating down on him as he watched the people filing out the front doors of the treatment facility. *Sheep*, he thought to himself. They live a life full of deceit and degradation. Then, after their high-risk lives catch up to them, the taxpayers pay for the rakehells' mistakes. And it didn't end there. Oh, no. He was sure it was genetic. The infection passed on to the spawn of the unholy combination of drugs and sex. The blood-borne pathogen would infect their children. Some of the spawn overcame the affliction and learned to live normal lives, though he doubted they were happy. How could anyone be happy when they constantly fought off demons and the urge to be bad? He felt them nonstop. If it hadn't been for his work, he might also have given in to the powerful pull of the invaders in his blood. But *he* was stronger than most. He could take it. And there would soon be a cure. He just needed the right person with the right combination of pathogens and what he named the White Knight Cell.

The White Knight Cell was a white blood cell that contained high amounts of a specific disease-fighting material he discovered through his work. The cell would find the invading pathogens attached to the red blood cells. Like a lion stalking its prey, the White Knight would wait for just the right moment and then attack and devour the invader in nanoseconds. Killing its foe and ridding the system of the worst disease known to man. He had seen it work under his microscope. It was like an avenging angel striking down a wretched demon from hell. He even tried to take his discovery to the hospital to let them know he had a cure for the affliction that caused his mother to commit suicide and leave him alone in the world. A twelve-year-old boy.

No family. No friends. Nothing but heartache and pain.

But the doctors wouldn't listen to him. In fact, the only one who agreed to see him was the coroner. She was nice, but she dealt with the dead. He needed someone specializing in people still on this plane of existence. Someone with clout. If he could get ten minutes together in a room with that person, he could show them what he had found. A person with unlimited resources could take what he discovered and improve on it. Then mass-produce the cure and hand it out. Maybe in pill form or possibly in shots. They could start with these sheep standing around the front doors of the treatment center, smoking cigarettes, pretending to be something they weren't. On second thought, give it to the innocent first. Like a vaccine. These people dug their own graves.

Then he saw her. He thought she had made eye contact with him as she exited the building. She still had a glimmer of hope in her eyes. She smiled at the others as she passed. Then she turned and entered the alley. He started his car and pulled out onto the street. He tried to turn in after her, but a line of cars had lined up along the curb waiting for their disease-ridden families to come out. By the time another driver waved him in, he had lost her.

"Goddamn it!" he screamed. "Where the fuck did she go?"

His head flung from left to right. He had to find her. She could be the key to unlocking everything. Maybe she got into a car and left while he waited in the street? If he failed because of all the damn people back at the clinic who were incapable of controlling their desires, there would be hell to pay.

"Weaklings," he grumbled.

No, she couldn't have gotten past him. There was only one way out, and he surely would've noticed her. She still had to be in the alley, or maybe she had ducked through a back door into a business. He stopped the car and shut off the engine. His driver's window rolled down as he sat quietly, listening. It took a moment to zone out all the street traffic behind him, but with a little concentration, he quelled the background noise. Then he heard something. It sounded like a groan.

He opened the door and stepped out into the alley. The crunch of broken glass under his shoes sounded like exploding fireworks in his ears. Then he heard it again. He turned his head slightly and focused. Concentrating on where the sound came from. It must have been from in front of him, but he saw nothing. Just an old blue dumpster. Mounds of trash and rotting food spilled out from its open top. His gag reflex kicked in, forcing him to fight back the urge to vomit. His heart raced. Then he moved closer. Each foot carefully placed one in front of the other. He stopped short and peeked around the corner.

He found her. She was on her knees with a man's dick in her mouth. The sight shocked him so much—he froze. Unable to move. He had never seen that in real life. Only on television and in movies. He couldn't look away, though he knew he should've.

It took the couple only a few seconds to realize someone had seen the two of them. The man with his pants around his knees smacked the girl on the side of her face, knocking her to the ground. She landed on her back in a pile of garbage that some wild animal had rooted out during the night. She looked up at him. Utter horror spread across her face. The man quickly pulled his pants up and lunged at the man he thought was a peeping tom.

"What are you staring at, you freak? This ain't no peep show."

He didn't even see the punch coming. The hard knuckles on his right hand landed on the side of his face. Then tore like sandpaper as they skidded across his ear. He felt as if something tore his ear from his head. His head pounded and ears rang. Then his knees gave out, and he fell to the ground. The man stood over him, his pants still unzipped.

"You want to watch something, pervert? I'll give you something to watch."

As he looked up, trying to regain his senses, the guy reached into his pants and pulled it out, and began pissing on him. He dug his heels into the pavement, trying to get out of the way, but it was too late. The urine soaked into his shirt. And the smell. It reeked of ammonia. He was sure some got in his mouth, forcing him to gag.

The guy finished and zipped up his pants. He had a smile on his face as he turned back to the woman, who was now standing next to him, rubbing her cheek.

"Where are you going?" he said to her. "Get back down there and finish what you started, or I'll cut you off. For good this time. No one will sell to you in this town, and you'll have to go to DC and blow homeless guys for a hit off their used crack pipe." He glanced over at the man on the ground and smiled.

In that instant, he felt the blood in his veins warm. A rush of adrenaline surged through his body. His vision narrowed. All he could see was the man standing in front of him. He could see the man's lips moving, but there was no sound. Like a mime. A bottle touched his hand as he pushed himself up from the ground. Then something in him snapped. He didn't even remember picking up the broken bottle. The entire attack took less than ten seconds. When it was over, he stood there, staring at what he'd done. He glanced down at the woman now sitting against the dumpster—her mouth open in horror. Unable to make a sound. Blood spatter covered her face and clothes. The man who had just hit her lay on the ground. Blood spurted from his mouth like a fountain starved for water with every labored breath. He was dead in less than a minute.

The liquid he had taken so much time in the past to save and handle as a rare element spewed onto the ground from a gaping hole in the man's neck. Part of him wanted to fall to his knees and scoop up every drop. It was a finite resource. The scene was surreal. His muscles tightened as he found himself unable to move again. He didn't even notice the broken bottle still clutched in his right hand until the pain in his fingers from his tight grip on the bottle's neck started creeping up his arm.

The woman who sat crumpled on the ground managed enough composure to blurt out a few words. "What did you do!"

He looked at her and dropped the remains of the broken bottle to the ground, and ran back to his car. The engine was still running. He threw the transmission into reverse and pressed the accelerator. As the tires squawked and spun, rocks shot out from under the car. Some of which hit the side of the faded blue dumpster. He gazed over the hood of his car and saw the woman squeeze her body between the dumpster and the building's wall to shield her from the flying debris. The rear of his car slid into the street, which was now mostly empty, and the few addicts still smoking in front of the treatment facility paid little attention to him. Once all four wheels were in the street, he cranked the wheel to straighten it out and sped away. He made the first right he came to and then an immediate left. His eyes flashed in the rearview mirror, checking to see if anyone was following him. There were no red and blue lights closing in. He heard no sirens, and nothing around him caught his attention. Once he felt he was a safe distance from the alley, he slowed and pulled into a fast-food restaurant. He put the car in park and shut off the engine. His blood-covered hands shook.

The yellow arches out front meant there would be a bathroom he could use to clean up. He looked at his hands. Blood that settled in the areas surrounding his fingernails formed a crust and cracked when he bent his fingers. He reached down to wipe his hands on his pants, but quickly pulled them back. More blood smeared on his clothes would only draw more attention to him. His eyes darted around the car, searching for anything he could use to clean up a little before heading inside the restaurant. There was an old t-shirt lying on the passenger-side floorboard. He reached for it and then noticed the cap of a bottle sticking out from under the seat. His hand quickly snagged the shirt and wiggled the bottle free from its prison. Then he twisted the cap off and tossed it on the floor before emptying the remaining water in the bottle onto the shirt. The bottle fell to the floorboards, coming to rest next to its cap. His hands worked the cotton shirt back and forth until most of the blood was gone, except for the dried blood embedded in his nails. He looked in the rearview mirror. Blood dotted his face, which he wiped with the stained shirt.

Once finished, he stuffed the blood-soaked shirt under the driver's seat. His eyes scanned the parking lot for a spot away from the main entrance, but still a quick jaunt to the side entrance, nearest the bathrooms. Chain restaurants were all laid out the same. An entrance at the front by the counter where customers place their orders and another further down the side of the building. Sometimes a sign labeled the door as *Exit Only*, but you could pull the door open and enter the dining area. He had been to this restaurant a few times as a teen and knew the bathrooms were located just to the right of the side entrance. Ten strides max. No one paid attention to someone rushing to use the restroom. He imagined it was a common occurrence in a place that served fried and processed food as its only menu options. Not to mention the idea of someone being in gastrointestinal distress probably made people uncomfortable, forcing them to look away. A reminder of a time when they barely made it to the restroom before losing control of their bowels.

He found a parking spot near the dumpster. *How appropriate*, he thought. Once out of his car, he made it to the bathroom in short order. No one sitting inside gave him a second glance. He grabbed a handful of paper towels from the dispenser and wet half of them in the sink. Then he went into the stall, closing and locking the door behind him, and sat on the toilet. Not even bothering to make sure the seat was clean. His hands were shaking as he used the wet glob of paper to wipe the dried blood from his hands and arms. Once he finished cleaning his hands; he flushed the red-stained ball of tissue down the toilet.

He took a deep breath and opened the door, glancing in the mirror as he passed by. There was no blood on his face. His shirt was black and wouldn't show any red spots. The patrons seated when he came in had since left, and the restaurant was empty. Once back inside his car, he let out a sigh and rested his forehead on the steering wheel. He'd made a huge mistake. His emotions took control of him for the first time. It must be an infection of his blood. Had it gotten worse? Is that what caused him to react out of pure rage, then thrust that shard of glass into his attacker's neck? As he replayed the scene in his head, he thought about the girl. She could identify him. *Fuck.* She certainly saw his car. He needed to ditch it. Somewhere no one would find it. Then destroy it in a way that makes DNA retrieval impossible.

Fire. Fire was the answer. He needed to torch the car. Fire destroyed everything. If it burned hot enough, even the metal tags holding the vehicle identification number would melt. That's what he would do. He would take the car to a neighboring county and torch it. He could then walk a few miles and catch a bus home. But first, he would need some gas.

Chapter 9

With two out of three of his underlings out trying to dig up as much information as they could on victim number four, Renquest needed to find something to keep Flaherty busy and out of McNally's office. As he flipped through the other six files on his desk, his phone buzzed. He recognized the number on the digital readout. The call was from inside the station. He thought about not answering because he hadn't talked to Flaherty yet, but decided that dodging his boss's calls after only two days on the job wasn't the best strategy for job security. Besides, he was already playing a game to secure his investigative independence from the politically appointed chief. He picked up the receiver.

"This is Renquest," he said.

"Bill, I need you to come to my office. There has been another murder," Chief McNally's voice boomed.

"Another victim? Do you think it's related?"

"I'll fill you in. Just get to my office ASAP."

Renquest clicked off the call and grabbed an extra loaded magazine out of the desk drawer and clicked it into the empty slot on his belt. Then he slid out from behind the desk and made his way down the hall to McNally's office. When he stepped through the door, he saw Detective Flaherty seated in a chair facing the chief's desk.

"Bill, come in. I hope you don't mind, but I asked Flaherty to join us," McNally said.

Renquest opened his hands in front of his chest and said, "You're the boss."

Flaherty didn't turn to acknowledge his superior; instead, he remained focused on the chief. The man in charge. The veteran detective pulled a second chair out and sat next to Flaherty.

"Now that both of my detectives are here," his eyes darting from Flaherty to Renquest, "I want to fill you in on the latest body."

"Are we sure it's a murder? Not a suicide or overdose of a junkie?" Renquest asked.

A glare from McNally made Renquest realize his summoning wasn't to ask questions, but to listen and keep his mouth shut.

"As I was saying, a 911 call came in about twenty minutes ago. A woman called screaming about a dead body in an alley downtown. She was hysterical, and it took dispatch a few minutes to calm her down enough to get a location."

Renquest nodded but said nothing. Flaherty remained motionless. Like a child in the principal's office.

Chief McNally continued, "Dispatch sent a unit to the scene to check out the complaint. The body was in an alley next to a local treatment facility in the Bailey's Crossroads neighborhood."

Flaherty finally spoke. "Hype central."

"That's right, Ryan. There is a huge heroin problem in the area, and that is the lone methadone treatment facility in Arlington County. So, there's a good chance this is a drug-related homicide and not related to our other problem."

"But you want us to make sure they aren't?" Renquest asked.

"Yes, it's a murder, and I want you to investigate. However, our priority is still the multiple-victim case. I want most of our attention and resources allocated to that case. Understood?"

Flaherty nodded.

McNally looked at Renquest next. "Detective?"

The new chief of detectives wasn't happy about anyone telling him how to run his investigation. Chief or not. This was the exact reason he had made it clear to Sanchez and Brooks about talking to the chief about the case. He was against treating one homicide as more important than another. All victims mattered, and he didn't place value on a murder victim's life because of how they lived. Once they were dead, none of that mattered anymore. How they lived was just a starting point for finding the killer. He needed to think quickly.

"Brooks and Sanchez are running down leads on the fourth victim. The coroner printed the vic and, when she ran them for an ID, they hit against a Samuel Pratt."

"Who is Samuel Pratt?" McNally asked.

"Nobody," Renquest answered. "He caught a charge for marijuana possession about fifteen years ago and received a deferred prosecution."

"So, we were talking about a college kid with a joint?" Flaherty asked.

"It couldn't have been much more than that. Hell, he wouldn't even catch a charge today," Renquest said.

Flaherty spoke up. "Probably shouldn't have caught one then."

Renquest turned to his junior detective and smiled. Strangely, the statement made him proud.

"Then what are Brooks and Sanchez looking for?" the chief asked, leaning forward, his hands crossed on top of the desk.

"It's the freshest lead we have. I don't know if there is a connection between Pratt and the other vics or not, but we need to look into it," Renquest said. "Sanchez is running the BMV records for a last known address. Brooks is going down to the treatment place where he did his court-ordered substance abuse evaluation to see if they'll share anything."

McNally pushed back from his desk and stood. "Where does that leave you and Ryan?"

Not one likes to be towered over; Renquest stood to match his boss's posture. Not wanting to be the only one still seated, Flaherty popped out of his chair and joined the two men.

"Well, I'm headed down to the coroner's office to speak with Johansen." He decided not to say why. There was no reason, at least not a good one, other than it was an old habit. Sometimes talking to the boss was like being on the witness stand in court. If you can give a yes or no answer, then do it. Make the other person be as specific as possible with their questions. When the chief didn't follow up, he continued, "Detective Flaherty here can go down and check out the stiff in the alley. If he finds anything of interest, he can call me and I'll head that way."

McNally hesitated before answering. "Ok. Sounds good, Bill. Just keep me up to date on what's happening in both cases."

Renquest couldn't help but think his boss's statement about both cases came as a warning. He would need to tread carefully and give McNally just enough to keep him happy. When the case broke his way, he could then fill him in on everything.

"Yes, sir," Renquest said, and then he turned to leave.

The aroma of a freshly brewed cup of coffee filled the hall. Flaherty was standing at the counter, putting two sugar packets into a coffee mug. He glanced at Renquest as he started pouring the steaming brew into the cup.

"Shouldn't you get that in a to-go cup?"

"Nah, I'm pretty good at drinking coffee and driving. Besides, at this time of day, the traffic should be fairly light. It shouldn't take over ten to fifteen minutes to get to the scene."

"Ryan," the chief detective said as he moved in closer to the table, grabbing a paper cup from a stack next to the coffeemaker. Flaherty, with the pot still in his hand, filled the cup to the brim. "When you go down to the scene today, I don't want you to mention the other case. Not to anyone. If someone asks questions about the other murders, tell them this is your assignment and you aren't working on the other cases."

Head tilted and eyes narrowed, the less experienced detective glared at his superior. His face showed disdain.

"Am I being pulled off the serial killer case?"

Renquest said nothing and took a sip from his steaming cup.

"I'm the only other detective in this department. Sanchez and Brooks are command staff and don't know the first thing about homicide investigations. I should lead that case. Not those two."

Coffee in hand, the man's boss leaned in. Only inches separated the two men. Their eyes locked. Only Renquest wasn't playing the staring game. He was asserting his dominance. When he finally spoke, his voice was confident, low, and its tone relayed his seriousness.

"First, I'm running the investigation into the other murders. Not Brooks, and certainly not Sanchez. Second, I have a career's worth of experience working homicides. I've seen things that would make most people lose their lunch. So, don't question my command decisions or my investigative experience. We will find the person responsible in both cases, and we will either put them in a courtroom or the ground. It's their choice."

Flaherty blinked. "You think there is a relationship between the cases, don't you?"

"I don't know. That's why I'm sending my only detective to investigate."

The young detective eased his posture. The space between the two men widened. Then he noticed the pot of coffee still gripped tight in his right hand, and he placed the carafe back on the hotplate.

"I'll head over there now."

"Thank you."

Flaherty shrugged his shoulders and turned away.

The show of disrespect by his junior officer annoyed the old detective.

"Detective."

The words echoed down the hall, causing Flaherty to stop. But he didn't turn to face his boss. Instead, tilting his head slightly to the left. Lending an ear to his superior. Another show of disrespect in Renquest's eyes. It was an old cop rule, but you look at superiors when they are speaking to you. A common courtesy. Especially when they outrank you. But being afraid the conversation had already attracted unwanted attention; he let the contempt being displayed by his underling slide. For the moment. Dealing with it later was the best option.

"You report to me and me alone. Do I make myself clear?" Renquest reiterated.

Flaherty said nothing. He stood silently. Then, after a moment, he simply turned his head and walked away. He was going to be a problem. Sanchez now seemed like the lesser of the two weights around his neck. Giving him only one member of his team he could trust to have his back. Not an ideal work environment when people are trying to kill you.

The encounter forced the detective to question his management style and decision to push people's buttons to learn more about their motivations and loyalties. He had used the same technique many times in the past, but he had been an old head in his previous department. Now he was the new guy. An outsider barking orders and taking a job several of them felt they deserved. He sipped from his cup and revisited the interaction with Flaherty. After five minutes, he shook off any remaining doubts still lingering. It had been a full commitment from the very beginning, and too late to change directions now. Finishing what he had started was his number-one priority. Not to mention, he still had Brooks. She was his ace in the hole for getting the others to fall in line. And if they solved this series of murders, they would earn their respect. The team might not like his methods, but the results would speak volumes.

Chapter 10

The visit to the coroner's office turned out to be a waste of time. Dr. Johansen's assistant said she had left by three that afternoon. It was common practice for her to do so when she had more than one cut to make in a day. The young, college-aged medical student said Johansen came in early, usually around five in the morning, on days with multiple examinations.

"Who was the other person she worked on?" Renquest asked, remembering only one body in the room when he and Brooks observed Pratt's autopsy.

"There are always others that need to be examined. Today it was a woman who died on the operating table at one of the local hospitals," the assistant said, never looking up from his book. "The hospital asked Doctor Johansen to perform an autopsy to determine if the surgical team could have taken steps to prevent the premature death. It's a way for the hospital to head off a medical malpractice lawsuit."

Renquest threw up his hands. "So, what did she find?"

"The woman died of cardiac arrest because of an unknown heart abnormality she apparently suffered with her entire life. There was nothing they could have done differently to save her."

"I meant my murder victim?"

The assistant didn't even try to hide his disdain, rolling his eyes at the number of questions he was being asked. "I'm working on that report right now. You should get the results tomorrow. Now, if you don't mind, I need to get back to work."

Knowing he wouldn't gain any insights into his victims' cause of death, Renquest thanked the young intern and left. As he sat in his car in the parking lot, with the engine running and air blasting, he looked at the pile of folders on the seat next to him. Margaret had taken it upon herself to make copies of each of the files so that he could have his own to take home and study. Margaret was a good egg. Smart and on the ball. He hoped to remember to buy her lunch one day this week. A gesture of appreciation. From all his years working for local government, he knew how undervalued support staff are by management. A mindset he fought hard to change at his old job. It was a fight he'd continue in this position as well. It would just have to wait until he solved the murders. Too many battles on too many fronts could leave his flank open to attack.

The engine in the Dodge Charger fired up, and he pulled out onto the street. He looked at his phone. His thumb pressed the icon that looked like a map with a pin on it. Before he left the office, he'd programmed in the location of the latest murder so that he could find his way if Flaherty needed him. Now, because the doc was out, he had some free time and figured he would swing by and check on his second in command.

The electronic map noted that the trip would take about fifteen minutes. He made it in ten. Once on the scene, he found a place to park and flashed his badge to the officer manning the perimeter before ducking under the crime scene tape stretched between a telephone pole and the front bumper of the police cruiser parked at the head of the alley.

As he made his way up the alley, toward the group of people gathered next to a blue dumpster, he stopped. His eyes scanned the pavement in front of his shoes. He could see two sets of black tire marks. He knelt and lifted a piece of trash that the wind had blown in his direction. There didn't appear to be any rubber residue, which meant that the tracks were not from a burnout left from someone applying the brake and pushing the accelerator, forcing the tires to break free and spin, dislodging heated pieces of rubber from the tires tread. The tracks lead back to the street. When he stood, he looked toward the other end of the alley. Past the blue dumpster. Past the cops and medical personnel. A building closed off the alley at the far end.

The whole alley was less than 150 feet long and not over 15 feet wide. One way in and one way out. If someone pulled into this tight alley, turning around would be impossible. They would have had to back out onto the street to leave. And Virginia is a two license plate state. Meaning, anyone standing to the left or right of the alley's entrance might have gotten a look at the plate.

Flaherty noticed his boss lingering in the alley and made his way over to where Renquest was standing.

"What are you doing here?"

"The doc left early for the day, so I figured I would come down and see how things were coming along."

The junior detective stared at his superior. A gleam of distrust in his eyes.

"Take it easy. I'm not here to rain on your parade. I just had nothing else going on at the moment."

Flaherty glared a little longer before relaxing his posture.

"Why don't you walk me through what you have so far." The pair walked up to the dumpster. What was originally a white sheet lay next to the blue steel container. Blood had soaked through the fabric around the head area, leaving a dark stain on it.

Not wanting to appear to take over the investigation, Renquest stood silent. After a long moment, he turned to his lead detective, who was staring at the red-stained sheet. "Detective?"

The sound of his title appeared to snap him out of his trancelike state. He turned to face his new boss. "Sorry. It's a mess under there. This is like nothing I've ever seen before."

"You haven't been to a murder scene before?" Renquest asked, trying not to sound shocked.

"No, I have. Only not like this one. Most of the cases Chief McNally assigned me to were drug overdoses and simple shootings. You know, one to the ticker and the guy died instantaneously. There wasn't much blood, and they still looked human," Flaherty said.

The veteran detective simply nodded. He remembered his first homicide. A prostitute. Her body lay on the ground, gutted from head to groin. Like the deer he used to see hanging from a tree as a kid at his uncle's hunting cabin in the mountains of western Virginia during hunting season. Dirt and yard clippings replaced the organs that used to occupy her body. It was the most putrid smelling soul shocking sight he'd ever seen. When they finally captured the person responsible for her gruesome death, he turned out to be a religious zealot who couldn't control his yearnings for lustful pleasures. So, he went out and found someone no one would miss. A 23-year-old prostitute who went by the name Angel. Her real name was Krissy. Krissy Taloman. A girl who fled an abusive home at fifteen and bounced in and out of relatives' houses until she was eighteen. Then, like so many young girls with no education and no money, Krissy found herself on the streets. She made money in the only way she knew how. On her back.

He hired her for sex and, when finished with her, felt so bad about his transgressions against God, he strangled her. Then, horrified at succumbing to his rage, he remembered the Lord's Prayer. Ashes to ashes, and dust to dust. So, he filled her empty cavity with dirt and various plant seeds and splayed her out in a secluded section of a city park to blossom and return to nature.

Of course, that never happened. A poor woman and her dog stumbled upon the scene a few days later. Scavengers ravaged the body over the long winter nights. It was a scene straight out of a horror movie. Some nights as he lies in bed trying to sleep, he can still smell the putrid odor of decaying flesh.

"Put all that aside. It helps not to think of them as people at first."

"But they are people," Flaherty snapped back.

"Sadly, they are. But if you want to work homicides, you must have a coping mechanism. I see a number."

"A number? What do you mean, a number?

"This is number one hundred and forty-three." The words came out so nonchalantly, even he thought it sounded cold.

"One hundred and forty-three what?"

"A hundred and forty-three victims."

"You have worked on almost a hundred and fifty homicides? Jesus! How do you not eat your gun?"

"Because it's just a number," he said, bending down to pull the sheet back. "It's the other number that keeps me awake at night."

"Other number? What other number?" Flaherty asked as he knelt beside his boss.

"Fourteen."

His companion stared at him while he looked at the face of the dead man under the sheet.

"Fourteen cases I couldn't solve," Renquest said.

"Seems like a pretty good clearance rate to me."

Renquest ignored the comment because those fourteen cases had always been a sticking point for him. It wasn't about the clearance rates. It was about justice. Those cases symbolized the denial of justice to fourteen of his fellow citizens. And that is what they paid him for. It was his sole reason for being. His purpose in life.

The man's face was gray, and his eyes had sunk deep into their sockets. The blood loss was massive. Based on the size of the pool surrounding the head, two things happened. One, whatever pierced his neck must have severed the carotid artery, causing a quick and massive loss of blood. Two—death was not instantaneous. His heart continued to beat for at least a minute after the initial blow. He would know more after the coroner set the time of death.

"Tell me what you see?"

His junior detective stood, then walked the perimeter of the crime scene. First, he examined the body, followed by the surrounding area by the dumpster. He knelt and stood. Several times. Renquest wasn't sure if it was for any legitimate reason or because he thought that's what he was supposed to do. Either way, the veteran detective let his charge complete his rounds. Waiting patiently for his assessment. When Flaherty appeared to be finished, he returned upright.

"So, tell me what you see."

"It looks like..."

Renquest cut him off. "Tell me what you see. Not what you think. That comes later. After we have all the evidence."

A little shaken by the interruption, Flaherty continued. "We have a dead male. Likely cause of death: a stab wound to the throat."

"What else?"

"The knuckles on his right hand show signs of bruising."

"Good. What else?"

"No sign of the body being dragged. So, whoever killed him did not hide what he'd done."

Renquest said nothing.

After a moment of no response from his boss, the young detective continued. "I saw some tire marks down at the head of the alley. Loose gravel seems to show someone peeled out of here in a hurry."

"Anything else?"

Flaherty's head turned first left, then right. He examined the body once more. Satisfied that he had covered everything, he shrugged his shoulders and said, "No."

"What about his pants?" Renquest said.

Flaherty, obviously surprised by the question, bent at the waist and examined the dead man's waistline. He scanned them from head to toe and then back again. Satisfied that he had missed nothing, he stood straight and heaved his shoulders.

Renquest's outstretched finger pointed directly at the victim's waistline. "His zipper is down."

The befuddled detective immediately went into defensive mode. "Maybe he was taking a piss behind the dumpster and someone cut his throat and robbed him."

Renquest took a deep breath through his nose. "Do you smell that?"

Flaherty shot a glance at his superior and took in a snort of air. "Smells like trash."

"Exactly."

"It's a fucking dumpster."

Renquest looked at his underling, who appeared to be growing more annoyed by the second. "It doesn't smell like piss."

Flaherty froze and then took another deep breath.

"And do you see a wet spot anywhere near the body?"

"No."

"So, why else would someone be behind a dumpster, next to a drug treatment facility, with his pants unzipped?"

The young detective shook his head. "He was getting a blowjob."

"That would be my guess."

"From whom?"

"That's the million-dollar question. Find that person, and then we will have something."

"Where would we even start?" Flaherty asked. His head turned, looking in all directions. "It's a goddamn alley."

"If it were me, I'd start at the treatment center on the corner." His thumb hitched over his shoulder. "Tricks for drugs. One of the oldest forms of payment in the books."

"*Those people* will not cooperate. They care more about the people using drugs and breaking the law than they do about helping the cops."

Renquest nodded. "That's true. It's their job."

"Some fucking job. Bleeding heart liberals. They will pull some privacy bullshit and tell me to leave."

"Who said anything about asking the staff?" He gave his partner for the day the side-eye. "When I pulled up, there was a group outside the door, standing around smoking. Someone will know who hangs out after class and trades sex for drugs."

Flaherty looked toward the street. Pretending as if he could see the actual treatment center that was two storefronts down from the alley's entrance. He looked back at Renquest, nodded and shoved his hands in his pockets. "What are you going to do now?"

"I'm gonna get a cup of coffee," Renquest said.

With that, the sandy-haired veteran detective began the short walk back to his car. As he turned the corner and ducked under the tape, he noticed the unmistakable white van belonging to the coroner's office pulling up. The patrol officer lifted the yellow tape high above his head, allowing the body hauler to drive under. At one point, the tape hung up on the vehicle's antenna, forcing the officer to yell at the driver to stop so that he could untangle the tape barrier from the metal rod.

Once finished, the frustrated officer ushered the van through. The driver stopped short of the alley and next to the curb where Renquest stood. The driver's door opened, and Doctor Johansen stepped out. Her brown hair twitched in the light breeze. She quickly pulled it back into a ponytail and tied it off with a flip of her fingers. A quick glance in the exterior door mirror before she circled around to the back of the vehicle.

Standing a few feet back from the curb, he watched Johansen as she dug around in the back of the van. Again, he noticed she was an attractive woman. He waited until she took a step back out and closed the doors—her right hand grasping a black medical bag. The type that doctors on television in the fifties used to carry. Oblong, with a rounded top and two handles for easy lifting. A camera dangled from her left hand. The carry strap looped around her wrist, allowing the expensive piece of equipment to dangle freely, swaying left to right as she walked toward him.

"Need any help?" he asked, immediately wishing he could shove the words back into his mouth. She was a capable professional woman. Not in need of a man's help.

She smiled. "Detective. I figured I might see you here."

"I was in the area," he said. "But I thought you finished for the day, Doc."

A laugh blurted from her mouth, followed by a smirk. "I had just finished pouring a tall glass of wine. A delightful meal of freshly steamed vegetables sauteed in garlic and butter, paired with chicken breast cooked in a lemon reduction. It was going to be an early dinner, followed by a good book in bed."

"Sounds like you had it all planned out."

"Yeah. Planned out." Her voice carried a hint of resentment at being forced to miss much-needed downtime. "So, why don't you tell me what you got, so I can finish here and get back in time for a few hours' sleep before I have to wake up tomorrow?"

Renquest gestured toward the alley, holding out his hand. A chivalrous offer to help with the medical bag.

"Thanks, but I've got it. After twenty years, you get used to carrying this around," she said, hoisting the bag up past her waist. "Besides, you looked like you were ready to leave. I wouldn't want to keep you from anything else you need to do."

He tipped one shoulder, tilting his head to the side. "I was just going to get a cup of coffee."

"Coffee sounds wonderful."

"Cream and sugar?"

Without breaking stride or making eye contact, she said, "Black, one sugar."

Renquest nodded. "One coffee coming up."

The pair had almost made it back to the dumpster before he turned back toward the end of the alley and his car. Flaherty caught sight of him and waved a hand in the air to get his attention. Renquest raised his arm, patting the air, signaling he would be over in a minute, and continued around the corner to the cop standing guard at the perimeter.

"Hey, where can a guy get a good cup of joe around here?"

The uniformed cop pointed over his shoulder with his thumb. Renquest looked past the officer, down the sidewalk, and saw a folding sign propped up. On its face, written in different colored chalk, it boasted of freshly brewed coffee. He thanked the officer and, within fifteen minutes, was back at the murder scene with a cup of coffee in each hand.

Chapter 11

Renquest saw Flaherty eyeing him as he approached the scene. For the third time.

"I thought you were leaving?"

"I said I was going to get a cup of coffee. Now I'm back." He was watching Johansen work the body but directing his comments to the junior detective. "If there's nothing new, why don't you see what you can get from the treatment staff?"

"I thought you said to talk to the hopheads outside?"

"Talk to them all. Just do it now, please."

Flaherty's eyebrows parsed, then he looked over at the Johansen before heading down the alley toward the clinic.

"Not going to make many friends with that bedside manner," Johansen quipped.

"Good thing I'm not here to swap spit in the shower."

Done with her initial examination, the blonde, leggy doctor rose next to the veteran detective. "Being in charge is a bitch."

"He is a capable investigator. But he needs some work to be a good detective." He handed her the coffee with his left hand. "You about done here, Doc?"

She blew the steam off the top of the cup. "Yep. I have an intern coming down to take the van and the body back to the office."

"How are you going to get home?"

"I figured you could give me a ride?"

The old detective wasn't sure what to make of the request. Did she want a ride home, or was there more to it? So, he did what he always does in situations he isn't sure about. He asked a question. "If you want, we could stop and get some dinner? You mentioned something about yours being ruined."

Johansen smiled. "That would be nice. I should be ready as soon as that intern gets here."

"I'm gonna check on Flaherty. Come find me when you are done," he said as he began walking away. His mind turned with ideas about what to talk about while they ate. He was never very good at this part. Maybe she wasn't either. He looked back over his shoulder. No way a woman looking like that was bad at anything. He shook his head and turned the corner toward the clinic.

It had only taken the intern, the same one Renquest had spoken with earlier that day, about ten minutes to reach the scene. He arrived in a red and black taxi. Johansen met them on the other side of the taped-off barrier. She helped her medical student load the body into the van, then disappeared into the back with the body. She emerged a few minutes later, minus the lab coat and protective gear, wearing exactly what she had shown up to the crime scene in. Only this time, she was carrying a purse instead of a medical bag.

"Ready?" she asked.

"Just waiting on you," he said jokingly as the whole transaction from the intern's arrival to her appearance from the van took less than fifteen minutes. "Any place in particular you want to eat?"

"How about Italian?"

"It's your town," he said as he opened the passenger door to his car. Johansen slid in. He closed the door once she was inside, then he circled around the rear of the vehicle, piling through the open driver's door. "Where to?"

"Head back toward downtown. It's a few blocks from the courthouse."

Putting the car in gear, he maneuvered a three-point turn, then headed in the opposite direction. Johansen and he rode in relative silence for most of the trip. She spoke only to give him shortcut directions to help avoid some of the heavy rush-hour traffic settling in. He used the time to call Brooks and see if there were any developments with Samuel Pratt's case. The call went to voicemail, so he left a brief message directing her to call him later that evening with any updates.

As he ended the call, the restaurant came into view. He found a parking space opposite the restaurant on the other side of the street. The two got out of the car, then jaywalked across the street. The waiters knew Johansen by name and took them to an empty booth immediately.

"Been here before?"

"Once or twice."

Johansen ordered a glass of Chardonnay and Renquest a local cider. Both of their glasses were empty by the time the food came. Both looking at each other, wondering where this was going before ordering another drink. Renquest took some of the pressure off and tipped his glass to the server, who then glanced at Johansen, who nodded approvingly.

The food was good, served family-style and entirely too much for two people. Renquest had the server divide the leftovers into two boxes, but Johansen said she didn't want any as she still had the food from before the call sitting in her refrigerator. That was fine with him. He guessed Custus wouldn't mind some takeout when he got home.

The doc lived on the opposite side of town, and the drive would take a good half hour in late evening rush hour traffic. Uncomfortably full, the detective used the time to see if he could get a feel for the department, namely Chief McNally, from an outsider. Someone with no loyalty ties but a working relationship with the man in charge of the police department.

"So, how do you like being the coroner?" he asked. His eyes remained fixed on the road ahead of them.

"Why don't you ask me what you really want to know?" Her eyes were on him.

The question caught him off guard. He continued to stare at the road in front of the car. "What do you mean?"

Johansen let out a sound. Which sounded more like a snort and less like a laugh. "There is no Mr. Johansen. I mean, there used to be, but not for a long time."

Truth was, Renquest wasn't even thinking about that. He had noticed her outer beauty and the intellectual attractiveness of a professional woman surviving in a field dominated by men, but until she mentioned it, the thought never crossed his mind. Though her bringing up the topic moved the thought to the foreground of his mind.

"What about you? Is there a Madam Detective Renquest?"

"Officially, that would be Chief Detective Renquest. But no, I'm afraid it's just me and Custus."

"Custus?"

"My old hound dog. I got him from the police after he failed out of the bloodhound program. They couldn't find him a suitable home, and I couldn't let him go to the shelter, where they would euthanize him if nobody adopted him."

"That's sweet. How long have you been together?"

"About eleven years now. Honestly, I don't know what I would do without him."

She reached over and touched his arm. He flinched. An automatic response from being a cop for over twenty years. A scuffle often followed someone touching you as a cop. Few people reached out to shake a cop's hand. No one casually laid a hand on a cop's arm for no reason. She must have noticed because her hand pulled back almost as quickly as she made contact. There was a noticeable change in the vibe inside the car. He felt awkward, and she was no longer staring at him; instead, her face had turned toward the passenger door window. The silence made him want to talk. But the words escaped him.

Luckily, Johansen broke the silence of the car's interior. "What was it you wanted to ask me?"

His hands tightened around the steering wheel. "I wondered what your opinion of Chief McNally was. Professional to professional, of course."

Johansen turned back to face the side window. She said nothing for a moment, as if trying to organize her thoughts. Assembling the words so as not to say anything wrong. After a moment, she faced him.

"He's okay. I mean, there was a lot of suspicion throughout the community when the county council selected him for the position. Many people in the department weren't happy about it. I mean, an outsider coming in and taking over. It pissed off a lot of folks. Good cops. Some had been with the department for years and felt they deserved to occupy that chair."

"Wait. McNally wasn't a local guy from the force?"

"No, half of the county council wanted to draw from the force. The other half wanted to bring in fresh blood from the outside. Someone who wouldn't be beholden to anyone. Willing to make tough decisions and not swayed by certain members of the council's political agenda."

"Huh?"

Johansen twisted in the seat. She was now looking right at Renquest. Her legs tucked up underneath her. "What?"

"I had assumed McNally had come up through the ranks. But it makes sense of a lot of things I've picked up on in the office. Especially the three under my charge."

"Like what?" Johansen leaned back a touch. Creating some distance between the two.

"The hostility from some officers on his bringing me in from the outside. I mean, I expected some pushback, but a few of them have been outright rooting for me to fail. Now I know why."

"Turn right at the next light," she said.

He moved over into the turn lane and veered the car to the right, which was sharper than he had planned. He was not paying as much attention to the road as he should have been, and his passenger slid a little closer to him as the car rounded the corner.

"So, what do *you* think of the chief?" he asked again.

"He seems like a decent cop. He says all the right things at the county meetings."

"What about as a person?"

"Turn left on the next street," Johansen said.

He slowed this time before the turn. She didn't move an inch as the car swung around the corner. He remained quiet, waiting for her to respond.

"This is me, straight ahead."

He hadn't even noticed she had directed them into a cul-de-sac. Her house was a small, two-story brick house that sat at the end of the street. A post-Second World War home. Like many of the homes in the area, contractors built them for returning soldiers who had money from being overseas and a new government program providing $10,000 for a down payment on a new mortgage. Houses went up all around the country. Neighborhoods formed. Schools and parks followed. Grocery stores and gas stations popped up at the corners. The new neighborhoods became small, self-sustaining communities.

Johansen's home appeared to be the only original structure left. The neighboring houses were all craftsman-style monstrosities, declaring the wealth of their owners to all passersby.

"Last holdout?" he asked.

She shook her head. "They pay half a million to buy these old houses only to tear them down and build these McMansions. It's kind of sad, really."

He nodded. "There's a lot of history being erased."

"Yeah. For an area so steeped in keeping history alive, they do a terrible job of preserving it sometimes."

He hoped she would answer his question about his boss, but let it go for now. She pulled her legs out from under her and gathered her purse from the floorboard. She turned to face him again.

"Thank you for the dinner. Would you like to come in for a drink?"

As tempting as the offer was, he needed to get home. "I really need to get home to Custus. He's going to be dancing a jig if I don't get back soon to let him out."

"Poor boy. You need to get a walker for him," Johansen said.

"I know. I just haven't gotten around to it yet."

She leaned over and kissed him on the cheek before getting out and closing the door. Nobody said another word. She simply walked to the front door and entered, closing it behind her.

He had to admit—he liked the style of it. The encounter brought to mind a line a famous comedian once said, *Always leave them wanting more.* He sat for a minute, thinking about the conversation. He couldn't help but feel as if Johansen had gone out of her way not to answer his question about Chief McNally. It gnawed at him. It was a simple question. Either you liked the guy or you didn't. He's a nice guy, or he's an asshole. Why not just say it? Unless.,.

He spun the car around in the cul-de-sac and headed back downtown. Custus would have to wait a little longer.

Chapter 12

By the time Renquest arrived home, Custus was lying next to the door. A small pool of water beside him. The old dog slowly got up, his head hung and ears lay back.

He looked down at his friend and patted him on the head. "It's okay, buddy. It's my fault. I should have come home first to let you out."

Custus' tail wagged a little, and he followed his master into the kitchen, where he grabbed some paper towels and tossed them down on the wet spot by the front door. "Thanks for not shitting on the floor."

The dog's nose nudged his arm as he finished wiping up the urine. He tossed the soggy paper towels into the trash. Hooked the leash onto the collar around his friend's neck and led him outside. As much as he wanted to get back inside to dig into the reason he had been late getting home, he wanted to let Custus take his time and be a dog for a few minutes. Being locked up in that condo must have been hard for him. Renquest had installed a pet door in the old house, allowing the dog to let himself out into the backyard whenever he wanted. He never worried if he had to work late, or his old partner, Paul Dodge, got himself into a spot of trouble and the night drug on into the morning. Thinking about it made him slightly homesick. After a few minutes, Custus finished his business and looked up, telling his owner he was done and ready to go back in to lie down.

After disposing of the waste in the dumpster, the two made their way back upstairs. The old dog made his way straight to the bedroom, where he plopped down on the oversized, round pet mattress. Renquest grabbed the file off the kitchen counter. Popped the cap off a cold beer and eased into the recliner. He took a pull from the bottle and placed it on the end table next to him. A file splayed open across his lap.

The pictures stared back at him. They all comprised the subject. A man, a woman, and a room. Someone outside took the photos, possibly from across the street. Peering in from a window of an adjacent building or a car parked along the street. Casually snapping photos of what appeared to be two consenting adults engaged in sexual activity. The man donned a mask in each photo. The woman in a submissive pose on the bed or floor. Kneeling. Looking up at her partner. He flipped through the stack of color prints. The room never changed. The angle of the camera remained relatively the same. Almost as if the shooter used a tripod but never took it down or moved it out of its hiding place. Leaving it for the next round of photo opportunities.

He didn't recognize any of the women. He hadn't guessed he would, having been in town for less than a week. But the man. There was something familiar about him. His posture. The way he towered over the women in the room. A command presence. One he had seen in his old partner, Paul Dodge, frequently. Born from years of service in the military. Reinforced in a quasi-military style environment after service. Something law enforcement and the prison system prided themselves on. Since whoever took the pictures sent them to him, he assumed the man in the pictures was a cop. Most likely from his department. And the way Johansen went out of her way to not answer his question about Chief McNally's personal life but spoke at length about resentment from others in the department about his being hired, led him to believe the man in the photos was his new boss, Chief McNally.

It wasn't a long shot, nor was it uncommon for men of power to have kinks. Many high-ranking officials, businesspeople, and billionaires get exposed for things they enjoy in the sanctum of their own bedrooms. It wasn't illegal. Some would say the behavior was immoral, but as a cop, he wasn't in the business of morality. That was a matter for the soul savers and Sunday morning televangelists. Kinky sex wasn't something he would partake in, but if both people were willing participants, he found no actual harm in cosplay.

As a cop, he also understood that the public would see it much differently.

Something like this hitting the papers could end a police officer's career. The headlines would be salacious, and reporters would camp out on his front lawn, fighting for a sound bite. It was a dangerous game. One he didn't wish on his worst enemy.

His thoughts wondered. He wondered if he should've opened the file propped on his lap. He had no evidence of a crime, and as far as he could tell, everything appeared consensual. Yet someone felt strongly enough about what was in those pictures to get the file to him. Only a person with access and the ability to roam freely in the station could have placed the file on his desk unnoticed. An inside job meant to sully the reputation of one of its members. The man who had hired him. Chief McNally. He wasn't sure how he knew the man in the photos was his boss, but it all fit. The timing. The motive. Bringing in an outsider for the new Chief Detective position. An outsider isn't an enemy if they don't know what you've done. But at this moment, it was all just a gigantic jigsaw puzzle. Like someone had flipped the box over and dumped all the pieces onto a table too small to hold them. A big, jumbled mess. And all he could see were the inner pieces. When working a puzzle, you need to find all the corner and edge pieces. Puzzles are best put together from the outside in. If you try to start in the middle, you could jump to conclusions, get tunnel vision, and wreck any chance of keeping an open mind. Start broad and narrow down. That's the rule.

As he brushed his teeth, he wondered why someone would want to expose McNally in such a publicly humiliating way. Why not just approach the man with the file? Make a demand for his resignation, or they'll release the files to the press. Blackmail. It works. There is a reason it's still popular with politicians and government workers holding security clearances. Blackmail puts people on the defensive. Then, when approached, they think about ways to protect themselves, when they should go on the offensive. And once they compromise, it gets harder to turn back.

But having worked in a medium-sized police department for most of his career, Renquest also understood the politics involved. Having served over two decades in one gave him insight into the political backstabbing that could go on, even amongst the rank and file. Add to that a leader brought in from the outside, and you've got yourself a pot ready to be stirred. This whole thing seemed personal to him. More about professional humiliation. Losing the job would just be the icing on the cake.

The room went dark with the flip of a switch. Custus groaned and sighed on the floor next to the bed. Renquest patted the mattress beside his leg, signaling to his friend that it was okay to climb on up. Custus jumped up and curled up at Renquest's feet. It had been a long day, and the tired detective closed his eyes and tried to clear his mind of the case and the photos. He soon faded off to sleep. Dreaming of his old house. His friend, Dodge, and he were having a glass of bourbon, hashing out the details of a case. He fell asleep with a smile stretched across his face.

The next morning, he took the quickest shower in the history of showers. He wasn't sure if he had even gotten all the right areas clean, so he rubbed a little extra deodorant in his armpits and dabbed a little extra cologne on his neck just in case. His epiphany the night before had given him a newfound sense of confidence. He wanted to get to the office first thing and get to work on the open cases.

First, he needed to check in with Brooks and find out how the records search went at the treatment facility. He still hoped the staff cooperated and had turned over any records they might still have regarding the fourth victim, Samuel Pratt. Next, he would have Sanchez brief him on any information he received from the search for state driving and vehicle registration records through VCIN, the Virginia Criminal Information Network. Hopefully, the search yielded a driver's license or an identification card for Pratt, listing a physical address. They needed to start somewhere, and having a point where they knew Pratt had been at a particular time in his life was as good a place as any.

An accident at Fairfax Drive and 10th Street North slowed the drive to work. A compact car tried to turn left in front of a dump truck loaded with construction debris. Everyone looked to be free of injuries, but the poor compact car, designed for gas mileage instead of impact resistance, wouldn't be seeing the pavement again. Patrol officers were on the scene directing rubbernecking drivers past the pile of twisted metal. He could hear the sirens of an ambulance echoing between the buildings. The emergency vehicle was no doubt being hampered by the snarled traffic he had the displeasure of sitting in.

After waiting his turn to negotiate the disabled vehicles, it was a straight shot to the office. He pulled into the garage a little past seven. The reception area was empty, and Margaret had not yet arrived. The halls were quiet. He could see Chief McNally's door was closed, and the windows were dark. He had beaten everyone to the office.

As he approached his office, he could see the morning sun spilling out into the hall through the open door. His ears picked up a noise from inside. Right as he stepped through the door, he noticed Brooks sitting at the conference table. There were two cups sitting in front of her. Steam lofted from the lidless mugs. She peered up from the table as he entered.

"Morning."

Renquest rolled his eyes and shook his head. "Do you ever sleep?"

She pushed a mug across the desk toward him. "Do you?"

"I'll get all the sleep I need when I'm dead," he said as he plucked the hot beverage from the tabletop and took a sip.

"All they had out front was artificial sweetener. So, I left it black."

"Black's fine," he said, pulling out a chair across from Brooks and taking a seat. "So, what did you find out at the county health department?"

She let out a sigh and shook her head. "Not much, I'm afraid. His counseling took place over ten years ago, and the county destroys the records after seven years. All they kept was his name, confidential file number, and court case number."

The chair squeaked as he leaned into it. "Do you think there is anything to glean from tracking down the court file? I mean, there could be some contact information and reports, or notes, from the probation officer assigned to the case."

"He wouldn't have met with a probation officer. If the judge had received no negative reports from the treatment center and he had completed his sessions on time, probation wouldn't be involved in the case. And honestly, after talking to one counselor, it sounded like Pratt received a deferred sentence because he wasn't an addict. He would have taken a few classes and completed some homework centered on a better decision-making process and given a completion certificate," Brooks said.

"Is that a common practice for a drug arrest here?"

"It all depends on the amount of drugs possessed. I wasn't on the force back then, but I recall there were a few officers who liked to run up their numbers by making questionable arrests."

"What do you mean?"

Brooks took a sip of her coffee. "Back then, the department liked to give out personal recognition to line staff who were putting in the work. One way they accomplished this was by highlighting and rewarding collars."

"Personal incentive to write as many tickets, or make as many arrests as possible in a particular time period," Renquest said.

"Exactly," Brooks answered. "I heard tell of a few officers using shake to put them ahead in the race for personal glory."

Renquest rolled his eyes. He hated the term shake. It was a bullshit charge cops used to tow a vehicle they knew they would find something in when inventorying the contents of the car for the *owner's* own protection.

"So, they make a stop on someone they know uses marijuana. During the stop, the officer *smells* the aroma of burned weed emanating from the open window."

"Exactly," Brooks said. "Then they get the person separated from the vehicle so they can investigate further."

"Next, they take a tiny brush, usually one of those plastic brushes that comes with your child's doll, and run it through the carpet on the floor mats onto a piece of paper," Renquest said.

"Dump the contents into the test kit and shake it up."

"If the water turns blue, it's off to the shoe," Renquest quipped.

Brooks cracked a smile. "The shoe?"

"Leave me the fuck alone. I'm old."

"Anyway," Brooks continued. "Judges were tired of their dockets loaded with bullshit shake charges and started giving out deferred prosecutions."

"No need to waste time or money on someone who doesn't need the attention," Renquest said. "Hold off on the court records for now. Let's see what Sanchez found from the license check."

The pair sat quietly for a few minutes. Sipping coffee and staring at the table. Doing anything to avoid making conversation. It wasn't long before Sanchez popped his head into the office.

"Boss, I'm gonna grab a cup of coffee and I'll be right back."

The two nodded at the same time.

Sanchez soon returned, carrying a manila file folder in his left hand. He squeezed into a chair next to Brooks and pushed the file out in front of him.

"Tell me you've got something."

The young officer grinned. He opened the folder, which contained a single piece of paper. He pulled out the sheet and slid it across the table to Renquest, who stared at it after donning his reading glasses.

"You've got an address," he said, wanting to sound complimentary. "Alright. Now we can do some actual police work."

"So, what's our play, boss?" Sanchez asked. A smirk crept across his face.

Renquest looked up at the whiteboard mounted on the wall behind the two officers. "A map."

Brooks and Sanchez shared a glance, then turned back to Renquest, who was still staring at the wall behind them. After a moment, Brooks turned to face the whiteboard and clapped her hands together. The sound of her hand hitting echoed throughout the small room.

"I can throw up a map of the county on the whiteboard using the projector. It should take only a few minutes."

"Good. Have plenty of dry-erase markers. We don't want to ruin this thing by scarring it up with permanent ones."

"On it," she said. "Then what?"

"Well, Sanchez and I are going to track down this address for Pratt. Maybe we can find something useful or talk to someone who knew him."

Sanchez nodded approvingly.

"What do you want me to do while you two are gone?"

Pushing himself out of the chair, he walked to his desk and grabbed the other files related to the murders and assaults in the case and tossed them on the table in front of Brooks.

"Once you have the map on the wall, I want you to mark every attack and all the murder locations, as well as the treatment facility and county health office. Add any personal addresses of the victims. Use whatever method you like. Just make sure that when anyone looks at the board, they should be able to decipher what is on it."

"Will do, boss."

Sanchez shot a glare at his fellow officer for the use of a term he must have felt he had coined. Renquest let it go. Better to let the two of them work out their personal issues. Besides, he kind of liked the name.

Chapter 13

Sanchez drove a marked pool car. It had a full complement of lights across the top and a laptop mounted between the driver and passenger compartments that officers could use during traffic stops to look up the driver's records and plate information. Within a few blocks of leaving the garage, Renquest noticed the mobile license plate reader attached to the trunk of the cruiser. Every few minutes, the shrieking alarm from the laptop would go off, alerting the pair to a potential match to a stolen or wanted vehicle. After the fourth alert, Sanchez tipped the lid of the in-car unit down, putting the computer into hibernation mode.

"Sorry about that, boss. It's annoying for people not used to it."

"I forgot how loud those alerts are. I'm not sure they could have picked a more horrible noise if they tried."

Sanchez snickered. "I know. And most of the time, it's total bullshit. A partial match to a plate from Maryland or DC reported stolen and thought to be in Virginia. Honestly, I'm not sure I have ever made an arrest based on an alert."

"Sometimes they are right," Renquest said, thinking back to a case he recently worked with his old partner, Paul Dodge. A patrol officer used his plate reader to locate a plate-swapping scam used by a serial killer to remain undetected. "Keep it on, just tone down the volume a bit."

Sanchez lifted the lid of the computer and, with a few taps of a button, he lowered the volume to a low roar.

Traffic was unusually light for that time of morning. Not wanting to show up at the address too early, forcing people awake with pounding on their door, Renquest had Sanchez pull into a donut shop so he could buy a cup of coffee and use the restroom. The young cop said he didn't want more coffee, as he'd cut down on his caffeine intake over the past year.

"I'll be right back," the veteran detective said with a nod.

Ten minutes later, the pair were back on the road, headed to the Yorktown neighborhood on the north side of town.

Sanchez took Glebe Road north through the Ballston area, passing within a few blocks of the detective's condo. Renquest thought about asking him to swing by so he could check on Custus, but decided against it. He could always make him stop on the way back after getting what they could from Pratt's listed address. Deep down, he knew the old dog would be fine for a few more hours. He just didn't want a repeat of the previous night. It wasn't about the mess, but more that he didn't want his oldest friend to feel bad about not being able to hold his bladder for an entire day. He saw the disappointment in the dog's eyes, which nearly broke him.

Five minutes later, they pulled up in front of a small brick house, not unlike the one Doctor Johansen lived in on the opposite side of Arlington. A small foreign model car sat under the carport next to the well-maintained yard. A "For Rent" sign donned the front yard with a phone number listed. Sanchez retrieved a pen from the cruiser. Renquest watched as he wrote the number down on the back of his hand.

"I forgot my pad. I'll write it down on some paper when we finish," he said after noticing the detective watching him.

Renquest smiled and turned his attention to the house in front of them. From where he stood, it was hard to tell if anyone was home. The three windows facing the street all had blinds pulled shut. The car looked as if it hadn't moved in months, based on the amount of dirt and debris lining the gap between the hood and the windshield. He bent over and peered inside the passenger window. Newspapers, junk mail, and empty fast-food soda cups filled the interior. He noticed the keys were in the ignition, cementing his belief that the car wasn't roadworthy and had sat unmoved for months.

The young cop sidled up next to his boss. "Well, that's disgusting."

"I've seen worse," Renquest said as he straightened and faced the house.

"Let's see if anyone is home."

The two men walked down the narrow path to the front door. Renquest climbed the three steps, rapped on the door with the back of his hand and stepped back to the level pathway. Sanchez had retreated to the corner of the house to cover their six if anyone tried to approach from the backyard around the corner of the house. *Good instincts,* Renquest said under his breath.

A few minutes passed, but no one came to the door. As he was about to step back up onto the stoop, he heard a frail voice trying to escape from the other side of the door. It was low and gravelly. He couldn't make out what the person was saying and moved to the first of the three steps, leaning in, trying to see if he could make out what was being said. Nothing.

"It's the police," he yelled at the solid wood door. Pulling his badge from the belt around his waist, and thrust it up to the peephole.

The sound of the security chain being pulled from the door rattled against the wood. Then he heard the deadbolt disengage. A moment later, a crack appeared in the jamb. A small, thin face, its cheeks caved in and punctuated with tobacco-stained teeth, peered through the gap between them. The much larger detective mustered his friendliest smile, then took a step back to seem less threatening.

Sanchez heard the door open and saw Renquest back up and make his way over to where he would have a better view of his partner and the old man standing in the now half-open door. Renquest signaled his backup to stay back by patting the air with his hand, low and at his side. He didn't want to draw too much attention to himself. The move worked because the thin-framed old man took one step out onto the porch.

"What do you want?" he asked. Eyes darted between the old cop and the younger one in uniform.

"Good morning, sir." Renquest saw no reason to approach until the old man felt more comfortable with their presence on his property. "My name is Detective Renquest, and this is my partner, Lieutenant Sanchez. We would like to ask you a few questions about one of your old tenants."

The frail, gray-haired man squinted and stared at Sanchez. The expression parked on his face led Renquest to believe the man had a past with law enforcement, making him suspicious of anyone in uniform. Or he didn't like Hispanics. Either way, the veteran detective wasn't about to play those games. He took two steps forward, and the old man's eyes darted back to him.

"Sir, we are here about one of your tenants."

"I don't have any tenants. Didn't you see the sign in the yard?"

"We saw the sign. That's why we're here. Your previous renter, Mr. Pratt. Do you remember him?"

The man tried to straighten up, but he had a permanent curvature of his spine that made him hunch forward. He puckered his lips and spat over the railing of the steps. A small trickle of foam stuck to his chin. Renquest couldn't help but stare at it as the old man refused to wipe it off.

"Is that the one that got himself dead over at that druggie park?"

"It is, sir. You didn't notice he hadn't been back in a couple of days?" Sanchez said as he took two steps closer to stand next to his partner.

The man glared at the lieutenant. Silent. Like he was deciding if the man in uniform was good enough to converse with him. When he finally spoke again, his gaze was back on Renquest.

"I pay little attention to the comings and goings, as long as they pay the rent on time."

It was a statement Renquest found hard to believe. He imagined the old man knew everyone on the street and watched out the window as his cash cows came and went about their days. Waiting to see if they brought a friend over, so he could try to get a few extra bucks if someone stayed the night. A genuine patriot in the community.

"Did he?" was all the detective asked.

Defiantly, the old man shook his head. "Nope, he was late last month. I told him if he was late again, I would kick his ass out and sell all his stuff to get the money he owed."

Sanchez stepped closer. His expression was one of disapproval. "Sir, that would be against the law."

The old man's head spun toward the young Hispanic officer. "It's in my house, so I can do with it whatever the hell I want."

Before Sanchez could move again, Renquest stuck his arm out. Blocking his junior partner from engaging any further. Sanchez glanced at his boss and then relaxed his pose and took one step back.

"Sir, we are going to need to see the room Mr. Pratt rented."

The request to examine the room clearly took the old man aback. Renquest noticed his posture straighten, and he could see the man's Adam's apple move up and then down the loose skin that made up his neck. But the man said nothing.

"Sir, I'm requesting your help in a murder investigation. Now, I can leave Lieutenant Sanchez here standing guard at your door while I'm gone, and you can wait outside until I get back in an hour or two. But it's turning into a hot day, and I don't think you want to stand out here in the sun and get all red and burned while I get a search warrant. Do you?"

The slender elderly man glared at Sanchez for a moment and then eyed Renquest. Then, he threw his hands in the air and mumbled something incoherent before opening the door and going inside. The two officers watched the door, waiting for the grumpy man to return. When he reappeared, he tossed a key to Renquest. It landed well short of his feet, in the grass to the right. Sanchez crossed behind his boss and picked the key out of the dying lawn.

"It's around the side," the man said, pointing toward the car in the driveway. "I'll know if anything is missing. So, you'd better leave well enough alone."

Before any words could escape Sanchez's lips, a nudge from his superior told him to let it go.

The old man followed the men around the corner before Renquest turned and said, "We'll let ourselves out." Sanchez continued along the path worn in the grass as his boss waited for the landlord to head back inside the house. Once out of sight, he met Sanchez at the side of the house and spotted a small stairwell and a door at the bottom that led to the basement. Renquest stepped aside and let the younger Sanchez lead the way. He inserted the key and with a quick twist of his wrist, the door swung open. Their eyes instantly watered as the pungent smell of ammonia pummeled their senses. The still air was now being sucked in their direction by the open door. Renquest shook off the attack. Sanchez wasn't faring so well. His eyes were full of tears. He used his shirt sleeve to keep the noxious smell from entering his nose.

"Why don't you step out and get some air?" Renquest said. "See if there are any masks and gloves in the cruiser's trunk. We're gonna need them."

Sanchez didn't need to be told twice. He bolted for the door to escape the smell. Renquest laughed to himself, then returned his attention to the small basement flat. As he took in his surroundings, the openness of the room struck him. Aside from the odor, the place was clean and organized. There were no dirty dishes in the sink. Someone swept the floor. No dust on any of the surfaces. It appeared Pratt took some pride in his personal space. Not the condition one would expect to find in the home of a rampant drug user.

As he ventured deeper, the brightness from the open door faded. The odor strengthened. The only light besides that from the open door was from two small windows at each end of the combined living and dining room. All the curtains were closed, keeping out any semblance of the outside world. He made his way to the far window, situated over a small, two-person dining table. With a whisk of his hand, he pushed the thin curtains to the side and slid the window open. The room instantly flooded with light as the window faced the morning sun.

Renquest spun around in time to see Sanchez step through the door. He was donning an N95 mask and black rubber gloves. He extended his hand and offered his boss a mask and a pair of matching gloves. Renquest took the gloves, but waved off the mask. The newly introduced fresh air had cut the odor to a tolerable level. Sanchez erred on the side of caution, deciding to remain masked.

"I'm a dog guy, but I believe our vic had a cat."

"Do you think it's still in here?" Sanchez asked as he scanned the floor for signs of the feline. "I mean, it's been a few days, and if it didn't have any food or water."

"I smell nothing but the litter box, but if it's in here, and it's alive, it will find us."

The young lieutenant lifted a couch cushion and peered into the gap. "And if the thing is dead?"

"Well, I suppose we will find it."

After a quick look around in the brightened surroundings, the two men split up. Renquest took the bedroom and bath, which were situated down a short hall, bounded by closets full of clothes. Storage space was obviously at a premium in the small rental. Pratt had jammed as many of his belongings into the cramped quarters as he could fit. The bedroom was small but used efficiently. A twin bed sat in the middle. The corners of the sheets creased at forty-five-degree angles. Renquest couldn't help but remember back to his time in the police academy, where they taught you to make your bunk on day one. Every corner a 45-degree angle. The top blanket tucked under the mattress so tightly that a quarter would bounce almost to the ceiling when dropped on the bed. There was a small closet at the foot of the bed. Shirts and jeans, neatly folded, lined its shelves. Rolled socks and boxers filled a basket on the floor. A small lamp sat on a nightstand, with a charging cord spread across its top. Nothing was out of place. Nothing seemed strange, except that nothing seemed strange or out of place.

Sanchez yelled from the other room. "I found the cat."

Renquest took one last look at the room before heading to see what he guessed was a dead cat. When he got to Sanchez's location, he was standing in front of a small enclave housing a stackable washer and dryer. In his arms, he was holding a white cat, which appeared to be in good health, but not too happy about the intrusion into its space.

"I think it's hungry." Sanchez said as he searched for something to feed the animal. "I think I saw some containers of cat food in the cupboard."

The older detective shook his head. "We will need to call animal control to come and get it."

"Really?"

"We can't leave it here with no food and water. Unless we find a family member to contact to come and get Fluffy and all his other possessions, the landlord upstairs will get to keep and sell everything."

A sour look took over Sanchez's face. "So, that old racist piece of shit gets to keep everything?"

Renquest nodded. "That's how I see it."

The cat, completely over being held by a stranger. Struggled against his captor and, with a twist of his body, broke free and fell to the floor. Its paws barely hit the ground as it raced for the open door and disappeared into the outside world. Sanchez turned to his boss.

"I think it heard you," he said as a smile curled on his lips.

"Problem solved," Renquest said and turned his attention back to the room. "Alright, we need to find anything that can give us information about anyone who might miss this guy. Family. An old girlfriend. Anyone he had extended contact with."

"I don't see any mail lying around. Do you think the old man is keeping it or tossing it in the trash after he goes through it looking for any checks or money?"

Renquest said nothing. He continued to search the apartment for anything that could help them gain a better insight into the last victim. After half an hour with no new leads, the pair left the basement, locking the door behind them. Renquest handed the key to Sanchez.

"Place the key into evidence. Then get the crime scene techs down here and have them seal the door."

"Yes, sir."

As Sanchez made for his cruiser, Renquest headed up the walk toward the front door. As he approached the steps, he remembered something about the rental unit. He didn't see a door or stairs leading from the upstairs unit to the basement.

He spun around and yelled at his partner. "Hey, make sure they also seal any doors they find that lead in from the rest of the house."

Sanchez, who was already on the radio with someone at the station, gave him a thumbs-up.

The detective then climbed the three steps and rapped on the door with his knuckles straight on. No retreating down the stairs this time, as intimidation was the purpose of this meeting.

Renquest stood silent, one hand near his holster and the other firmly on the tattered screen door to prevent it from flying open and smashing him in the face. Then the interior door swung inward, and the frail old man, his mouth open, ready to spew hatred at whomever was disturbing him for a second time, peered up at Renquest. A hint of fear was present in his eyes as he stared at the looming presence before him.

"Officer...," the old man stuttered.

Renquest wanted to mess with the old man. Put the fear of God into him. Slowly. Methodically. But he had things to do. Not to mention, the old man had rubbed him the wrong way from the second he and Sanchez first knocked on his door. Frankly, the old detective wasn't in the mood for nonsense.

"Shut up," he said in a condescending voice. "Go inside and get the mail you took from your former tenant."

The old man stammered as he tried to answer. "How dare you," cut off before he could finish his complaint.

"I don't want to hear it. You go inside and get any mail you haven't already tossed in the trash or burned. Bring it to me this fucking second. I'll check his and your bank accounts. If I find anything that causes me pause, I will come here and tear your house apart. I'll bring ten cruisers and the Postal Inspectors. If I can prove bank fraud, hell, I might even call the FBI."

The stoop fell silent, then the old man retreated into the house and returned with a small stack of envelopes, which Renquest snatched from his shaking hands. The old man stepped back, trying to close the door.

"Remember what I said," the detective shouted before he could get the door shut all the way.

Once back in the confines of the car, he looked at Sanchez, still with a hint of a smile on his face. He tossed the mail onto the back seat.

"Shut up," Renquest said.

Refusing to wipe the smile from his face, Sanchez started the car and pulled out into traffic. He jammed on the brakes, causing Renquest to nearly hit the dash, as he hadn't finished fastening his seatbelt. He looked at his partner, who was staring over the hood of the car at something on the road. It was a white cat. Sitting in the lane of traffic, staring at them. Refusing to budge. With a turn of the wheel, the lieutenant guided the cruiser around the obstinate feline. Renquest watched as they passed. The cat stared, ignoring everything but him. The detective watched in the mirror until the animal disappeared into the distance.

Chapter 14

After a few diversions because a small house fire forced the Arlington County fire department to close a few intersections, and a quick stop by his condo to let Custus outside to take care of his business, the pair made it back to the station in time for lunch. Flaherty and Brooks were waiting in his office. A colorful box sat in the middle of the conference table. Its top overflowing with tacos and fresh chips, filling the office with the smell of Mexican food.

The two had laid out paper napkins to use as plates along with several cans of soda. Brooks spoke first.

"We got some tacos. I hope that's alright."

Renquest sat down. Sanchez followed his lead, pulling out a chair beside him and scooting up to the table. Brooks dished out two tacos for everyone, and each of them grabbed a soda from the center of the table. No one said anything. They all ate and drank until all the food was gone.

After each of them wiped the desk in front of them and tossed the trash into a container, Flaherty broke the silence.

"What did you guys find out at Pratt's house?"

"The owner is a dick," Sanchez said.

Brooks and Flaherty looked at Sanchez, then at Renquest. Not sure how to respond to his comment.

Renquest jumped in. "He had an aversion to Sanchez's ancestral lineage."

Sanchez let out a roaring laugh. "And you served me tacos!"

Brooks continued to wipe the table down, even though it was clearly clean. Renquest knew the comment from her fellow officer made her uncomfortable, so he changed the subject.

"What we found was a very tidy apartment. Everything had a place. Everything was in its place. His bedsheets even had angled corners."

Brooks stopped wiping the table's surface and sat back in her chair. "You mean like they teach you in the military?"

Renquest nodded.

Flaherty said, "That's an avenue we haven't investigated. But I can look into it. I got a friend at Veterans Affairs in DC. I can make a quick call."

"Good idea," Renquest said, now staring at the whiteboard in front of him. "Tell me what I'm looking at."

Brooks stood and studied the board for a few seconds. Then she passed out a sheet of paper to each of the men at the table. The paper was a smaller version of what lay in front of them, except there was a notes section at the bottom and on the back. She then grabbed a laser pointer from a small box attached to the wall beside the whiteboard and turned it on. A little red dot flashed on the ceiling. Her hand directed the dot to the board and rested it on the first name, Donald Deevers.

"Who is Donald Deevers?" Renquest asked, even though he recognized the name from one of the murder files.

"Donald, or Don as his friends apparently called him, is a small-time thief and part-time drug hype. He has no permanent address and sort of couch-surfs with whoever will put up with him for a few days. It appears he wears out his welcome rather fast and moves frequently."

"Where does he stay when no one will let him stain their couch?" Renquest asked.

"The homeless shelter right next door," she said, pointing at the wall without windows across the room.

"What else?"

The red dot darted to the next section below Deevers' name.

"He has some mental health issues," Brooks said.

"What are we talking about here? Is he slow in the head or full-out Cybill?"

"Who is Cybill?" Sanchez said.

Renquest shook his head. Brooks smiled.

"He is somewhere in the middle. Not completely batshit crazy, but definitely not the brightest crayon in the box."

Request shifted his gaze to the next name on the list. "Who do we have next?"

Brooks spun and stepped back to make sure she wasn't blocking any of the team's view of the board. Her hand pointed, and a red dot appeared over the next name.

"This is the second victim, Cynthia Lewis."

Brooks told the same story about Lewis as she did about Deevers. Then she told the story two more times. Everything about the victims appeared to be similar. Starting with their transient lifestyles and drug use. While the first two victims favored heroin, the last two, Robert Harrington and Mary Chao, were meth users. But they all used a needle to inject their chosen poison. The last thing all four victims shared was that they lived. Unlike the next three.

The old detective leaned forward in his chair. He propped his elbows on the edge of the table. Hands clasped in front of his face. His eyes moved from one name on the board to the next. Then back again. Saying nothing, but his mouth moved ever so slightly. After a minute, he spoke.

"Ok. Now tell me about the dead ones."

Brooks handed the pointing device to Flaherty, who stood, and Brooks took a seat. Renquest liked the teamwork and felt a little proud that his personnel strategy might be working. Then he realized Flaherty was already talking, and he missed the opening. A little embarrassed, he focused on his lead detective, who was mid-sentence.

"...runners found the body in a small, wooded area west of Crystal City and the Pentagon. Ms. Youst was very similar to the previous vics. She was a drug user, though. And from what we can tell from her criminal history, her use appears to be more than recreational. She had multiple arrests for possession, disorderly conduct, and solicitation. Though I don't believe she was a prostitute. I looked up the solicitation charge, and it stemmed from an arrest for one of the possession busts. Apparently, she offered the cop a hand job if he let her go. So, I'm not sure that piece of info is relevant."

"I agree," Renquest said. "Can't fault her for trying to get out of a jail sentence."

Brooks and Sanchez both nodded in agreement.

"What about the next two? Is the pattern repeated with them?" Renquest asked.

The red dot shook a little as it hovered between the last two names on the board. Wallace and Kemp. Both had the same drug habits as Yoast and most of the other traits tied in with the four vics that lived.

"So, what have we got?"

Sanchez started. "All the victims are drug users."

Brooks chimed in next. "The four live ones appeared to be recreational users."

"The last three, the dead ones, were heavier users," Flaherty said.

"Good," Request said. "What else?"

All three of his subordinates turned and gazed at the board. He could almost hear the gears in their collective minds turning. Working out the problem in front of them. None of them spoke. That was a mistake. They needed to work together as a team. Four individual minds clicking as one. Sharing thoughts and ideas. He leaned back and watched for a moment longer. Then he broke the silence.

"Look at it from a different perspective."

All three glanced back at him. Blank looks were on their faces. He smiled.

"What's missing?"

The three turned back to the whiteboard. Shooting an occasional, *I don't know,* glance at each other. Renquest gave it another minute. Then, just as he was about to tell them what he was thinking, Brooks spoke.

"We are missing a victim."

Renquest nodded but said nothing.

Brooks continued, "We didn't include the guy Flaherty found behind the dumpster."

Content that his captain mirrored his thought process; he tipped his hand toward her.

Flaherty appeared confused, as did Sanchez, about what their co-worker had suggested.

"Wasn't the last vic stabbed in an alley getting sucked off?" Sanchez said, still with a look of befuddlement on his face.

"Yes," Flaherty responded. "A broken bottle to the neck. I mean, he bled out, just not through a tube."

"Yeah, so how is that related to the others?" Flaherty asked.

"I don't know," Renquest said.

"Then why add it to the board?" Sanchez asked.

"Because we don't know that it's not related at this point," Brooks finally answered.

Renquest pointed at his female captain. "There it is."

The other two men in the room just stared at each other. Then a voice from the doorway boomed in.

"You can't rule it out, so you rule it in." Chief McNally stood in the doorway. He'd been there long enough to hear at least the last part of the conversation taking place.

Renquest stood up. "Chief. Sorry, I didn't know you were standing there."

McNally waved his hand, signaling to the others in the room that it was okay to return to their seats. Everyone except Renquest sat.

"What can I do for you, Chief?"

Chief McNally eased off the door jamb and stepped into the room.

"I see someone is finally using that whiteboard I bought."

"We were just finishing up. Something I can help you with?" Renquest asked. Not being a fan of people listening to conversations they weren't part of; he was a little irked at the chief for sideling in and not announcing his presence.

"No. I was just getting a cup of coffee and heard you all in here talking about the murders. Thought I would stop by and see how things are coming along."

"Well, we're almost done here. I can come down and fill you in once we're finished." He hoped his boss would get the hint without being too obvious.

McNally stood still for a moment, then nodded before leaving the room. Renquest was nervous the intrusion may have been enough to alter the team chemistry he'd been working hard to foster. He had no intention of allowing them to return to personal grievances and pissing contests for the chief's approval. He looked at his team. They all seemed relaxed.

"So, where were we?"

The room fell silent. After a moment, Brooks spoke up.

"As the chief said, we can't rule the last victim out, so we rule him in," Renquest said. He noticed the blank faces of two of his underlings.

"Think about it. When we are investigating any crime. We start tabula rasa. A blank slate. No assumptions. That's how we will look at each of these murders," Renquest said. "I know what you're thinking. If we include Pratt with the other murders, aren't we assuming he is part of them and not something else?"

Sanchez and Flaherty glanced at each other and nodded.

"Wrong," Renquest said. "Let me ask you a question. How many murders were there in Arlington in the year leading up to the first one in this case?"

Brooks said, "One."

"How many the year before that?"

"None," Flaherty answered.

"Okay, then."

The three of them looked puzzled. Finally, Sanchez heaved his shoulders with a look of bewilderment.

Renquest continued, "You've had one murder in the last two years. Now, in the last two weeks, you have had four. And we know there is a relationship between the three dead victims and the four who survived. Do the math. What are the odds there's no relationship between Pratt and the others?"

"Almost zero," Brooks said.

"Hell, maybe less," Renquest spouted. "So, until we can rule out being part of the current series of murders, we rule him in."

The three officers nodded in agreement.

"Now I have to brief the chief. You all have your assignments. Let's see if we can break something loose today."

"What are you going to do after you talk to Chief McNally?" Brooks asked.

"I am going to head down to the coroner's office and see if we have a name to go with the latest body."

Renquest left the room feeling confident his team would find the killer before someone else ended up dead. As he approached the chief's door, he saw it was open. He knocked lightly on the jamb before entering.

"Come in, Bill," the chief said without looking up from his desk.

Renquest still didn't like being called Bill, but he figured the boss could do it if he wanted to. It wasn't worth bringing up right now with five unsolved murders hanging over his head. Instead, he took a seat across from McNally's desk. The chief continued to scribble something on a piece of paper before he pushed a button on his phone. A few seconds later, Margaret came in and took the form. She smiled politely at Renquest. He smiled back. When she left the room, McNally spoke.

"I hope I didn't overstep my bounds earlier. I passed by and couldn't help but notice the team working together as a unit. Something I hadn't seen before."

"They are a talented group. Brooks is very capable," Renquest said.

McNally nodded. "She is. You know she applied for your job. I just couldn't pass up the chance to hire a veteran detective. Someone with your experience is scarce in this business. And frankly, we need to solve these murders sooner rather than later."

"Well, you wouldn't have been wrong to put her in charge, sir."

McNally brushed the comment aside. "So, how is the investigation coming along?"

Renquest summarized for the chief what he'd partially overheard through his eavesdropping minutes earlier. He described the visit to Pratt's basement apartment and the grumpy, racist landlord. Though he left out the details about the creased bed sheets, which made him believe Prat may have served in the military. He couldn't think of a good reason for his boss to insert himself into the investigation. McNally was ex-military. And like many veterans, he was proud of his service. As he should be. But former service officers always seem to know *someone who can help* with records and veteran issues. And he already had Flaherty working that angle. If the investigation confirmed that Pratt had, in fact, served in the armed forces, only then would he inform his boss. Even if Pratt turned out to be a veteran, Renquest didn't believe his prior service played a role in his death. But running down all leads and ruling out motives is how police solve crimes. There's no room for sloppy techniques in a homicide investigation.

"I would like to see more information about the prior victims. Have you been putting any manpower into that area of the investigation?" McNally asked.

That question from his chief only confirmed his decision to limit the information flow until he knew more about the attacks. Interviews with the first victims took place right after their attacks. The information they provided was right there, parked in the front part of their brains. It'd been weeks since the first attack. On the screen, they make it look like pivotal moments happen long after the crime that leads to the Perry Mason moment. In real life, that almost never happens. The gotcha moment is always at the beginning of the case. People who experience trauma want to put it behind them as quickly as possible. Making a choice for a victim to relive their trauma days or months later can force their mind to reset as a defensive mechanism. Sometimes it can even lead to unreliable information. When victims of a crime feel unsafe or vulnerable, they often say what they believe the authorities want to hear. It's not intentional, but one false statement could set an investigation back days or weeks while officers chase down dead ends. He'd seen good detectives make that mistake, forced to watch helplessly as their cases collapsed around them. Along with their careers. Not something a detective with his experience relished.

"As of right now, we are focusing on the most recent victims. Once I have an ID on the guy from yesterday, we can work through his timeline and maybe rule him out as unrelated. If not, we will work backwards and find the thing that links all of them together."

"Besides being dead."

Renquest said nothing. The question was certainly rhetorical.

"Anything else, Chief?"

Chief McNally shook his head and waved his lead detective out of his office with a swat of his hand. Renquest went back to his office, stopping at the coffee machine to pour a fresh cup on the way.

When he got back to his office, all three of his charges were gone. He stepped over to the whiteboard, studying the names scribbled on it. Then he turned his attention to the map, taking mental pictures of each victim's last resting place. He couldn't discern any pattern. It all seemed chaotic, but he knew one existed. He just needed to dig deeper. If he could get his team into the meat of each attack, he was sure they would uncover the missing piece that linked all the cases.

After ten minutes of staring at the pictures on the whiteboard and mumbling to himself, he grew tired. He checked his watch. The position of the hands told him it was almost nine in the morning. The coroner's office would open in a few minutes. He needed to talk to Johansen about the stabbing victim. The cause of death was obvious, but there were still a few unanswered questions bouncing around in his head. Like, was he an IV drug user? Was she able to locate a name? Did he have anything on him that might make identifying him easier? Tattoos or specialty dental work were always good leads. Were there any signs of sexual activity before his death? He needed to find whoever was in that alley with him. That person would be the key to solving this case.

Traffic was lighter than normal, so the drive to the coroner's office only took ten minutes. He parked the car in the garage. In fact, the same spot as the last time he visited Johansen. Once inside the building, he made his way through the maze of hallways, finding himself the only person in the reception area when he arrived. The secretary, her eyes momentarily distracted from her computer monitor, looked up at him, then buzzed the door open.

Johansen was in the cut room. She wasn't donning her protective gear, so he guessed the autopsy on the stabbing victim was over, or she hadn't started yet. The stainless-steel table was bare and clean. There was no sign anyone had used it that day. The air in the room hung heavy with the smell of disinfectant. Normally, a tinge of metal greeted him as he entered the room. Another reason he believed the doc hadn't started her day yet.

Johansen turned as he pushed through the door. "Detective, I was hoping to see you today," she said. "I haven't started on the last victim, but you are welcome to stick around and watch. I'll be ready in about twenty minutes."

Renquest stepped closer to the table in the center of the room. "As much as I'd like to stay and see you slice this fella up, I have some other things I need to get to today. I came down to check and see if you ran his prints?"

"I printed the hands and fingers this morning, and my intern entered them into the system. Though I haven't checked to see if they matched up to anyone yet. But if you give me a second, I'll see if anything popped up."

Johansen abruptly left, leaving Renquest standing in the cold, bright, sanitary room. He hated the cut room. It didn't matter that he'd been on the job forever. He never shook off the queasiness of knowing that the place was just an oversized filing cabinet for the dead. It was like a mausoleum, but without the pomp and circumstance that makes it seem less like death and more like moving on to a better place. The thought forced goosebumps to rise on his arms.

Johansen came back into the room. A smile spread across her face. Her hand gripped a thin file folder. She locked eyes with him as she crossed the room. He couldn't help but smile back.

"You got something?" he asked. A finger on his outstretched hand pointed at the file she carried.

She nodded.

"You have a name?"

She nodded again.

"Let me see," he said. His fingers wiggled in a *come-on give it to me* gesture.

"How much do you like me right now?" she said, slowly pushing the file toward him.

There was no mistaking the tension in the room. Tension unrelated to whatever was in the file or the pair being surrounded by death. He reached into his jacket pocket, fetched his reading glasses, and slipped them over the bridge of his nose.

"What you want is on the first page," Johansen said. Her long, slender finger pointed at the first page of the file.

His eyes darted over the brim of his glasses at her and then back down at the file.

Gender: Male. Height: 73 inches. Weight: 202.

Name: Sullivan, Travis. DOB: 05/05/1987.

Suspected Cause of Death (COD): Laceration to the carotid artery causing fatal loss of blood ending in cardiac arrest (pending official autopsy results).

He flipped the page over. It was blank except for Johansen's signature. He took off his glasses and stuffed them back into his inside jacket pocket. Then he closed the file. "Can you send me a copy of that?"

"Already did. Check your inbox."

"Thanks, Doc. This is good information." He looked back at the drawers that lined the far wall behind him. "Have you examined the body at all?"

"Just when it came in. Right before we placed it in that drawer," she said, pointing at the door with the number nine stenciled on it.

"And?"

"Well, I can't say anything for certain, but by the looks of his arms, Mr. Sullivan had a long history of IV drug use. My guess is when I get him on the table, I will find needle marks between his toes and fingers," Johansen said.

Renquest peered over at the number nine drawer and then back at Johansen. "That'll do, Doc." He stepped toward the door and felt Johansen reach out and touch his arm. He stopped and looked back at her. She was still smiling, and her deep blue eyes momentarily drew all his attention.

"I was wondering if you wanted to have dinner sometime again," she asked.

The question caught him off guard. He liked her, but honestly, he'd been concentrating so much on the cases that he'd thought little about anything else except Custus and the stack of mysterious photos someone had sent him. But he didn't think it was a bad idea. He wrote his personal number on a scrap of paper and told her to call or text him with a time and place. She took the paper and stuck it in her pants pocket. He thanked her again before heading through the doors and back to his car. He had something to go on now. IV drug use was the one thing that tied all the victims together. It could be a coincidence, but eight people, half of them murdered, all with histories of IV drug use. All living in the same community. He'd stake his career on every single one of them, having sought drug treatment at the county clinic. He needed to find the address for Sullivan and then check to see if his team had had any luck locating whoever was in that alley with the guy in drawer nine. The witness was pivotal. The puzzle was coming together.

Chapter 15

Renquest made a quick trip back to his condo to let Custus out and give the old boy a few ear scratches before returning to the station. The detour home cost him about twenty-five minutes. Before leaving, he grabbed a few items from the fridge. He figured eating lunch at his desk was an effective way to make up for the lost time. It was something he had grown used to working on the Sex Crimes Task Force at his old job. In fact, the only time he ate out during work hours at his old gig was when he and his previous partner were returning from a long stint at a crime scene that forced them to miss a meal. But even then, they usually spent the time working out details and dividing up the workload of the case. Lunch was an afterthought, usually the contents of a plastic bag in the fridge or whatever sugary offering the vending machine in the breakroom held behind its glass door.

The lights from the Dodge Charger illuminated the wall as the front end swung into his parking spot in the garage. Thoughts about the case whirled in his head. He was used to it. It was something his mind did when he worked on a murder. His mind's eye scoured every detail. Refusing to let go. Like a dog with a bone. He sat quietly in the car for a moment, taking a deep breath before snatching his hastily prepared lunch from the front seat and exiting the car. He then took the elevator up to his floor. Once inside the station, he made his way past the reception area and to his office. His lunch went into a mini-fridge Chief McNally had supplied him after his first day. A reminder that during his interview McNally told him that sometimes the job of Chief of Detectives could command long hours that drag into the night. Renquest mainly used it for soda and the occasional leftover lunch he wanted to keep fresh until he could get home to Custus.

He sat at his desk and stared at the names and dates scribbled on the whiteboard at the far side of the room. The writing on the board seemed to flow better now. Apparently, the information Johansen gave him filled in some gaps. As he focused on each name, thin lines linking the victims materialized. Weak at first, but the longer he looked at them, the stronger the imaginary lines appeared, forming a bridge between the victims. However, things changed as his eyes moved to the last victim, Travis Sullivan. The lines blurred again. Eventually disappearing altogether before reaching the black, oversized letters that made up his name. This reminded him that the things he didn't know still outweighed the things he knew. The team had filled in a lot of details, but Sullivan's murder had a direct connection to the others. That he was sure of. Once he had the missing pieces, those lines would become clearer. But right now, he didn't have enough to link Sullivan to the rest of the victims. Drugs and the clinic were clear frontrunners, since the other victims met that criteria. But that didn't mean it wasn't there. They would simply have to dig deeper. If something else were out there, his team would need to get it the old-fashioned way. By knocking on doors and talking to people. Renquest was a little jealous that he couldn't help more in that area. He missed the game.

His arms flexed as he pushed his chair back from the desk. The cracking of his knees as he stretched made him wince. Once he finished, he looked at the files on his desk, grabbed the pile, and walked to the whiteboard. Using a dry-erase marker, he underlined the name Travis Sullivan under the last victim's entry on the board. He punctuated the name with a question mark. Retracing the symbol several times to show the team, unanswered questions remained. He thought about the criminal records of the other victims.

Now that he had a name and date of birth, he could run a criminal history check through NCIC. Dates and locations of arrests could provide a timeline of where the subject lived and hung out. The team could cross-reference Sullivan's old charges against the other victims to see if anything stands out. Maybe there was a common location where they purchased drugs. The arresting officers could be the same. Though he doubted that point would bear any fruit. He needed to speak with Margaret at the reception desk. Since he was new to the department, he wasn't sure if anyone had created login credentials for him yet. Margaret told him his old username would suffice, and he just needed to reset his password. Once completed, he'd have full access to the NCIC system.

In a hushed tone, Margaret added, "Now that you have an account, every search and every login attempt gets linked to this department. All that information is reviewable by the chief."

Her tone made him think this was a warning not to use the system for personal reasons.

As he walked away, he turned back toward the young receptionist.

"You know what? I don't have the faintest idea where the terminal room is."

Margaret laughed. "It's on your computer, in your office."

His head canted to the side. "What do you mean? When Brooks ran a criminal history for me the other day, she used a specific computer."

"That's right. There is a terminal in the basement for officers and command staff to use. However, the chief and his lead detective — that's you — have access installed on their laptops. There should be an icon on your desktop. Click it and you'll be able to perform searches."

"My personal VCIN terminal." Renquest laughed, but it came out more of a snort.

He thanked Margaret and then headed back to his office. After lifting the lid of his laptop, the screen flashed on, and his fingers tapped in his username and password. A little circle spun in the center of the screen for a few seconds while the system logged him on, and then his personal desktop configuration appeared. An audible ding let him know he had an email waiting for him. He muted the volume with the click of the mouse; found the icon for the program Margeret told him about; and double-clicked it. More spinning wheels and permissions to agree to followed. He clicked off each one as it appeared. Then, the system directed him to enter a new password.

It took the detective four tries to get a password that the system would accept. The breadth of which was no simple task. The password requirement included a series of capital letters, lowercase letters, special characters, and numbers. And the password could not contain known words, repeating letters, or repeating numbers. After creating one that the system would accept, he immediately wrote it down in the notepad he kept in his pocket because he knew he would forget it the moment he signed off. He surprised himself by remembering it long enough to write it down.

It took him only a few clicks before he had the system figured out. He located the menu and clicked on the tab for criminal history. A new window opened, prompting him to enter a name and date of birth.

Sullivan, Travis

1987/05/05

He hit enter. This time, a spinning hourglass replaced the spinning wheel. A few seconds later, the results of the match appeared on his screen. He copied the unique number assigned by the FBI to every person in the database and opened a new search screen. Then he pasted the number into the box labeled "UCN#." The hourglass returned for five seconds, and another window opened on his screen. This one contained a detailed report of Travis Sullivan's criminal record. It read like an after-school special on public television from the 1980s.

His first arrest was as a juvenile for theft, but because of state laws concerning juvenile records, the record contained few details. He moved past that section to the next entry in the report. Based on the date of that arrest, Sullivan's next police contact occurred at age nineteen. Drug possession and trespassing. Following a trial, the court convicted him on both charges, and he received a two-year sentence. But the judge suspended all jail time and placed him under probation supervision.

Sullivan's time on probation was a good indicator of where he was going to go in life. He had at least three probation revocation hearings over the next two years. At one point, the judge in the case even extended his supervision time by six months for failing to report to probation on multiple occasions.

The pattern repeated several more times. New arrests, then probation, followed by years of non-compliance. It was a vicious cycle. Until about three years ago, when the arrests stopped. Not a single entry. He had become invisible. Until he turned up dead.

Renquest reviewed the report again, wondering if he was missing something. Sullivan hadn't gone more than a year without getting into trouble since he was nineteen years old. Then one day, he just woke up and quit the lifestyle. There are many reasons that force people to change. Number one on the list is marriage and kids. Once a person has a family, other priorities take hold. Kids need clothes and food, and insurance. Spouses need love and attention, and stability. Families are demanding and leave little time for other activities. A close second, just behind growing up and having a family, is the consequence of not doing that. A long prison sentence. If you stay and play in the criminal arena long enough, you'll get busted. And if you keep getting arrested, eventually you'll do some real time in a state facility. Put out of circulation. But Sullivan seemed to have no family. And since he was still dealing dope and getting blowjobs behind dumpsters from junkies, that meant there was one more possibility for his miraculous turnaround. The detective knew that nothing happens in a vacuum. Sullivan could've been an informant. He may have been working for the police. Maybe even the DEA. Both of which would've kept him safe from harassment by patrol cops and clear of the drug task force's radar.

Renquest thought a DMV check would be the next step to see if Sullivan had a driver's license and an address. He moved the mouse back over the menu and clicked on the tab to query driver's license records. The cursor danced across the screen as he typed in the name and DOB, then hit submit. The hourglass flashed briefly on the screen before the system spat out the search results. Sullivan never received a driver's license but had a state ID card issued a little over five years ago. Renquest brought the screen showing the criminal history results back up. The issue date on the ID coincided with a short stint of incarceration at the county jail. It made sense. A decade earlier, the state pushed a program to get driver's licenses or ID cards issued to people while in jail. The thought process being that newly released inmates with a valid ID could drastically cut the waiting times for county services. Making it easier to secure food assistance, housing applications, and job searches. Though recent federal ID requirements made the process more complicated. As a cop, Renquest thought the program was a great idea. Nothing was more frustrating to a police officer than dealing with a suspect who wouldn't talk and had no valid identification.

He stared at the address reported on the ID listed in the system. Something looked familiar. He stood straight and peered over his shoulder out the window. His eyes focused on the large brown building across the street. 401 sat centered above the front entrance. He looked back at the report. The address matched the homeless shelter. The ID turned out to be a dead end.

He printed copies of Sullivan's criminal history and placed them in the file in chronological order. Once he finished, he closed the lid of his laptop and leaned back in his chair, contemplating where to take the investigation from here. A moment later, he looked up. Flaherty hovered in the doorway.

"Detective?"

Renquest pushed himself upright and leaned forward over his desk. "What can I do for you, Flaherty?"

The younger detective entered and approached the desk.

"I have some news on the vic from the alley," Flaherty said

Renquest pursed his lips and nodded. Gesturing toward the chair beside Flaherty, who pushed it back and sat before continuing.

"So, after looking at the board this morning, I went back down to the treatment center. I wanted to follow up with staff about the person we think may have been in the alley when our guy..."

Renquest interjected. "Sullivan. Travis Sullivan."

"You've got a name?" Flaherty said, a bit surprised his boss already had that information. "How did you find it?"

"Doc got a hit off the fingerprints today," Renquest said.

The answer appeased the detective, and he continued with his story. "So, anyway, on my way down to the treatment center, I thought maybe we're asking the wrong questions. I was focusing on the person being a witness to the murder. But I got to thinking, there is a better-than-average chance the person is someone who is in treatment at the clinic."

"Keep going," Renquest said.

"Well, a hooker might stand around a treatment center waiting for johns to come out so she can turn a trick. But everyone knows most people who go to the clinic don't have any money and are only there because probation orders them to go. So, why would a prostitute spend any time trying to get money from people who don't have any?"

"Unless she was a user too," Renquest said.

"Exactly. And if she is a client there, the staff will want to protect her and throw all kinds of privacy bullshit at us until we get a subpoena, which will be tough because we would be on a fishing expedition. Judges here have been reluctant in the past to sign off on those types of requests," Flaherty said.

Renquest's right hand rubbed the back of his neck. "You said something about changing tactics. What did you have in mind?"

"At first, I thought I'd hang out front and try to talk to the addicts as they left, but there are two problems. One, they don't like cops. And two, talking about other people in the group could get them kicked out of treatment. That would violate their probation supervision agreement and could get them thrown in jail." Flaherty paused for a moment. "I realized I needed to ask about the dead guy. I don't think he is part of the program, and the staff will be more than willing to talk about a predator taking advantage of their patients."

"That's good. If you can get them talking, they may slip and give us the name of our witness. When are you going to go back to the center?"

The younger detective stood stoic. A smile crept across his face.

"You already did?" Renquest asked.

"Yes, sir."

"What did you get?" Renquest stood and maneuvered around the desk.

Flaherty pulled a slip of paper from his pocket and handed it to his boss, who had sidled up right next to his chair. Renquest took the paper and pushed his thumb across its face, unfolding it into his hand. Written in black ink on the paper was a name. Travis Sullivan. The moniker *pimp* written behind it. He looked down at Flaherty, who was making a circle in the air with his index finger. Gesturing for Renquest to flip the paper over. Renquest turned the paper in his hand, and another name appeared: Kim Norman.

"You got an address?"

Flaherty stood from his chair, proud of his accomplishment. His hands smoothed the front of his jacket as he adjusted the cuffs of his sleeves. "She rents an apartment in Seven Corners."

Renquest patted his detective on the shoulder. "That's good work, Flaherty. When are you going to go pay her a visit?"

"I planned on heading over as soon as we finished here."

"Good," Renquest said. "But I'd wait until tomorrow morning. You're more likely to catch her at home before breakfast. And I want you to bring her back here. She is a material witness to a murder. We need to make sure we control the interview and that she is safe. If she did witness the murder, she could be next."

"I'll get on it," Flaherty said as he spun to leave the room. He stopped in the doorway and glanced back at his boss. "I think we might have this one."

Renquest nodded. Then Flaherty disappeared out the door and into the hall. Renquest's phone buzzed and shimmied across the surface of the desk. He picked it up, and a little rectangular shape with a point at one end flashed on the screen. Then, with a series of swipes of his finger, the screen unlocked and a message from Johansen appeared.

My place. 7 pm. Don't be late- Bec

Renquest read the text again. He realized he didn't know her first name. He had just been calling her Doc. *Bec,* he thought. Short for Becky. Which was usually short for Rebecca or some variation of that name. Rebecca Johansen. He liked the sound of it. He said it again in his head. *Doctor Rebecca Johansen.* He put the phone in his pocket and looked at the whiteboard one more time. They'd made good progress. He felt the cogs were all spinning smoothly. It wouldn't be long before they identified a suspect. At least he hoped.

Chapter 16

As he maneuvered the corner, he glanced at the clock on the radio on his dashboard. Its menacingly large numbers flashed 19:15. He'd gone home to let Custus out and to make sure the old boy had eaten his dinner. The smell was immediately noticeable as he stepped through the front door. There'd been another bathroom incident. This time in the bedroom. The cleanup took about five minutes, followed by another ten to let Custus sniff around outside in the pet yard. A feeling of guilt hit Renquest for leaving his loyal companion alone again. So, he sat on the bench and let him wander the fence line until finally stopping at the gate and looking back at his master with tired eyes. Custus then waited patiently while Renquest snapped the leash to his collar, before opening the gate and leading him to the elevator. The thought of texting Johansen and canceling their dinner weighed heavily on the detective's mind. But once back inside, Custus went straight to his bed and lay down.

After filling the water bowl and placing a treat at the edge of his bed, the guilt-ridden detective reassuringly patted the dog's head.

"I'll be back before you know it," Renquest said.

Custus didn't move. His heavy eyes peered up at his friend. Renquest sat with him until he fell asleep.

A soft chime came from inside the house as he released the doorbell button. Light shone through the large window to his right. The urge to retreat down the stairs to the sidewalk to give himself room if something went wrong was hard to fight off. But this visit was personal, and he needed to learn to separate his work and social lives. Not an effortless task for a veteran detective closer to retirement than to the academy. He took a breath and tried to relax. It had been a long time for him. Honestly, he couldn't remember the last time someone had invited him over for dinner. Nervous energy pulsed through his veins. The moisture in his hands increased. Any remaining saliva in his mouth quickly evaporated. He took a deep breath and chuckled to himself. He'd stared down killers without flinching. But dinner with a beautiful woman had him feeling like a seventeen-year-old on prom night.

"Get a grip," he mumbled.

Through the reflection in the door's glass, he saw himself and realized he hadn't changed his clothes since their meeting that morning. Trying not to be too obvious, he reached up and loosened the tie around his neck and slipped the loop over his head. He folded the neckwear in half, then once more, and stuffed it into his inside jacket pocket just as the door swung open. He took a step back and straightened his shirt collar.

Johansen stood in the doorway. She wore a short, light blue skirt, not tight and fitted like part of a suit, but pleated and flowing. A warm-weather piece of clothing. He knew nothing about women's fashion, but he felt the skirt conveyed a more relaxed vibe. Taken from the night-out with the girls' section of her closet. Their eyes met. She smiled. He forced a smile. Then she slid aside, allowing him to step inside and close the door behind him.

"I brought a couple bottles of wine. I wasn't sure what we were having." The aging detective's voice cracked a little as he handed her the two bottles. One white. One red.

"Thank you. But I figured you were more of a beer guy," Johansen said.

"Most of the time, but I'll drink what's available."

Johansen took the wine from his outstretched hands. The distance from the front door to the dining room table was about five steps for him. It took her seven. She placed the wine on the table and disappeared through another doorway. He imagined she had gone to the kitchen to fetch a couple of glasses. A few moments later, she returned with one glass and an open bottle of what looked like beer. She handed him the long-necked brown bottle.

"It's a local cider."

He nodded.

"Glass?" she asked.

"No, thank you," he said, waiting for her to open the wine and pour a glass for herself before taking a pull of his beverage.

The shirt she wore flowed in the breeze as she trekked to and from the kitchen, carrying plates of roasted meat and vegetable dishes. When satisfied with the appearance of the table and all the food was out, she pulled out the chair next to him and sat down.

They each took bites and made small talk in between chewing and sips of their drinks. Once they both had made an acceptable dent in the food on each of their plates, Johansen slid her chair back and stood. She offered her guest a seat in the living room while she cleaned up, but he politely offered to help with bussing the table and washing the dishes.

She said, "Thank you," and the two went to work clearing the table.

As Johansen cleaned the plates, instead of throwing the scraps into the trash, she put a small to-go package together for Custus.

The bachelor smiled and said, "Thanks."

"How old is he?"

"I'm not sure. He was a shelter dog. The staff wasn't sure when he was born. So, we celebrate his birthday on the day we met each year."

"That's sweet." She touched his arm. "How is he doing with the move? I know it can be stressful for people. I would assume the same applies to pets."

He looked down at the floor and shook his head. "I'm not sure it was the best move for him."

Johansen stopped drying dishes and faced her guest to better see his face. "Is he alright?"

"I don't know. But he is old, and he shouldn't have to be home all day by himself. I wanted to hire someone to come and sit with him during the day, but I just can't get used to having someone in my house when I am not there." He shook his head in shame. "It's a cop thing."

She said nothing.

"It's selfish, but I can't have someone in my house all day. Eventually, I wouldn't be able to find something and accuse the sitter of stealing. Then everything would turn to shit."

Johansen turned back to the sink and picked another glass out of the rinsing sink. She slowly wiped it with the towel in her hand.

"You could bring him down to the office while you are at work," she said. Her eyes focused on the glassware in her left hand.

He looked over at her. He wasn't sure he'd heard her correctly. "What?"

"For centuries, coroners and funeral homes have had cats roaming the halls. I think it comes from some ancient superstition passed down from the Egyptians. But to this day, if you visit a funeral parlor or mortuary, you stand a good chance of leaving with cat hair on your pants," Johansen said.

Renquest was quiet.

"I mean, he could lie around, and my intern could make sure he gets out to the bathroom. He would have plenty of company, as people come in and out all day."

Renquest saw the concern on her face. "What do you think it is?"

His host stopped drying the dishes. "I'm not a veterinarian."

"I know."

"But based on his age and the bladder issues, I'd say Custus is in kidney failure. Soon, he won't be able to go at all," she said. A smooth and sympathetic tone in her voice.

"How long?" Renquest asked. He didn't want to look at her. Showing his vulnerability was not something he was comfortable with.

She placed the glass in the cupboard and picked a plate out of the sink. "Six months, if I had to guess."

Silence engulfed the room.

"How long have you had him?" she finally asked.

"Eight years," Renquest answered.

"That's a long time."

"Longer than my first marriage," he quipped. A half-hearted chuckle broke from his lips.

She smiled at him.

"Are you sure about this?" he asked.

"It would be nice to have some company again," Johansen said.

He nodded. "Thank you. Again."

Ten minutes of silence followed as the pair finished the dishes.

Once they had put everything away, his second beer in the rearview mirror, Johansen offered to adjourn to the living room. It was a tempting offer, but he felt he needed to get back to Custus. His host offered no argument. She appeared happy to know he cared so much for his friend. She gave him a goodbye kiss on the cheek and gently touched his arm. He got into his car and made the short drive home. Custus was waiting at the door when he arrived.

* * *

He'd dumped the car. Someone would eventually find it, but when they did, it'd be nothing more than a rusted, burned-out shell. He painstakingly ensured that no useful information remained to connect the remains to him. He stripped the VIN tag from the frame in front of the driver's side of the windshield. The second one would burn along with the plastic and thin metal body panels. He felt comfortable with his decision to destroy any evidence that might link him to the car. But something else was on his mind. The girl from the alley. She had seen him. Up close. He remembered the faces of every person he had experimented on. He knew she wouldn't forget the rage on his face when he killed that degenerate in front of her. How much she would talk if the cops found her is what he didn't know.

He opened the refrigerator door. Only three bags of precious red liquid remained. Seeing the last few bags surrounded by so much emptiness ignited something deep inside him. It was a feeling he hadn't known for decades. Pushed down deep in his gut since he was a child. Panic. Almost immediately, he felt the evil contaminating his blood attacking his healthy cells. A warm sensation shot up his right arm. His eyes hurriedly searched the room for anything to help him stop it from spreading. On the far wall, he saw a piece of medical-grade rubber hose. He quickly grabbed it, putting one end in his mouth, then looping the other around his bicep, slipping the end between his skin and the tightly wrapped hose. A few minutes passed, and the burning sensation slowed, then faded completely.

His hand was numb by this time, and his fingers turned a pale blue color. He held tight for another fifteen seconds to be safe. Then he slowly released the tension on the hose and felt the blood flow back into his hand. The burning sensation didn't return with the color to his skin. He'd won this battle. But it almost cost him his hand. He knew fighting without the regular treatment was useless. That is why the guy in the alley was dead. It wasn't his fault. The contamination of his blood took hold and transformed him. Changed him into a killer. Not just any killer, but a rage killer. The biggest worry he'd had all these years was that he'd end up like his mother. She fought it as long as she could, but in the end, it invaded her body. Saturating every cell. Until one day a bullet to the head ensured the end of her suffering. He had found her. Lying on the cold kitchen floor in a pool of her own blood. To this day, he swears he could see the virus dying as he watched the blood coagulate and dry. For hours he sat cross-legged by his mother's corpse. Staring at the pool of thick red liquid. Only the sound of sirens broke his trance. Police officers pounded on the door, screaming, before bursting through. Shards of wood spewed across the floor. He later learned the mailman had seen the tragic scene while placing junk mail into the box mounted beside the front window and notified the police.

He needed to find another donor. He still liked the girl. The one who saw him kill the guy in the alley. Finding her could solve two problems for him. He had noticed her for a reason outside the treatment center. The infection ran through her, but she differed from the others. He didn't know why, but he had developed an eye for such things over the past year. The more he practiced, the more he learned. Practice makes perfect, one of his old science teachers used to tell him. He never paid much attention to the whimsical yammering of the old man. But as it turns out, the man who always smelled of tuna was right. Well, partially, anyway. His test subjects were dying. But sometimes people die for the sake of progress. Natural selection. Or manifest destiny. Or whatever applied. The point was, he knew he was closer than he'd ever been to a cure. He couldn't let anything get in his way now.

The infection repelled him from the healthy. Instead, choosing to push him toward those infected worse. The tiny invaders were trying to survive. Contact with the most seriously infected seemed to feed their appetite. Strengthen them. Hanging out around the clinic had taken a toll on him. He could feel the battle turning against him after each visit. But it was the only place he knew to find the right people. The ones he was sure had the disease coursing through their veins, but whose bodies were still fighting. He needed to find the girl before she was unsavable. Like his mother.

The night was dark. A new moon. Time to go hunting again.

Chapter 17

Custus was fast asleep at the foot of the bed when the squelch from Renquest's alarm pried his eyes open the next morning. He showered and shaved, pulled on a pair of slacks and slipped a button-down shirt over his shoulders. His favorite tie remained on a hook in the back of the closet. A decision he'd made right before he slipped off to sleep the night prior. A choice to be a smidge less formal at work. The tie's ends fluttered as a gust of air pushed past as he closed the closet door.

The coffee pot had finished brewing by the time he finished tying his shoes. He poured a cup into a travel mug and took the first sip of the day. It was hot. Almost burned his tongue as the black liquid passed over it, carrying its load of caffeine to his stomach and eventually to his veins.

Custus wandered into the room and looked up at his friend.

"We are going to try something different today, old buddy," he said, reaching down and patting the dog's head. "I think you will like her. I do."

The old dog nestled up against his leg. His droopy eyes masked his joyful mood. Renquest knelt and scratched behind Custus' ears and looked around the room. He noticed the manila envelope on the end table. The one containing the bondage photos. He stared hard at the thing that could end his career. He even considered taking them back to the office for safekeeping. But in the end, he felt it was best to keep as much physical distance between the contents of the envelope and his boss as possible. Someone intended the pictures to be a political hit job, and he was still at a loss on how to handle the situation. He made copies and stashed them in his gun safe in the bedroom closet. His motto was never to be too cautious. There was at least one person out there who knew he had those pictures. And that was one person too many when he didn't have a plan.

Heavier than normal traffic had cars stacked up bumper to bumper on Fairfax Boulevard. Congestion was as bad as he'd seen since moving to the area. As he waited through the third cycle of the stoplight without moving, he tuned the radio to the local news station, hoping they might provide some insight into what the hell had traffic so snarled this morning. Just as the cars in front of him crept through the now green traffic light, the newscaster said there had been two accidents on Fairfax Boulevard near George Mason Law School. Construction was bogging down cars on Columbia Pike and US 50. The congestion on three of the main roads through town forced him to take side streets to get to Johansen's office. It wasn't something he'd planned on doing, but the detour allowed him to scope out more neighborhoods he wouldn't normally have time to see on his way to work. One of the first things he learned was that the county had replaced many of the four-way stop intersections with roundabouts. Something he himself favored, but people unfamiliar with the circular traffic patterns stopped as they approached the intersection. And that defeated the sole purpose of roundabouts, which was to keep traffic moving. He often wondered how people lived as long as they did in America with their unwillingness to adapt to change. He shrugged and tapped his horn at the driver who'd stopped in front of him. The agitated driver gave him a New York thank you as he sped away.

Custus' drop-off with Johansen went according to plan. She had an old dog bed, likely used by one of her previous pets, laid out behind the receptionist's area. Custus sniffed around the lobby for a minute and then made himself comfortable. He got plenty of attention from the staff and appeared content to rest the day away in his new surroundings. A sight that lifted a heavy burden from the detective's shoulders. Knowing Custus was in excellent hands helped make the short commute to work a little less worrisome.

Renquest sat behind the desk in his office and stared at the whiteboard. It'd become his ritual over the past week. Something he did to start the day. The names and backgrounds all seemed to come together. Except for

Pratt. As a victim, the young man didn't fit the profile of the others. He was clean. Had his own place. It was neat and organized. He even had a pet that seemed to be cared for. But it was the lack of IV drug use that stood out to him the most. Illicit drug use was the one thing that tied all the victims together. He ran through the timeline in his head. Putting the murders in chronological order, then pairing them with the crime scene photos. Specifically, the pictures depicting the placement of bodies. Once everything was in order, he went through them separately. He spread the pictures out across his desk. Each photo underwent in-depth scrutiny. His eyes scanned for similar details. One thing stood out above all others. The directional placement of the bodies. All the bodies appeared to be lying with their heads and feet facing east to west. All near wooded areas or just off heavily used pedestrian trails. Often yards from the road or path, partially covered in leaves or brush. Except for Pratt. Walkers found his body on the side of the path in a public park. It would've been next to impossible for someone not to find his corpse. The hair on his arms tingled. Nothing about Pratt's crime scene was like the others. Which made the keen detective wonder if his team had stumbled onto another murder. Maybe a copycat.

A rap on his door snapped his concentration. It was Brooks. He waved her in.

"Good morning," he said.

"Morning, Detective."

"You're up bright and early today. What's on your mind?"

Brooks stepped into the office. "I was thinking last night."

"About what?"

"The victims," Brooks said.

"Oh?" His hand rose to his chin and rubbed his bristled skin. "All of them, or one in particular?"

His captain moved closer to the whiteboard she had spent hours working on. She walked from left to right, stopping at each name on the board. She said nothing, but stared for a moment and then moved to the next name. When she reached the end, she glanced back at all the names and pointed at one.

"I was thinking about this one," she said, her fingernail tapping Pratt's name on the board. "I think this one is different."

Renquest pushed his chair back. Slipped out and made his way over to the conference table. He propped his rear up and sat half on and half off.

"Tell me what you're thinking."

"I'm not sure. Something doesn't feel right. The dump scene is different. He wasn't a heavy user. Add to that, both you and Sanchez said his place was immaculate. I was at the other victim's home during the interviews. They lived in squalor. It was like an episode of Hoarders, only times five. These people were not clean and didn't have beds made with square corners. Hell, I bet most of them had nothing more than a stained mattress on the floor covered in old Doritos bags and smelling of piss," Brooks said.

She pulled out a chair and plopped down. Renquest looked at the board and then back at Brooks, who was now biting a nail on one of her fingers.

"I was thinking the same thing," he said.

She looked over at him. "So, I'm not imagining things."

"Well, we could both be imagining the same thing," Renquest said.

He could almost hear the thoughts churning in her head.

"You think? I mean, what are the odds?" she said.

"Hundred to one at best."

She nodded. "What about the last victim? The guy with his throat cut in the alley?"

The older detective shook his head as he ran his hand through his thinning, grayish hair. Then he leaned forward, his eyes staring at Travis Sullivan's name.

"I'm not sure yet. But we will know more when Flaherty brings in the witness today."

"Are *you* going to question her?" Brooks asked.

The way she said *you* made Renquest think she wanted to take a crack at the questioning. Not that he was against the idea, but Flaherty had done all the legwork on this one. His work, his witness. "I'm going to let Flaherty handle it. Breaking the lead means he should get first crack at her." Renquest paused for a moment to gauge Brook's response. When he felt comfortable that she was okay with his decision, he continued. "But I want you in the room. She may be more likely to open up with another female present."

"Sure thing, boss," Brooks said.

"I want you to let Flaherty ask the questions. You can come up with a list of your own, but you should run your questions past him first. This is his lead, and I want him to handle it. I'll be watching from my desk. If I see something I don't like, I'll buzz you both out. Then you can have a crack at her. Do you understand?"

"Yes, sir," Brooks said.

"Alright. Make sure and let me know when Flaherty gets back with the witness. I want to talk to him before he starts," Renquest said.

Brooks turned and left. Renquest was happy he and his captain appeared to be on the same page about Pratt. The concurrence from his second in command solidified his thoughts about the case and Pratt's lack of similarity to the other victims. But he knew they were still swinging at some wild pitches. There was much more they needed to figure out, and he hoped the witness interview would clear some things up.

He picked up the phone, and Margaret answered on the first ring.

"What can I do for you, Detective?" she said. Her voice sounded raspier than normal.

"Do you have access to LexisNexis?" Renquest asked.

LexisNexis was a massive internet-based scraping tool that compiled tens of millions of addresses, phone numbers, work histories, and court cases on millions of Americans. The program was a favorite of criminal investigators and attorneys, who used it to locate witnesses and to uncover derogatory information about individuals suspected of involvement in criminal or civil matters. But the feature Renquest was interested in was the ability to provide possible relatives' names with addresses and phone numbers. If he could locate a sibling or a parent, or an ex-spouse, that could break this thing wide open.

"Margaret, I need you to run a name for me."

"Send me the information in an email, and I will get back to you as soon as I have any results." Margaret rang off as quickly as she'd picked up.

He hoped the background check would reveal more detailed information about Pratt. Where he had lived. Employment history. Service in the military. Credit reports. If the program returned nothing useful, he would then have his team dig deeper into the man. Including door-to-door interviews with neighbors and anyone they thought might have known him. While they did that, he would start with the grumpy landlord. Renquest had been champing at the bit to talk to him one more time since he and Sanchez first had the displeasure of meeting him. Only this time, he would send a cruiser to pick him up and bring him down to the station for an official interview. He'd let him stew in a soundproof room for an hour with ample water to drink. A full bladder is a powerful motivator. Renquest wasn't a fan of all the old tricks, but he would sleep just fine if the man who insulted Sanchez was uncomfortable for a bit. *Karma's a bitch*, he thought to himself.

Just as he was about to get up and get another cup of coffee, his desk phone rang. It was Margaret. She had the reports on Pratt printed and told him, "You can pick them up when you are ready."

Before he could stand, the phone rang again. This time the voice belonged to Sanchez. They had Kim Norman in the squad car and were about to pull into the garage. He thought for a second. He needed to keep in mind that Norman was a witness and not a suspect. Did he want to use a less formal setting, like the conference table in his office? A witness might be more willing to cooperate if she didn't feel like she was being interrogated. His eyes turned to the murder board. He'd need to cover the board if the interview were to take place in his office. Letting a witness see the board would be an enormous breach of policy and could damage the case. The station only had two interview rooms, so he told Sanchez to place Norman in room number one. He also told them to make sure not to leave her alone and to make sure she didn't have any weapons on her. He also reminded the two to leave the door open. It was important for the witness to feel she could leave at any time.

"Make sure you leave the door open until the interview begins. Then explain why you're closing the door for her privacy. If she says something that incriminates herself, we don't want some defense attorney objecting that she wasn't free to leave."

"You think *she* might have done him?" Sanchez asked.

"No, but the one thing I have learned over my career is we don't know shit about anything until we do," Renquest said

Then he hung up the phone for the second time in five minutes. Things were really beginning to pick up. If Kim Norman could provide an appropriate description of the person who stabbed Sullivan, then he could issue a BOLO and have patrol units actively working the neighborhoods for anyone matching the assailant's description. It would be a wide net to cast, but he didn't have a choice. They were still gathering information, so using a net was better than casting specific bait at this point in the investigation.

On the way to the interview room, he made a stop at Margaret's desk. She printed, stapled, and stuffed the Pratt report into a manila folder, then shoved it into his mailbox. When he pulled the file from the hole, it felt unusually heavy. He opened the folder to find a stack of papers at least an inch thick. It reminded him of the Christmas catalogue he used to thumb through as a kid, marking his wish list for Santa. His thumb fanned across the pages' edges like shuffling a deck of cards. There must have been 100 pages of information in his hands. He could feel his heart race at the idea of knowing more about one of his victims. Then he glanced up at the clock on the wall. The report would have to wait. The Kim Norman interview was now the priority.

He took the elevator down to the basement, where he found Flaherty and Sanchez standing outside the door to interview room #1, which they had left ajar, as he'd instructed them to do. Renquest snuck a quick glance inside the room. He was curious about her appearance. A steaming paper cup of coffee sat on the desk in front of her. She was wearing shorts and a tank top. Tennis shoes with no socks. All of which appeared to be the clothes she'd slept in before being rousted out of bed by two cops. She didn't wear makeup, and her hair was in a ponytail. But even in her current condition, she was an attractive woman. In her late twenties. Fairly tall, between five-six and five-eight. Brown hair. Hazel eyes. A light complexion. If he had seen her on the street, he wouldn't have guessed she was trading favors for drugs behind a dumpster in an alley a few days ago.

He looked at his lead detective. "Any problems?"

Flaherty peered over his shoulder at the cracked door, then back at Renquest. "No. It was almost as if she was relieved when we showed up at her door. Like she was expecting someone else."

"That's good. We can use that. Did she say anything in the car on the ride over?"

"Nope," Sanchez said. "She just stared out the window. Relaxed. It was as if something lifted an imaginary weight off her shoulders."

"Alright. Sanchez, you come with me. Brooks is going to assist with the interview. I think a woman in the room might make her feel more comfortable and willing to talk. Especially about the sex stuff."

He looked at Sanchez, who nodded in agreement.

"Good. We are going back to my office to watch from my desk. Call Brooks and get her down here." He pointed at Flaherty. "Let's get this thing wrapped up with a nice little bow."

"Yes, sir."

With that said, Renquest and Sanchez headed back to the office. Once inside, Sanchez called up the video from the computer on the detective's desk and diverted the feed to the projector. In a few seconds, the two watched as Kim Norman sat nervously behind a table in the interview room. The writing on the board was a little distracting, but it kept the two men from sitting shoulder to shoulder, staring at the small video screen on his laptop.

Flaherty and Brooks entered the room after about five minutes. Flaherty took the chair on the right, the seat of power, and Brooks, the one on the left. After sliding her chair out to sit, his Captain left herself a little behind her partner. The move left no doubt about who was in charge. Renquest liked it. The witness's subconscious would notice the subtle difference and, if the two needed to go good cop-bad cop, it put Brooks in position to come in as the rescuer looking out for her fellow woman. *She was good;* he thought to himself. He wondered if he had made a mistake by not making her the primary for the interview. That doubt lasted only a few seconds once Flaherty started talking.

Flaherty introduced himself and Brooks. His voice was steady. Like the low hum of an idling engine. He thanked Norman for coming in to help them try to clear up what had happened in the alley that day. The statement carried a tone of sympathy—an *"I'm sorry for your loss"* vibe. So far, his lead detective was doing well.

"Miss Norman. It is Miss, isn't it?" Flaherty asked.

"Yes," the witness answered.

"Do you mind if I call you Kim?"

She shook her head. Her eyes focused on the steel table in front of her.

"Okay, Kim, do you remember the afternoon in the alley?"

She nodded.

"Kim, I'm going to need you to answer with your voice. The voice recorder can't pick up gestures. Can you do that for me?"

She nodded again. Only this time, a low "Yes" followed the head movement.

"Alright then. Thank you for understanding. Now, can you tell me what happened that day in the alley behind the treatment center?" Flaherty asked. "Try starting with the moment you left the center that day."

Renquest noticed her hands shaking. She pulled them off the table and onto her lap. He and Sanchez watched as she fidgeted with her clothes. Her lips pressed tightly together, and her shoulders hunched over a bit. Not wanting to push her away, Flaherty sat patiently.

After a minute of silence, Kim Norman looked up at Flaherty and sobbed. Renquest watched as his lead detective reached across the table and touched her on the arm. A small touch to reassure her she was safe. Brooks stood and grabbed a box of tissues from a table just outside the door. She put the box on the table in front of Norman, making sure to hand her one. Then, she placed a reassuring hand on her shoulder, letting her know everything would be fine.

After a rash of nose-blowing and deep breaths, Kim Norman let out what she'd been hiding. She said, "I've struggled with my sobriety for a few weeks now, and meetings weren't helping." So, she set up a time to meet with her old dealer after her treatment session. "But during the session, I admitted to the group that I'd thought about giving in to my addiction. The others in the group really let me have it. They told me I'd been clean for almost six months. Throwing it all away now would mean starting over. The meetings, drug tests, and maybe a probation violation from the court."

She didn't tell the group she'd already called her dealer, but since she'd changed her mind, she'd just avoid him. But that plan went sideways almost immediately because Travis Sullivan was waiting around the corner when she tried to use the door in the alley as an escape route.

"He was so angry that I didn't want to buy from him." Her eyes focused on Brooks. "Then he said, since he came all the way down there just for me, I owed him something for his time."

"What did he want you to do?" Flaherty asked.

Her head dipped as she looked away.

"He wanted you to perform oral sex, didn't he?" Brooks asked.

Kim Norman bit her bottom lip and nodded. Tears filled her eyes again. A momentary silence filled the interview room.

Watching from his office, Renquest felt pity for Kim Norman. Victims of rape and sexual assault live with a pain unimaginable to most people. Their entire existence becomes about a brief moment in time. He often thought that murder victims had it easier in the end. At least the dead get peace. It's the living who suffer the most.

It was at that moment that the veteran detective witnessed Flaherty's first and only mistake during the interview. He leaned in to comfort her. When someone's traumatized by an assault and is giving details about the attack, the interviewer should maintain physical distance. Any attempt to touch or invade the victim's space could cause a protective wall to go up. Especially if the victim is a woman and their attacker was a man. Renquest watched Kim Norman's reaction. She flinched. Flaherty seemed to realize his mistake and withdrew his hand. After a moment, Norman continued her story. *No harm, no foul,* Renquest thought.

She went through the details of the sexual encounter. Flaherty let her speak and didn't interrupt. Her assailant was dead. They wouldn't file charges against her, so why make the victim of a horrible crime relive all the gory details? But then she described the murder.

"He…"

"So, it was a man?" Flaherty asked.

"Yes. We were beside a dumpster, and I was, well, you know, giving him what he wanted. And this guy just walks up to us. Travis goes berserk on the guy and knocks him to the ground. Then he turned back to me and told me I needed to finish what I started."

"What happened next?" Flaherty asked.

"Well, the guy on the ground got up. I didn't see him because of where I was kneeling, but the next thing I knew there was blood all over me. Travis was lying on the ground. Blood was squirting out of his neck. I just started screaming."

"Did you get a good look at the man who stabbed Mr. Sullivan?" Brooks asked. "I mean, after he stabbed Travis?"

"I'll never forget his face. He looked as shocked as I did at what he'd done. Then he turned and ran. I heard tires spinning and a car racing away. Then I just took off. I've been hiding in my apartment ever since."

Brooks got a detailed description of the assailant from Norman. Once the pair was sure they had everything, Flaherty ended the interview. Brooks offered Norman a ride home, and Flaherty handed her a business card, followed by a quick reminder to call if she ever saw the man again or thought of anything else that might help the investigation. Norman nodded, then she and Brooks left the room.

A few moments later, Flaherty appeared in the doorway to Renquest's office.

"Are we keeping that POS Sullivan on the board with the others?"

"For now," Renquest said.

"You still think it's connected to the others?"

"I don't know what to think. The stabbing is obviously a departure from the other murders. But something just isn't sitting right with me. This guy turns into an alley with no way out. Then gets out of his car and strolls up to see who is getting a BJ behind a dumpster? Something's off."

Flaherty looked at the whiteboard. "Okay. We'll get patrol to look for this guy. I'll take his description to the shift supervisors for the second and third shifts. They can distribute it to the units. He'll turn up." He paused, noticing the extensive file on Renquest's desk. "What about yours and Sanchez's guy? Where are you on Pratt?"

Renquest picked the file off his desk that Margaret had prepared for him and held it up. "We've got some work to do."

Sanchez smiled and took the file from the chief detective's outstretched hand. Placing it on the table in front of him. He opened it and began leafing through its contents.

Flaherty turned and disappeared into the hall. Sanchez divided the file in half and gave Renquest one of the two stacks. The pair began reading background information about Pratt. Sanchez took notes. Renquest kept it all straight in his head.

Chapter 18

After two hours of flipping through hundreds of pages containing credit reports, vehicle registrations, and family details, Sanchez needed a break.

"I need to get some food and check my emails," he said as he stepped out of the office.

Renquest sometimes forgot that each of his officers had other duties to perform outside of this case. Mostly administrative, like approving leave for line officers or overseeing civilian complaints.

He said, "Okay," as Sanchez turned the corner out of view.

The old detective wasn't sure he was gaining anything of value from the pages of information spread out before him on the desk. The financial data pointed to a normal life. He had had a few late payments over the past few years, but there were no accounts turned over to collections, and Pratt had never filed for bankruptcy. A local company employed him as an IT specialist, and he received a $700 monthly disability payment from the Department of Defense, which was automatically deposited into his savings account. The account contained a little over ten thousand dollars, most of which appeared to come from government payments over the past year. That Pratt was saving the disability money instead of using it for bills showed a sound financial footing and pushed the detective away from the possibility that his death resulted from an unpaid debt. Drug-related or otherwise.

He was back at the beginning again. No motive for the murder. Everything uncovered thus far pointed to the same, yet unknown, suspect they believed responsible for the other victims. But he just couldn't shake the feeling that something was different about this victim. The apartment, his financials, and the location and condition of the body bothered him.

The detective glanced at his phone. It was well past 3:00pm. He rewatched the Kim Norman interview, this time taking notes he felt would be helpful when his officers interviewed friends and family of Sullivan about his personal life and employment history. Somehow, a relationship existed between Sullivan and the other murder victims—he just wasn't sure Sullivan was the target in his own killing. Deep inside his cop brain, something told him the intended victim may have been Kim Norman. Sullivan, being in the wrong place at the wrong time, may have led directly to his gruesome murder. Though his actions that day, as disgusting and misguided as they were, might have saved Kim Norman's life. Of course, everything he was thinking was pure speculation. He needed more information about both Sullivan and Norman.

As he stood to stretch, Brooks poked her head into the doorway. Her usual smile had given way to a straight-lipped frown. The corners of her mouth wrinkled, revealing an expression of dismay. Even her posture had changed. Shoulders slumped forward; her back hunched.

He waved her in.

"What can I do for you, Captain?" he asked as she slipped through the doorway and toward his desk.

The stocky captain didn't sit in the chair; instead, she turned and stepped over to the window. Staring through its streaked glass at the buildings across the street. She said nothing. Renquest watched her as she stood quietly, gazing at the plain brown façade of the shelter opposite his office. He knew something was bothering her. He just didn't know if it was about the case or a personal matter, so he didn't push. She would talk when she was ready.

After a few minutes of silence, Brooks spun on her heels to face him. Her eyes showed confusion, but they also held a glint of determination.

"Detective," she said. "How do you filter through all the bullshit about this job?"

He straightened his back and leaned against the corner of the desk. "I'm not sure what you mean. But usually, I try to start by saying what's on my mind."

The captain's eyes darted to the floor. Her hands found their way into the pockets, still stiff from starch and ironing. The fabric detailed the outlines of her fingers as they burrowed deeper into the small cloth caverns.

"What's bugging you?" he asked in a low, soft tone.

She looked at him. She forced her hands deeper into her pockets—the fabric bulging out as her fingers reached the termination point inside the cloth pouch.

"Never mind. I'm just being ridiculous," she said. A fake smile snaked across her lips.

Renquest nodded. "When you're ready, I'll be here."

The corners of her mouth turned up slightly as she bit her bottom lip. "Sure."

"So, tell me about the interview with Kim Norman," he said, not wanting things to get more uncomfortable than they already were.

"You were watching from in here, right?"

He made his way around his desk to the high-back leather chair and gestured at the seat across from his before he sat down.

"Both me and Sanchez. But it's always different when you are in the room. Those untimed blinks, or finger twitches, don't always show up on camera. And you can't smell fear and desperation through a computer monitor."

"Are you suggesting that you can smell fear or when someone is lying?"

"That's exactly what I'm saying."

"That's total bullshit," the captain blurted out. Only after the words escaped her lips did she realize she'd just called her boss a liar. "I mean, with all due respect."

Renquest snorted a laugh. "It's okay. I thought the same thing when I first heard it. But over the years, it seemed to manifest itself as truth."

With a puzzled look on her face, Brooks asked, "What do you mean?"

"It's hard to explain," he said. "It's not like people emit an actual odor when they lie. That's not what I'm saying."

"So, what are you saying?"

"It's more like an association. When I was a kid, my mom liked to bake. She would make the most amazing chocolate chip cookies. They were so soft and packed full of chocolate chunks. We could have only one cookie a day. And believe me, she always knew how many cookies remained at the end of each day," Renquest said. "Well, one day I came up with a plan to get more cookies for myself. I told her I needed a batch made for another student's birthday we were celebrating at school." He noticed the quizzical look on Brooks' face. "This was before anyone really knew about food allergies, so parents would bake things for their kids' class parties. So, my request was perfectly normal. Of course, mom baked the cookies and placed them in a Tupperware container for me to lug to school the next day. Instead of taking the treats to school, I hid them in a paper bag in my closet. I even put a piece of Wonder Bread in the bag to help keep them fresh longer."

"What happened?" Brooks asked.

"Well, as I found out, cookies and bread are favorites of mice. When I got home from school, I raced to my closet to get a cookie. When I opened the bag, the mouse leaped out. It hit my face before scurrying off into a corner and disappearing. It scared the hell out of me. As I got older, when people lied to me, I'd smell..."

"Chocolate chip cookies," Brooks said.

"That's right," Renquest responded.

Brooks stared at her boss. "It still seems, I don't know, kinda silly."

The detective leaned back in his chair. With his hands cupped behind his head—he simply said, "You'll see," and laughed.

Brooks didn't appear to be impressed with his answer. Rolling her eyes, she stood. Her hands pressed the wrinkles out of her uniform, which had formed from sinking her hands deep into her pockets and stretching the fabric.

"Where are you going?"

She finished patting down the front of her trousers. Then, she pulled on a strand of hair that had worked free from the ponytail, snugged tightly against the back of her head, and tucked it behind her ear. Once finished, she turned on her heels and blurted over her shoulder as she left the room, "I'm going to get some answers."

Renquest smiled to himself and couldn't help but think once again that his captain was going to be a good detective one day. She continued to show good instincts and tenacity in wanting to get to the truth. It wouldn't take a lot of effort on his part to help get her to the finish line. He needed only to provide encouragement and nurture the natural traits that existed in her. She would do the rest.

His stomach gurgled, and he looked at the clock on his phone. He was feeling a little light-headed. It was time for something to eat. He wondered how Custus was managing at Johansen's office. After he got a sandwich, he would make the short drive to see how Custus was faring with Johansen at the coroner's office. While he was at it, he figured he would grab an extra sandwich for his old friend.

When he stepped into the reception area of Johansen's office, Custus, who seemed to know he was coming, instantly greeted him. Or maybe he could just smell the odor of corned beef emanating from the bag he carried at his side.

The medical student manning the reception desk looked up for a moment, then buried his nose back into the textbooks splayed out across the desk in front of him. Renquest picked a chair and sat down. His friend pushed against his legs, trying to get closer to him, or maybe it was the sandwich wrapped up in the white deli bag perched on his lap.

After he and the old hound dog finished eating, Renquest patted his friend on the head and tossed the empty bag and wrappers into the trash can by the reception desk.

"Is the doc in?"

"She had to go to Manassas for a meeting. Won't be back until later tonight," the intern said, never looking up from his books. "You want me to tell her you stopped by?"

"No, that's all right. I'll see her when I come by to pick up ole Custus here."

"Suit yourself."

Renquest bent over and rubbed the dog's long, floppy ears for a minute, then straightened upright and headed back to the office. He found Chief McNally waiting in his office for him when he returned.

"What can I do for you, Chief?" he said as he removed his jacket and slipped it over the back of his chair.

"I hadn't had a briefing yet today, so I thought I would come down and see for myself how the cases are coming," the chief said.

Renquest extended his hand, offering a seat to his boss. "Things are coming along. We found a witness to the latest murder. Flaherty and Brooks finished interviewing her a few hours ago. I'm waiting for the final report."

"Brooks and Flaherty did the interview?"

"Yes," Renquest said.

"And you weren't in the room with them?"

The way his superior asked made him feel some apprehension. "Something on your mind, Chief?"

Being the Chief of Police meant challengers to your authority were few. And they almost never came from inside the ranks. Renquest picked up on the subtle changes in his boss's body language. A tightened jaw. Straightening of the spine. Tensed shoulders. And a small drop of sweat on his forehead, just below his hairline.

"I'm wondering why I brought you in. If I had wanted Brooks and Flaherty to lead the investigation, I would have kept things the way they were. But I didn't. Do you want to know why?" McNally said.

Renquest knew a rhetorical question when he heard one. He remained silent.

"Because I went out and found a detective with a track record of closing cases. I hired you." The chief also leaned in. His face was close enough that Renquest picked up the scent of coffee on his boss's breath.

"And I must tell you; I took a lot of shit for bringing you in. The County Council wasn't excited about some reports from your previous employer."

"Anything in particular?" Renquest said, only half-joking.

"Your attitude, for one. Your superiors reprimanded you several times throughout your career for insubordination," McNally said.

Renquest again said nothing.

"Then there is institutional control. You allow the men and women under your command too much leeway. Some at your previous position believe your lax supervision style led to the serious injury of your partner."

Renquest remained silent.

"As leaders, we must set a good example. We must lead from the front, so to speak. We must never take a backseat. The troops under us take orders. They don't give them. And we don't let them fend for themselves," McNally said.

Renquest had heard enough. Patience was something he valued, but even he had his limits. Micromanaging every aspect of his command style was a bridge too far. The revelation that his former employer shared their concerns about him with his new employer made him feel uneasy. It contradicted the assurances provided to him when he left their employment. He straightened, grabbed his jacket from the back of the chair, then carefully slid it over his broad shoulders.

"You hired me to find the person responsible for the attacks and murders taking place in your city. Something you couldn't do. With all due respect, I don't believe failing to solve this case rests on the shoulders of the officers under your command. In fact, they've shown me to be highly intelligent and driven investigators. The only things missing were proper guidance and a push in the right direction."

Renquest paused as he noticed the expression on the chief's face change from one of concern to anger. His cheeks were flushed, and a slight twitch appeared in his right hand. He thought about shutting his mouth and leaving. But his ego got the better of him. If he were going down, he'd go down in flames.

"The only commonality I noticed here was a lack of strong leadership," he continued. "You could have promoted Brooks or Flaherty to chief detective, but you looked outside. Not because the people under you weren't ready, but simply because you didn't have the foresight to see the quality and competence in your own department."

The chief, his bottom lip pinched so firmly between his teeth Renquest thought he might bite clean through it, appeared close to exploding. To the detective's surprise, his boss took a deep breath. His teeth released the death grip on his lip.

In a calm, insular tone, McNally said, "You have until the end of the week to solve these murders. The county council meets again next week. At that meeting, I will recommend your termination for gross insubordination, dereliction of duty, and behavior unbecoming a law enforcement officer." Turning to face the door, he finished, "You were right about one thing. Hiring you was a command decision I failed at. Pack your bags, Detective. This will be the last case you work in Arlington." Then he marched out of the office—the door slamming behind him.

The timetable his superior set left Renquest two workdays plus a full weekend. Four days to finish the job. It wasn't a lot of time to catch a serial murderer. Even less time to apprehend an intelligent one. But he had never quit a case in his life. Sitting there, he thought to himself, *this one wouldn't be the first.*

Chapter 19

The elevator doors opened, and the newly energized detective stepped into the parking garage. As he maneuvered around the elevator banks, he looked toward his car parked along the south wall. Three figures stood next to his car. It took a moment for his eyes to adjust to the dim lighting of the garage, but then quickly recognized the three officers. It was Brooks, Flaherty, and Sanchez. They stood huddled at the rear of their boss's ride, quietly discussing something among themselves. As Renquest approached, all three stopped talking and simultaneously faced him. Their backs straight, with hands pressed against the seams of their trousers. The same form the academy drills into cadets.

Renquest stopped short of his car. "What's going on here?"

Brooks stepped forward. "Sir, we heard most of your conversation with Chief McNally."

"You really shouldn't eavesdrop. It's not polite," Renquest said.

"I apologize for that, Detective. But it was hard not to overhear the two of you. Your door was wide open and, well, it's right next to the coffeemaker."

"You all ran out of coffee at the same time?"

Brooks glanced back at her co-workers before answering.

"Just me and Flaherty, and we left before you and the chief finished. After," Brooks pointed to Flaherty and herself, "we went and found Sanchez. After a short meeting, we all agreed to come down here and wait for you." She looked around the half-empty garage. "This is as safe a place as any to talk. The chief's parking spot is outside near the side entrance, and the uniforms don't pay any attention to anything happening down here."

Renquest nodded. "What's on your mind?"

Flaherty stepped forward to stand next to Brooks. "The three of us have been working on this case from the beginning. No one wants to catch this psycho more than we do."

Sanchez nodded in agreement. "So, what's the plan, Detective?"

Renquest caught himself smiling. He tried to fight it, but failed. He gave his three officers a once-over, then said, "My house. Nineteen hundred hours. Bring everything you have on the abductions and murders."

In unison, the three officers chimed, "Yes, sir."

The taillights flashed as his fingers depressed the door-unlock button on the remote in his pocket. As Renquest slid into the driver's seat, he watched the three officers make their way to the elevator bank. He glimpsed himself in the rearview mirror. What he saw staring back pleased him for the first time since leaving his old department for this job. During the short time he'd been in Arlington, feeling like an outsider was the norm. Not anymore. The response he witnessed from his officers flipped the script. He hadn't become part of their team. Nor had they joined his team. It was the shared experience of battle that forced them to forge a new team. One working toward the same goals and expectations. Something in his experience usually led to success.

The car's engine roared to life with the push of a button. As he shifted the car into gear, he reflected on what had transpired only a few minutes before, and his chest swelled a little, knowing he had been right. All they needed was a leader. Someone to bring them together instead of fostering divisiveness by driving a wedge between them, using competitiveness instead of motivation and trust. He looked at the empty seat beside him and thought about the file of photos he'd received, sure of what he needed to do.

The front tires grabbed the sealed surface of the parking garage floor and squealed as he turned the wheel and backed out of the parking spot. In less than a minute, the car was on the street, headed south towards home. But first he needed to stop at Johansen's office and pick up Custus.

Even with the slight detour to grab Custus, he walked through his front door less than a half-hour after he left the office. Once inside, he took off his jacket, tossed it over the back of a chair, and then made his way to the bedroom to change into a fresh set of clothes. Donning a pair of blue jeans and an old t-shirt he'd received at a training event several years back, he knelt over the gun safe in his closet. His fingers danced the code out on the keypad, forcing the lid to snap open. After reaching in, he removed the copies of the pictures he found on his desk. He looked at every photo. Examining the man in the mask. Going over every detail. He needed to make sure his hunch was right. The extra attention only confirmed what he already knew to be true. The man wearing the mask in the photos was Chief McNally.

Brooks was the first person to arrive. She was wearing a pair of shorts and a tank-top with running shoes.

"I just came from the gym," she said when Renquest opened the door.

He stepped to the side and motioned for her to enter.

"Where are Flaherty and Sanchez?"

Brooks took a swig of water from the metal container she held in her right hand. Custus nestled up next to her leg, and she patted him on the head.

"They're coming. Both live in Fairfax County. Flaherty has kids. It's easier to find houses with a yard outside of Arlington." Brooks took another drink of water. "Sanchez still lives with his mother, I believe."

Renquest cocked his head to the side. Brooks must have noticed because she laughed before continuing.

"The cost of housing is so high here, it's not uncommon for people to live with parents or share a house with total strangers to help split costs."

Renquest was aware of the skyrocketing real estate market in the DC metro area. Hell, he'd paid twice as much for the condo they were standing in than single-family home he owned further south. He had just assumed a young man like Sanchez would want his privacy and a place to entertain female guests without a parent peering over his shoulder.

"I just thought…" he paused. "Never mind."

Renquest offered Brooks a chair at the small dining room table. She pulled up close, placing her water bottle on the table. Then she noticed the file splayed out in front of her.

"What's this?"

The experienced detective placed his hand on top of the file. Pulling it towards him. "This is why you are here."

"What's in it?" Brooks asked.

"Are you sure you want to know? This is one of those career moments where knowledge is irreversible. If I open this file to you, there is no going back."

Renquest could see the skepticism in Brooks' eyes. The hesitation in her gaze was unmistakable.

"Look, I get it if you don't want to get involved with what lies within this folder. Even having this could blow up in my face. Finish my career even. There is no need to take anyone else down with me." He paused and took a sip of beer before continuing. "But I could use your help. I've already decided I'm not bringing Flaherty or Sanchez on the inside. They have too much to lose."

"Why me?" Brooks asked.

He answered her in one word: "Trust."

The young captain smiled, then nodded. "Show me."

His hand pushed the file across the table. His palm turned upward, inviting her to open it.

Brooks pulled the file closer, opened it, and then closed it. She turned her attention back to her boss.

Renquest shrugged his shoulders. "There's still time to stop."

With a look of resolve on her face, Brooks opened the folder again. Renquest watched as she studied the images. Her fingers pushed each picture aside as she moved to the next one. When she finished with the last photo, she straightened the stack and closed the file. At first, she sat silently. Her eyes focused on the manila folder in front of her. After a long moment, she spoke.

"It's him, isn't it?"

"Yes," Renquest answered.

"How can you be sure?" Brooks asked. "The man in these pictures is wearing a mask. There isn't the slightest glimpse of his face in any of them."

"The same way you knew it was McNally the moment you looked at the first picture," he said.

Renquest placed his hand on the folder and slid it back to him. The revelation affected Brooks more than he had expected. "I have to ask..."

When their eyes met, he could see a fire burning behind them.

"The hell you do!" she said. Her hands clenched on the table.

The veteran detective leaned back in his chair. "I do, and you know I must ask if you were ever involved in a relationship with him. Consensual or otherwise."

All the blood in Brooks' body must have diverted to her brain, because her cheeks flushed red as an apple in a matter of seconds. Just as she appeared to want to scream at him, they heard a knock on the door. Renquest looked at Brooks, then back at the door.

"It's okay, I believe you. Why don't you splash some water on your face while I get the door."

Clearly still angry, Brooks stood from the chair and took a step towards the hall bathroom. Renquest grabbed the folder from the table and pushed the folder over in front of her. "Can you put that in the safe in my closet on your way to the bathroom?"

She stared at the file for a moment, then came another knock at the door. This time it was louder and a few raps longer.

Renquest tipped his head toward the bedroom. "Go ahead. I trust you."

The words seemed to ease her anger a little. She scooped up the file and disappeared into the bedroom. Renquest made his way to the door, opening it to find Sanchez and Flaherty standing on the other side. Flaherty had a large pizza box in his hands, and Sanchez was carrying a six-pack of a local bottled microbrew. One Renquest recognized from an earlier trip to the grocery store. He wasn't a microbrewery kind of guy, but he would try one. It was still beer. Kind of.

The table was a chair short, so Renquest suggested they all move into the living room. He pulled a chair from the table and placed it facing the couch and recliner. Then he sat down. Sanchez chose the recliner. Flaherty eased onto the couch. About that time, Brooks appeared from the bedroom. As she entered the room, the other two glanced at her. The usually perceptive detective hadn't considered the visual of Brooks appearing from the bedroom. As she entered the room, he said the first thought that entered his mind.

"The toilet in the hall runs non-stop," Renquest said quickly. "If you need to use the restroom, please use the one off the master bedroom. But please try not to wake Custus."

The two men nodded and returned to talking among themselves.

Once Brooks sat next to Flaherty on the couch, Renquest cleared his throat. The room fell silent as all three of his guests turned their attention in his direction.

"As you know, the chief and I had a brief discussion today about this case. I want to be clear. I truly believe Chief McNally wants us to catch this guy. His intentions are in the right place. However, I believe his motives are self-serving."

"I'll say," said Sanchez.

"He knows the County Council will fire him if we don't have a suspect in custody soon," Flaherty chimed in.

"Maybe," Renquest said. "But I can't control that. All we can do is work the case with the evidence in front of us. That's the job. That's what they pay us for." He paused and looked at each of his guests. "So, what do we know?"

The officer's eyes darted from one to the other. No one spoke at first.

Brooks broke the silence. "We believe that a single person is responsible for all the murders and abductions. One person working alone."

Flaherty spoke up. "Except for Pratt."

Brooks nodded. "Correct. Except for Pratt."

"Okay. So, we have two separate cases. Let's start with the victims who survived. How many were there?" Renquest asked.

"Four," Sanchez said.

"So, four abductions and four murders," Renquest said.

The three officers nodded simultaneously.

"What does that tell us?" Renquest asked.

Flaherty answered, "There was an escalation in his behavior."

"That's right. Something made him change his pattern from an abduction to one that resulted in murder," the detective said.

"But what was it that made him change? What made him snap and start killing his victims?" Brooks asked.

"That's what we need to find out," Renquest said.

Sanchez had sat quietly for most of the meeting while the other three tossed out ideas of what could have forced an escalation in the suspect's behavior. The lack of input from the young lieutenant didn't go unnoticed.

"You've been awfully quiet, Sanchez," Renquest said, reaching down to pet Custus, who'd come out of the bedroom to see what all the fuss was about. "You have nothing to add to this conversation?"

Sanchez, who wore an Arlington Police polo shirt, stood from the chair and walked over to the kitchen counter and opened another beer. The bottle, covered in condensation from being left out of the cool refrigerator, left a water ring on the countertop. He wiped the water with his hand and used his pant leg to dry his hand. Then he took a long swig. Swallowing hard and exhaling as if he had just consumed the most refreshing drink of his life. When he finished, he turned and spoke.

"What if there is no connection between the murders and the earlier abductions?"

The statement caught Renquest's attention. "What do you mean?"

"If we consider the Pratt murder unrelated to the other cases, what leads us to believe there is a link between the other murders and the earlier abductions?"

Flaherty shook his head. "There are too many things in common with the victims. A connection between all the victims must exist."

Brooks pushed herself off the couch.

"No, Marco is right. We just assumed the killings were all related to the abductions because of the blood draining. But all of that was in the news and readily available to anyone following the case in the press," her voice raised an octave as she spoke. "Hell, the chief even went to an emergency county council meeting and gave an update on the investigation."

"Press and the public were at that meeting," Sanchez said.

Flaherty wasn't buying into the idea and showed it with a shake of his head.

"Think about it," Brooks said, turning to Flaherty. "Someone has a beef with someone else. Albeit money, drugs, or a cheating spouse. They lose their ever-loving as the knowledge eats at them day after day. Then, these crazy abductions hit the news. Someone is out there drugging people. Their blood drained from them, only to be turned loose alive and otherwise unharmed."

Renquest watched as his team worked. A sense of accomplishment welled up inside him.

"Right," said Sanchez. "Easy for a guy to set up a couple of murders to mimic the abductions. Then, he used the other murders as misdirection for his own killing. We assume we are dealing with one serial killer when, in fact, there could be two killers and two separate motives."

"Okay. Let's say you're right. But what about Travis Sullivan and Kim Norman?" Flaherty said. "Right, there was an attempted abduction and a murder."

Brooks and Sanchez looked at each other and both sat back down, a little deflated. The theory they'd built, possibly torn down in seconds. The question for the team now was how Sullivan and Norman tied into the other murders and abductions?

Renquest had an idea.

"I believe the Sullivan murder is attributable to the person responsible for the earlier abductions."

"How do you figure?" Flaherty asked.

"I think Kim Norman was an intended target. But when he tried to take her, Travis Sullivan surprised him. The two men fought. He killed Sullivan and then ran without taking Norman. They found a burned-out car down in Prince William County the other day, and I will bet my left nut it belongs to whoever killed Sullivan."

"The problem is that fire and evidence don't mix well. We won't be able to get anything off the car," Brooks said.

"True. But we haven't had another attempt since Sullivan. Maybe that's because he no longer has a car."

"Or he is just scared and hiding out in a basement somewhere in town," Flaherty responded.

"Or he left town," Sanchez added.

"I don't think either of those is true," the veteran detective answered, his right hand rubbing the old hound dog's head. "A person with that type of compulsion can't quit hunting for long. It's a desire buried deep in their psyche. It's relentless. Unforgiving. The urge is so strong it'll overpower any attempts to subdue it."

"So, first we need to figure out who the person is. Then, figure out how to catch the guy?" Brooks asked.

The four officers sat in the small living room and discussed each case in depth. Together, they pored over every detail in each abduction and murder. After they extracted all the information from the files, they ate the remaining pizza and drank diet soda from Renquest's refrigerator, since they had finished the last beer hours before.

It was a little before midnight when they finally settled on a plan of action. The last details still needed to be hammered out on an aggressive and risky construct. Some of the finer points would have to fall into place as the investigation unfolded. Both because of the time constraints Chief McNally placed on Renquest earlier that day and what they didn't know yet. But it was a start. And that would have to do for now.

Chapter 20

Sanchez and Flaherty left together. Both men appeared energized and champing at the bit to get to work. Renquest wondered if either man would sleep much that night, remembering how he felt as a young cop on the verge of solving a big case. There was very little you could do to keep your mind from racing. Unable to think of anything else. It was a good feeling—for the younger officers. Old detectives needed their sleep.

Brooks hung back. She announced she needed to use the restroom before hitting the road. Once the front door closed, she re-emerged from the bedroom, making her way to the couch, where Custus had taken up residence shortly after the others left. The old dog lifted his head and repositioned it on her lap. She gently scratched behind his ears.

"He likes you," Renquest said.

"I had a dog just like him once," Brooks said.

Custus nestled his head deep in her lap as she continued scratching.

"What's on your mind?"

She stopped scratching, and the old dog looked up at her. She sighed.

"I knew about the chief," she said.

"Knew about him?" Renquest sat on the chair in the middle of the room. "Are you talking about the photos?"

She nodded.

"How long have you known?" he asked.

"The first time I heard anything about it, I was on a call. A woman had made an accusation concerning someone in the department, and it was my job to meet the complainant and interview her. Initially, the interview was just to get a feel for the person lodging the complaint. We get so many of these things a year, we must sort through them to figure out which ones are credible and which ones are just pissed-off folks who got a ticket for something."

"Makes sense," Renquest said. "What were your conclusions on this one?"

Brooks reached into her lap and resumed rubbing the old dog's ears.

"At first, the woman didn't want to provide any names. She only wanted to let us know that there was someone in the department involved in activities she felt were inappropriate for a police officer. There was something about her that made me believe she was telling the truth. I can't explain it. But deep in my bones, I knew she had information, and it was bad for the department."

"So, you pushed her?"

"Yes, hard," Brooks said. Her eyes focused on Custus.

"Did she crack?"

"She did. And then she told me something. Something I didn't want to believe."

Brooks took a deep breath, looked down at Custus, then told Renquest everything the woman had said in her interview. According to her, she first met McNally at a local event shortly after the county council appointed him chief of police. In fact, the meeting took place at an official gathering that the county council scheduled so other leaders in the community could meet the new chief of police. A chance to voice concerns they feel the new head of the police department might want to know about. The woman was a longtime volunteer at county events and fundraisers. She enjoyed attending the annual 5k run, where she handed out water to the runners as they passed the finish line. Later in the year, the county council put out a call for help from the community on election day. As always, the good samaritan happily dropped what she was doing to devote her entire day to assisting elderly voters with their ballot questions. She felt tremendous pride in her hometown, which drove her sense of duty to help when she could.

So, when someone from the county offices called her directly, saying there was a need for volunteers to work the ceremony honoring the new chief of police, she once again happily agreed to help. That became the day Linda Bevins first met the devil. The interactions at first were casual enough. A handshake at first. Followed by a request that she volunteer at police functions. A sideways glance here and there. A hand on her back as they parted ways. An awkward glance from across the room. Then one day, she received a personal invitation to dinner.

She made no apology for her part in what transpired. Her new caller was charismatic and handsome. An accomplished ex-soldier, elevated to the chief of police of a county with slightly under two-hundred and fifty thousand people. What was there not to like? Things gained momentum quickly, and before long the two were involved in a torrid love affair.

In the beginning, he booked a room at a local motel. The couple met once every couple of weeks over the course of a few months. The rendezvous lasted an hour or two at most. But then things changed. As he became more comfortable, he made requests. Sexual requests. Simple things, like wearing costumes and masks. At first, Bevins was happy to play along. It all seemed so exciting, and role-playing added a level of intimacy she'd never experienced before. As time passed, the meetings became more frequent. And the requests became more bizarre. Sadistic even. He would change into leather garb. Whips and chains attached to dog collars hung from his sides. Obedience became more of a demand and less cosplay. McNally began making her call him Master and Lorde. Forced to kneel at his feet. Degrading her until she begged his forgiveness for whatever self-indulgent wrong he perceived she'd committed.

She wanted to stop, but he threatened her. Not with violence. No, he used something much worse. He would shame her. Sully her name and reputation. He videotaped every session without her knowing. If she didn't continue indulging his fantasies, or told anyone about the two of them, he would post the videos on the internet for everyone to see. She became so distraught—it affected her health. She stopped eating and lost thirty pounds, which led to her hospital admission and eventual escape. Once under the care of a doctor, the hospital admitted her to a psych ward, where she had daily meetings with a psychologist. Visitors were strictly off-limits. Not even her immediate family could visit for the first few weeks.

McNally had sent flowers once, but after several months of zero contact, he left her alone. She imagined there were other women out there he'd found to play his sick games with. But because she always feared he'd come back, she kept her secret for months. Until one day she met another woman who'd fallen into the same trap as her. The strength of this other woman doubled, even tripled, what she herself was capable of. This lady was a career professional. A real Type A personality. Someone able to recognize her mistakes and stand up to a bully. Brooks asked, but Bevins refused to provide the other woman's name. She referred to her only as the Doc.

The last statement sent a jolt through Renquest's nervous system. His ears filled with a ringing. His cheeks flushed as blood rushed to his head. The thoughts in his head drifted to Johansen.

"So, Linda Bevins never said who the other woman was? Never gave a name or a description?" he asked.

"Nothing," Brooks said. "But I kept nudging her. Right until she stopped returning my calls. Eventually, she moved out of town, and I never heard from her again."

"But you didn't stop looking?"

"No, I started following him. Just nights at first. But that spiraled into weekends and my days off before long," Brooks said.

"That's how you got the photos?"

His Captain nodded.

"Ever find out who *Doc* was?" The words conjured up images he didn't like or want swirling around in his head. Thoughts he didn't need.

She shook her head.

"What about the pictures? How did they end up on my desk?"

"I don't know," Brooks said.

"You didn't put them there? Hoping I might take the bait and challenge the chief?"

She looked square in his eyes. "No. I had put this whole thing to bed after Linda Bevins left town, and my efforts to locate anyone else willing to talk turned up nothing."

"You didn't turn the photos over to anyone else. Maybe in a last-ditch effort to save your case?" Renquest asked.

"No. I kept the pictures locked in the evidence room. I put them in an old case box from the nineties involving an unsolved bank robbery. No one had looked at that case for twenty years. I thought the pictures would be safe there," Brooks said.

Renquest grimaced. "So, what you're telling me is anyone with access to the case files room could have found the photos and placed them on my desk?"

Brooks said, "I guess I am. I should've stored them off-site. I'm sorry."

"We play the hand we're dealt. Nothing we can do to change it now, so there's no sense fretting over spilled milk. We'll figure something out."

The old detective rose from his chair. Custis groaned as Brooks stood, and his head slid onto the cushion.

"I think that's enough for tonight. I need to get this old boy outside one last time and get to bed. We are going to have a few long days ahead of us," he said.

"What about Chief McNally?" Brooks asked.

"We don't have time to worry about that right now. We need to solve the murders, or nothing else will matter."

"Why's that?" she asked.

"Because I won't have a job and you might not either," Renquest said. There was no reason to sugarcoat the situation for her. She needed to know how serious this could get.

Renquest bent over and clicked the leash onto Custus' collar and opened the door. Brooks stepped out and looked back and smiled as she disappeared down the hall. She was young and energetic, so she bypassed the elevator and took the stairs. Renquest watched her leave before taking the elevator to the lobby and out to the fenced-in area for pets to do their business. After cleaning up the mess and a quick elevator ride back up, Custus was resting on his bed. Renquest followed suit and slid under the sheets and closed his eyes. He didn't dream that night. Instead, he awoke with a sinking feeling in his gut.

* * *

The last couple of days had been terrible. He'd injected his last vial of blood the previous day, and he was already feeling the effects of non-treatment. The feeling of bugs crawling under his skin returned that morning. There was no amount of scratching that soothed the pain. It made him wonder if it was already too late. Doubt crept in. Would the treatment continue to work after a break in the doses? Or was he doomed to the same fate as his mother?

With the aid of a tiny step stool, he peered out the small, rectangular window high on the basement wall. If he slid to one side and cantered his head to the right, he could see cars passing on the street in front of the house. He watched as they drove past. One. Two. Three. They just kept coming. Everyone was out in the world's chaos except him. How could they go on with their lives as if nothing were wrong? Were they blind to what was going on? Or was it that most people didn't care? Maybe it hadn't affected them in the same way as it had him. His mother's death turned his life upside down. They simply didn't understand. They hadn't experienced grief like he had. The thought of that made him angry. He could make sure some of them would know how he felt. Even if that wasn't what he intended.

He stepped back off the stool and looked away from the window. His anxiety eased. But his thoughts quickly turned back to the outside world. The muscles in his arms tensed. He took a deep breath and visualized himself out amongst the people. Something simple at first, like eating at a restaurant. That was something he hadn't done in years. His mind visualized him sitting at a table. Interacting with the waiter and placing an order. The more detailed his thoughts became, the more at ease he felt. His breathing became more relaxed. He could feel his heartbeat slow. The thoughts in his head quieted. He would be back out in the world one day. Part of the chaos he feared so much. If he couldn't survive among people, what was the point of everything he'd done?

He turned to the small television perched on the wall in the back corner of the room.

"Might as well check the news before heading out," he said as he flipped on the television.

The screen lit up, and as the picture appeared, he saw a man standing in front of the courthouse. A gold badge hanging off his belt outed him as a cop, though he didn't look like any cop he'd ever seen. His hair grayed, and his waistline bulged. He wanted to say the man looked experienced, but he felt the term *aged* fit him better. He reached for the remote and pressed the volume button. The caption at the bottom of the screen read: Detective Renquest, Arlington County Police. Renquest spoke about a series of murders in the city that had taken place over the past month. Interested, he moved closer to the television.

From behind a podium, the detective said, "We are confident the earlier assaults connect to the murders. And we also believe the last victim, whose name is being withheld at this time pending family notification, died trying to stop an abduction he saw taking place."

His ears rang, burning as the cop's words passed through them. It was all lies. He had murdered no one. It wasn't his fault that his test subjects fell ill and died. In fact, it was their own lifestyles that led to their demise. Except for the guy in the alley. He'd killed that guy for sure. But that was self-defense. The man had left him no choice. Kill or die. And what was this talk about the dead guy walking in on an abduction and trying to help? It'd been he who'd saved the girl from that drug-dealing pimp. The credit belonged to him. Not some scum-sucking gutter shitbag who preys on women. The anger swelled in his body once again. He could feel it coursing through his veins.

Then the detective said something he couldn't believe. He had to pause and then back the scene up fifteen seconds to listen to it again. The lump in his throat rose and fell with the words coming from the detective's mouth.

"It is our belief that there is a sexual component to these crimes. The culprit behind this is a sexual deviant who uses violence to fuel his sexual compulsions."

A reporter shouted a question from the back of the crowd. "Are you saying the victims were raped or sexually assaulted?"

"No comment."

The remote fell from his hand, crashing onto the floor. The batteries popped out and rolled under the metal workbench. He couldn't believe his ears. Not only was he not responsible for the murders, but insinuating he was some kind of pervert was insane. He was not a sexual predator. In fact, he'd abstained from sex for years. Physical attraction was a distraction he couldn't afford. There was even a slight chance of viral transmission through sexual intercourse. That was not a risk he wanted to take.

He reached down and grabbed the remote off the floor. His fingers frantically pressed the power button. But the television stayed on. Its sounds reverberating through the room. Before he could stop it, his arm drew back and threw the remote. The glass television screen shattered. The picture went black, but the sound played on. He hung his head. In less than a minute, he'd lost everything. Just like his mother, he'd die from the disease. It was over.

Focusing on how he'd die became his singular focus now. He couldn't cure himself and would surely slip into the darkness over the next few weeks. Once the treatments stopped, the disease's progression was impossible to stop. The detective's voice on television played in his head. Then, an idea popped into his head. He knew how he'd die. It was the one thing he could control. And having the fat man there at the end would be poetic. Suddenly, the anger and tension surging through his body a moment ago had all but faded. A smile even appeared. Confident and calm, he turned, opened the basement door, and began planning his own demise.

Chapter 21

The press conference went off without a hitch. They had little time to prepare, and if it weren't for Brooks' ability to think on the fly, none of this would have happened. Renquest couldn't help but think that her knowing the chief wasn't fully on board with the plan was a small motivator. While Chief McNally was against the idea, he let Renquest and the team move forward. The detective knew his boss wanted him to fail. He could think of no better way to achieve that goal than a flock of news cameras recording his every word for a potential hearing in front of the county council to seal the deal. McNally even forced Renquest to use the county courthouse as a backdrop, not the police station. It was all designed to get the county commissioner's attention. If the investigation went south and he could not solve these murders, people would remember the courthouse and not the police station. That image could transfer poor public sentiment to the commissioners, elevating McNally's position of power and all but guaranteeing his request for Renquest's removal without objection. A political maneuver that could cement the chief's stature in local politics for years to come.

Renquest was no politician, and he hated how bureaucrats used the police to score cheap political points. But over the years, he'd gotten used to it, or numb to it anyway. His old partner, Paul Dodge, hated when politics impeded solving a case and would often spin out of control, landing both men in hot water at the conclusion of a case. It was times like this he missed having a partner and wondered where his old friend was and if he was doing okay. Last he heard; the parole agent was back in his home state of Indiana, recovering from a gunshot wound he received while working on the pair's last case together. The thought of not having him around to help when things got bad made him a little sad. Regretful even in the way things turned out.

After the press conference, Renquest made his way past the horde of shouting reporters, most of them local, but a few had made the trek from as far away as Richmond. He didn't even bother with the usual *no comment* as he disappeared into the courthouse. Once inside, he felt relieved to be out of the limelight, but that feeling didn't last long. As he cleared the security area, he saw a well-dressed Hispanic man waiting for him in the lobby. It was Ramone Diaz, the ranking member of the county council.

He stood a little over six feet tall with an athletic build. Wide shoulders and muscular arms made him look like a formidable man. Renquest couldn't help but feel a sense of dread as he approached; the man's hand outstretched in a politician's greeting.

"Detective," the councilman said. "I'm Ramone Diaz of the Arlington County Council."

"Councilman," the detective said.

"I saw your press conference."

"I guessed you would."

"In fact, the entire council watched it from right there in the boardroom," Diaz said, pointing to a set of closed wooden doors to the left of where they stood. "As you can imagine, we have been following these cases closely."

Renquest said nothing and simply nodded.

"It's no secret we're concerned about the lack of progress in these matters. That's why when Chief McNally asked to bring a chief of detectives on board, we voted unanimously to approve your position. But your press conference confirmed our suspicions. You and your team are nowhere near solving these murders," Diaz said.

"We needed to make a move." Renquest said. Though he found it hard to keep a calm tone. Being called incompetent is not something he tolerated. County councilman or not.

The athletic-looking councilman forced a politician's smile. One that is hard to know if the bearer is happy about something you did or if for an advantage they think they gained. He then pursed his lips, his head bobbing before speaking again.

"I was an athlete growing up. Football. Basketball. Basically, I tried out for anything with a ball. I even got a football scholarship to a small college in Florida. Unfortunately, I blew my knee out on a dirty chop-block my sophomore season, and that ended my playing days."

"Must have been hard."

"It was. But after six months of rehabilitation, I accepted the fact that I would never play ball again. That is when someone introduced me to what would become my genuine passion."

"Politics?" Renquest asked.

Diaz let out a boisterous laugh. "Not hardly. But it was what made me an excellent politician."

Renquest stood perplexed. Was this guy going to tell him, or was he supposed to guess? Then it hit him. This was all just a strategy. A look five moves into the future. That was the game.

"Chess," he said.

"That's right. Chess is a true strategy game. There are limited moves on a chessboard. That forces you to look into the future and visualize the entire board, seeing how your opponent may react to your move and the five moves after that."

"That's what makes you a good politician?"

The politician's smile returned. "That, and I trust no one."

And just like that, the councilman turned and walked away. Renquest wasn't sure what to make of Ramon Diaz. Other than that, he was a politician whom you couldn't trust to do the right thing. People like him would always choose self-serving interests over helping others. But people like Diaz were manipulable. The trick was figuring out which of their interests overlapped with yours. Then, all it took was a little shove in the right direction.

Renquest watched as Diaz slipped through the wooden doors to the meeting room. He could see others in the room through the gap between the doors as they were closing. Diaz most likely needed to report back what he had learned to the other members of the county council, who were waiting in the room. Renquest laughed inside his own head. Johansen was waiting for him when he returned to his office.

The greeting he usually received from her was one of smiles and of friends. He knew immediately that this visit was different. Her face carried the look of someone bearing bad news. Her eyes were red and her cheeks flushed, as if she'd been crying. He felt a shiver run down his spine and a deep pit open in his stomach. And just like that, he knew why she was there.

"Are you okay?" he asked, not sure he wanted her to answer.

She stood silent. Staring at him. He could see tears welling in her eyes.

"Whatever it is, Rebecca, you can tell me. I won't judge you."

Her mouth opened, and he braced himself for what he might hear. He wondered how he would react to her revelation. His hands tensed. His muscles ached. And just as he was about to ask her again, she spoke.

"It's Custus. He's gone."

Immediately, his heart raced. His stomach soured as acid filled the void. Beads of sweat pushed out of the pores on his forehead.

"What do you mean, gone?" His voice cracked as he could not control the tone.

She stepped closer. "I was working in the back, and he was lying on his bed out by the receptionist's desk. After an hour, I thought I should check on him. You know, to see if he needed to go out to use the bathroom." She paused and wiped a single tear that had formed and rolled down her cheek. "I called his name, and he didn't come. So, I went out to see what was wrong. When I opened the door, he was lying curled up on the bed. I figured he was sleeping."

Renquest stood quietly, not sure he wanted to hear what was about to come out of her mouth.

"But something didn't seem right. He seemed too peaceful. I knelt and touched his head, but he didn't move. I placed my stethoscope on his chest. There was nothing. He was gone. I think he just fell asleep and didn't wake up." She reached out and touched his hand. "I'm so sorry, Bill."

His heart sank. He didn't know what to say. He didn't know what to do.

Everything changed in an instant.

"Where is he now?" He mustered the words while fighting back any show of emotion.

"He is in the lab. I wrapped him in a blanket and put him in one of the cold lockers."

"I want to see him."

She took his hand. "I'll drive."

The old, tattered blanket Custus had slept on for years looked odd against the clean surface of the metal table. Its checkered pattern curved around the still body it covered. The old dog's head protruded out one end and rested on a blue paper pillow. For Renquest, the reality sank in.

"He looks so peaceful."

A solitary tear slipped down the old detective's cheek.

"I don't think he suffered, if that helps," Johansen said.

He approached his oldest friend. Slowly, as if not to wake him. Even though he knew the truth. He placed a hand on the dog's head and bent over, kissing him gently on the forehead.

"Goodbye, old friend," he whispered. "I'll never forget you."

His hand gently ran across the face and down the neck of his beloved dog one more time. Then he stood and wiped the moisture from his cheeks.

Turning back to Johansen, he asked, "What happens now?"

She took two steps in and pulled the blanket over the dog's head. "I have a friend who is a veterinarian. The same one that took care of my sweet boy. I can call her if you like?"

Renquest was silent for a moment. "That would be nice."

"This is going to sound insensitive, but she will need to know how you want the body dealt with," Johansen said. Her fingers caressed his forearm.

"I… I don't know. I had never really given it much thought." His head dropped. Eyes now stared at the floor. "I always knew this day would come. I just thought we would be home when it did, and I would bury him in the yard. Maybe place a nice little stone marker at the spot. You know, something I could see from the window and visit."

Johansen squeezed his arm tighter.

"There are cemeteries for pets. A place you can visit and mourn."

Renquest shook his head. He hated cemeteries. Both his parents were in graves in one of the nicest rest parks in their hometown. It had been over ten years since he had visited or placed flowers next to the headstone. He just didn't see the point. They were dead. Nothing he did would change that.

"I think I would like to keep his ashes. In a nice box, stored on the mantel. Maybe even someday spread them in a field or meadow out in the country."

"He would've liked that idea, I think," Johansen said.

The two stood and stared at the checkered blanket on the cold steel table. Neither saying anything.

The cold water felt rough, abrasive even, against his cheeks. He had used his shirtsleeve to wipe the tears from his face so many times that his skin had become irritated and flushed. His eyes were puffy, and his nose bore the signs of someone who had been blowing into a tissue for hours. Using both hands, he cupped cold water, pressing the liquid against his face and holding it for a ten-count. He repeated the ritual until most of the puffiness in his eyes and cheeks had disappeared. Now he looked only half-dead.

At his desk, he opened the files on Pratt and Sullivan. Victims four and five. He scoured the pages but found it difficult to concentrate. His thoughts kept turning to Custus, lying on that steel slab. Something he'd seen so many times before, but always with strangers. He closed the files. He needed to get out of the office. Maybe some fieldwork would distract him from reality.

The engine fired up in the Dodge Charger. His hand gripped the wheel, and the tires squawked as he pulled out of the parking garage onto the street. He didn't have a destination in mind, but after twenty minutes he found himself parked in front of a familiar house. Sitting there, the engine still running, he stared at the brick house. Something wasn't right, and he knew the answer was in that basement.

Chapter 22

The sound of the brakes squealing snapped him out of his trance. He looked in the rearview mirror and saw Sanchez step out of the driver's door and approach his car on the passenger side.

"Detective. I was driving past and thought I saw your car. What are you doing here?"

Renquest killed the engine. His gaze focused on the small, two-story brick home.

"We're missing something," Renquest said. His fingers tapped against the leather covering of the steering wheel as he re-hashed the conversation the two men had with the old man a few days ago.

Sanchez knelt next to the passenger door. "I keep having the same feeling. I can't seem to shake it."

"It's in there," Renquest said. His hand outstretched, with a finger pointed toward home. "I know it."

"Do you want to take another look?"

Renquest nodded. "I do."

"Me too," Sanchez said. "I'll see if the old man is home."

Sanchez rapped on the door two different times. But no one answered. He walked back and leaned in the open passenger window.

"Doesn't appear to be anyone home."

"You still got the key I asked you to make?"

A set of metal keys dangled and clanged from a rubber key holder Sanchez shook in his right hand.

"Yep."

Renquest slipped out of the driver's seat and closed the door behind him. The two men made their way up the driveway, past the old car, which was still sporting two flat tires, and around the side of the house to the basement door. Sanchez used the freshly minted key, then pushed the door open. The stench of rotten food and ammonia assaulted their senses. Sanchez turned to Renquest, who had taken a step back and turned his head away to get some fresh air.

"I forgot to bring masks," Sanchez said, with a hand covering his nose and mouth.

"Not sure they would have helped anyway," the veteran detective said and slipped past his junior partner. "Let's get this over with."

The pair entered. Renquest could see Sanchez holding his breath.

"You're gonna breathe it in eventually. Might as well get used to it."

His lieutenant exhaled and coughed.

"You start in here and I'll take the bedroom," Renquest said.

"Any idea what we are looking for?"

Renquest shook his head. "I'll know it when I see it."

"Yeah, but I might not," Sanchez mumbled, a half-hearted attempt not to breathe any of the foul air into his mouth as he spoke.

The bedroom was located down a narrow hall, which certainly didn't meet current building codes. The stout detective's shoulders brushed against both walls as he made his way to the bedroom at the end. He had looked in the room the last time the two men were there. A crime scene unit had also combed through the small basement apartment but found nothing of significance. The only prints in the place belonged to Pratt and the old man who owned the property. Which proved nothing. Even if Pratt deep-cleaned weekly, Renquest expected to find partial prints of the owner. It was inevitable.

A search of the closet yielded nothing. Renquest flipped over the mattress. Nothing again. He lowered to his hands and knees and looked under the bed. Clean. The nightstand had one drawer. Empty.

It was almost as if Pratt didn't live in the apartment. The cat was the only thing he saw that required taking care of. But a quick visit every couple of days to fill the food and water bowls and empty the litter box would suffice for a cat. He scratched his head and took one last look around the room. It seemed normal. Nothing was out of the ordinary. As he turned to the door, he noticed something about the hallway. He stepped back and looked at the room. He particularly looked at the wall that contained the doorway. It was easy to see three feet of wall space to the left of the door. He stepped up to the doorway and stared down the hallway. The left side of the hall had no doors or closets. But it sat only about six inches to the left of the door. He looked back at the wall in the bedroom.

He called out to Sanchez. "Come back here."

Sanchez appeared and immediately commented on the width of the narrow hallway.

"Man, this is one skinny-ass hall."

"Come in here for a second," Renquest said, waving him into the room.

Sanchez stepped past him and glanced around the now disheveled space. He looked back at his boss.

"This place is a mess."

"Not that," Renquest said. "Stand right here and look down the hall."

The detective pointed to a spot on the floor with one hand and down the hall with the other.

Sanchez moved to the place Renquest had pointed at and gazed down the hall.

"What do you see?"

"A skinny-ass hallway," the lieutenant said.

"Take your time and look around."

Sanchez took a breath and held it for a moment before exhaling. His eyes moved from right to left. Then floor to ceiling. Back down the hall and back to the left again. He took a step forward toward the doorway.

"This wall," he looked at Renquest, who stood nodding. "The hallway and this far wall don't seem to line up."

"Exactly," Renquest said.

"But there are no doors on that side of the hallway."

Renquest shook his head.

"And I don't remember any closets or doors along that wall in the living room either," Sanchez said.

"Let's take a look."

It turned out there was a door in the far corner of the living room. A small utility closet housed a water heater and old paint cans. As Renquest stepped into the compact space, he immediately recognized there was a space behind the wall that ran the length of the apartment to the bedroom. Big enough for a man of his size to stand in.

"There is a void back there, isn't there?" Sanchez asked, a hint of hesitation in his voice.

"Appears so," Renquest said as he turned to exit the room. "They might have just left it there when they converted the basement into a rental. A small area to run the plumbing and electrical wires. Might make it easier to fix things like broken water lines."

Sanchez nodded. "True. But how do you get back there? I don't see another door in the hallway or the bedroom."

The two men looked down the hall.

"There's no way in from here," Renquest said. Then he looked up.

"You think the entrance is up there?" Sanchez asked.

The old detective rubbed his hand over the back of his neck. He wasn't sure what, if anything, this meant. Then it hit him.

"No stairs."

"What?"

Renquest moved back to the center of the living space. With the outside door at his back, he examined every inch of wall space in the apartment.

"There is no basement access from upstairs."

Sanchez stepped back beside his boss.

"Maybe the only way in was from the outside? Sometimes they built old houses like that."

"I don't think so. That was usually something done pre-World War Two. When basements were more for storing food than for living in. After World War Two, builders put things like water heaters and coal furnaces in the basements. Then, to make it easier for the homeowner to service the units, they put stairs inside the house. Did you see any windows along the wall on the front of the house when we pulled up?"

Sanchez looked up toward the front of the house, as if he were trying to recall a memory. "I don't think I paid any attention. I remember a lot of shrubs. They were pretty overgrown. So, even if there had been a window, I don't think I could have seen it."

Just then, Renquest's phone beeped. The message on the screen read: *Custus is with the vet. You can pick him up this afternoon. I selected a nice box for the ashes. I hope you don't mind. Becca.*

The reality of the day hit him hard. The work at the house had helped him forget, but the thoughts of Custus were back in his head.

"Everything okay, boss?" Sanchez asked.

"Yeah," Renquest said. "Just something I've got to take care of when we get back."

He took one more look around before the two men left the basement. Renquest took a photo of the front before leaving. Sometimes online maps and real-estate websites show pictures of houses taken months and years earlier. Before he crawled around on the ground getting poked by the sharp leaves of the unruly holly bushes lining the front of the house, he thought he might see if he could locate some photos from when the yard was better kept. If not, Sanchez would have to come back and get dirty. He could do it, but being the boss had its advantages.

When the two men returned, Brooks was waiting in Renquest's office.

"You two have fun?"

"Not exactly. What can I do for you?" Renquest asked his captain.

"What is that smell?" Brooks waved her hand in front of her nose.

Renquest took off his jacket and tossed it over the back of his chair. "What do you need?"

"Okay. Well, Flaherty and I made it out to Sullivan's home. He lived about as you would've expected."

"What do you mean?"

"He is a drug dealer. His place is a mess. Dirty dishes in the sink. Clothes slung everywhere. Needles and pills on every table. A real shithole," Brooks said.

"Is the evidence team out there?" Renquest asked.

"Yes sir. Tech boys are bagging and tagging everything. Flaherty is meeting with the judge to get an emergency warrant signed for his car and the shed out back."

"Don't need one," Renquest said. "Legally, it's all part of our murder investigation. Plus, he is dead."

"I know. I thought it best if we covered all our bases on this one. No need to make the chief mad with something we could have easily avoided."

Renquest knew Brooks was right. Getting the warrant was the right play and served as a shield against a judge throwing out valuable evidence on a technicality at trial.

"Good thinking. Any leads on who may have killed him?"

"Not yet. We had a few calls come in, but mostly asking about a reward," Brooks said.

"We knew it would happen. I expect the calls will pick up over the next twenty-four hours. The press conference should help jar some people's memories."

Sanchez's chair moaned as he leaned back. "Do you think anything will come of the calls?"

Renquest shook his head. "I don't put a lot of faith in the public during a murder investigation. People are self-serving and do the right thing only if it benefits them. But you never know, so keep monitoring the phones and follow up on any leads that seem promising." Renquest slid forward in his chair and opened his laptop. Then he reached into his shirt pocket and pulled out his readers. "Anything else?"

"Are you alright?" Brooks asked.

"I'm fine."

"You seem a little off, that's all."

He noted the concern in her voice. "It's been a long day, and the press conference kind of drained me. I'll be fine," he said.

Brooks nodded and left the office.

Renquest took off his reading glasses. He rubbed his eyes and sat in silence.

His thoughts turned to Custus. The pit in his stomach expanded the more he thought about his old friend. It felt as if nothing in the world could fill its cavernous void. He took a deep breath and sighed. Then he returned his attention to his computer screen and continued the search for old photos of the Pratt house. Work was the best way he knew to help keep his mind off Custus. Plus, he'd just hung it all out there in the press conference. Now he needed a lead, or he'd have plenty of time to sit at home and mourn his friend as an ex-chief of detectives.

Chapter 23

The small wooden box sat on the counter. A little brown reminder of the pain he'd forgotten about while he slept. The previous day had been a roller coaster of emotions, and the moment his head touched the pillow, he was out. It was a deep sleep. He didn't remember any dreams. He felt rested as he pulled a coffee cup from the top shelf of the kitchen cabinet. A splash of creamer and two packets of sugar. Fake sugar, if he were being honest with himself. A ritual started several years ago after a consultation with his doctor ended in discussions about rising glucose levels and warding off the genetic time bomb that is diabetes.

Steam lofted from the rim of the cup as the hot liquid swirled clockwise. A small amount splashed onto the counter when he removed the spoon.

Renquest put on his jacket, pulling the left side out by the lapel and sliding his wallet and badge into the inside pocket. Next, he tapped his right hip. The hard frame of his weapon thumped under his fingers. He looked back at the round bed still lying on the floor in the living room. His gaze returned to the wooden box on the counter.

"Only a few more days and then I can take you back home, buddy. I just gotta finish this first."

His eyes filled with moisture as he closed the door behind him.

It was already 7 a.m. and traffic was heavy. Fridays were like that. Especially the closer to the courthouse. Fridays were sentencing days for almost all the circuit court dockets. Flaherty said it'd be standing room only as family members of the defendants, victims, and the entire probation department stuffed themselves into the confined courtroom.

"It was a zoo," Flaherty had said. So, Renquest made a trip past the Pratt house. He wanted to look for windows behind the bushes that lined the front of the house.

The three-mile drive took him a little under twenty-five minutes. It felt as if he had hit every red light in the city. By the time he arrived, the sun had risen above the tree line, shining over the roof of the house, directly into his eyes. The old man was standing on the front stoop. A beer can in one hand. A half-burned cigarette in the other.

"It's a little early for a beer, isn't it?" Renquest asked as he walked up the driveway, past the broken-down car. The trash on the passenger side reached halfway up the window. There was a clear increase in the amount of garbage stuffed inside the vehicle since the last time he had visited the house. He imagined that the city's trash collectors had little reason to stop at this house.

"What the hell do I have to do today?" the old man shouted as he took a drink. "And what do you want?"

"I had a few questions about the basement apartment. If you have a moment."

Renquest watched the old man closely. Looking for any type of reaction. A twitch of the hand. A sudden dart of his eye back toward the house. He saw nothing. The man didn't even blink. It was as if he were already drunk. Or possibly still wasted from the night before. The old man took another swig from the sweat-covered white can that had the word BEER in black letters inked on its face.

"When did you get the work in the basement done?"

"A couple of years ago. It's too damn expensive to live here anymore, thanks to all those tax-sucking government employees," the old man said between swigs from his can.

"You do the work yourself?"

Renquest knew the answer to this question but wanted to see if he could get the contractor's name, which would make it easier to look up the plans in the county permitting office.

The old man let out a snort. "You think I hired one of them overpriced contractors to work on my house? Hell, they only come by to pick up the check. The illegals do all the work. Work that used to be done by whites."

"Illegals?" Renquest asked. Again, knowing the answer, but wanting to keep the man talking.

"Don't act like you don't know. All of them wetbacks coming here and leaching off our system. Clogging the schools with Mexican mumbo-jumbo talk. This used to be a nice town. But now it's polluted with trash," the old man said.

Renquest found it difficult to hide the disdain he felt for this man. He felt his blood pressure spike every time he opened his hate-filled mouth. But he stayed composed, mostly.

"If you didn't hire a contractor, how did you get the work done?"

The old man tipped the can up and drank until the last drop ran down his chin. He wiped his mouth with his sleeve and tried to crush the empty can in his hand. A task much too difficult for his feeble hands. He barely made a dent in the sides. Then he tossed the can over the railing, where it landed between two shrubs.

"Not that it's any of your business, but I found someone on the internet. White guy too. Did the job cheaper and better than any of those brownies waiting for work down at the gas station every day."

The more the old man talked, the viler his sentiments became. Renquest decided he'd heard enough. He glanced at the empty can the old guy had discarded near the bushes a few moments ago. He stepped up next to the can and knelt. As he picked the can out of the tangle of overgrown shrubs and dead leaves, he scanned the basement wall for windows. He saw none. Then he stood and held the can up.

"This is recyclable. I'll toss it in the blue container on my way to my car."

The old man stared suspiciously at him. "Whatever." Then he turned and made his way inside. The screen door squelched as it slammed behind him.

Renquest shook his head. "What an asshole."

He tossed the empty can into the blue recycling container across the street before he climbed back into his car. He took one last look at the house. Why would the old man have closed off the stairway to the basement but left the void intact? Maybe the cost was too high to remove the stairs because of a structural component? And what good would a three-foot-wide room be for anyone? Maybe he used it for storage. But from what he saw through the open door the last time, the old man preferred to live embedded in his possessions rather than neatly stacking them in a makeshift closet.

As he drove away, he watched in his rearview mirror as the owner pushed the door open and stepped back out onto the porch. Beer in hand.

The line to get into the parking garage wrapped almost all the way around the building. He remembered Flaherty telling him that the county had recently opened two floors of the garage, which used to be strictly for county employee use, to the public on Fridays. It was an agreement reached between the court and the county council. Judges had been complaining for years that defendants were late for court because they spent hours circling the blocks surrounding the courthouse searching for a metered parking spot. The council finally caved after the court said it would use portions of its budget to help defray the cost.

Disillusioned by the massive number of people and vehicles, Renquest parked in a spot designated for patrol officers on the west side of the courthouse and close to the police employee's door. He placed the small placard on his dash, proclaiming it an official police vehicle, then made his way inside.

The receptionist told him that no one had called asking for him. He hadn't been expecting anyone, but he'd hoped Brooks or Sanchez or Flaherty might have checked in with a new lead. He went to the coffee machine to refill his mug before sitting at his desk to go over the murder files one more time before meeting with his team. The desk drawer caught when he tried to open it. It took an extra-hard jerk to break it free. Once opened, he reached inside, shuffled past the loose paperwork, and found the files he had hidden there. As he tossed the file onto the desk, a loud crack startled him. He looked up and saw Flaherty standing in the doorway. Renquest stacked and straightened the folders and slid the pile to the side.

"What can I do for you, Flaherty?"

"Just coming by to see how you are doing," Flaherty said.

"I'm good. Do you need something?" Renquest asked as he waved him in.

Flaherty stepped to the open chair in front of his boss's desk. "Mind if I sit?"

"Sit," Renquest said. "Now stop fucking around and say what's on your mind."

Flaherty pulled the chair back so that he could sit down. "I had to stop by the coroner's office this morning to check on some paperwork for one of the earlier victims. I needed a few things to clean up my report."

Renquest said nothing and simply nodded.

Flaherty continued, "When the Doc and I finished talking shop, she asked how you were doing. I told her you were fine. She seemed to be a little put off by my answer. So, I pushed her, and she mentioned Custus died yesterday."

Renquest looked down at his desk.

"Why didn't you tell us?" Flaherty asked. "I mean, I don't know what we could have done, but we would've been there for you."

"I'm okay," the veteran detective said. Though he wasn't sure, the tone of his voice relayed the message he was trying to send.

Flaherty paused before saying anything. He was unsure whether he was overstepping, so he let the matter go. "Well, if you need anything, we're all here."

Renquest swallowed hard, holding back the water he felt welling up behind his eyes.

"I appreciate the thought. But seriously, I'm good." Repeating the same lie. As if he would miraculously believe it if he just said the words enough.

The room fell silent for a moment. Not wanting to give Flaherty a chance to mention Custus again, Renquest said, "What did you get?"

"What?" Flaherty asked.

"At the coroner's office," Renquest said. "You mentioned you needed to pick up some paperwork?"

"Oh, yeah, I needed the toxicology report for the second murder vic, Wallace. I couldn't finish the report until Johansen signed off on the official report."

"Anything out of the ordinary?"

"No, he was a hype. Loved the needle," Flaherty said as he leaned forward in the chair and tossed the report onto the desk. "In fact, he probably wouldn't have lived much longer had someone not killed him."

Renquest stretched his arm across the desk and pulled the file in front of him. He flipped to the last page to check the cause of death.

"Looks like all the others. Heart failure because of exsanguination."

Flaherty stood, reached out, and pinched the top of the file. He turned to the second page. His finger pointed to a paragraph about halfway down from the top.

Renquest donned his reading glasses, then scanned to the part his lead detective had just referred to. He read the results aloud.

"Chronic liver failure most likely caused by extended drug use and Hepatitis C. Without a liver transplant, the patient would most likely have suffered massive organ failure followed by death." Renquest closed the file and dropped it on the desk. "Ominous."

"The doc said it takes years, sometimes decades, of hard drug use for the liver to evolve into that shape."

"I wonder if any of the other murder victims would've suffered the same fate as Mr. Wallace?" Renquest asked.

"We don't have the official results on the other cases from the doc yet, but based on the interviews we did with family and friends, they all lived hard lives," Flaherty took in a deep breath. "Lots of drugs. Lots of alcohol. And lots of partners."

The high-backed leather chair let out a low squeal as Renquest leaned back. His eyes wandered to the murder board.

"What about the ones our guy left alive? Any findings in that area that link them to the dead ones?"

Flaherty shook his head.

"Only the dead get an autopsy. And I don't think the others even had bloodwork done."

He tilted his head and squinted as he glanced at the murder board across the room. The names of all the victims in vertical rows across its breadth.

"Could be something to look at," Renquest said.

"We would need their consent to obtain blood samples. No judge in the world would sign a warrant to take the blood of a victim of an assault. And after this long, I'm not sure what we will get from the results. A month is a long time, and things change." Flaherty stared at his boss, still staring at the board.

"Sir?"

The question snapped Renquest out of his trance. "Why don't we go back and take a second look at the live victims?"

"This will be the third interview for most of them," Flaherty said. "Are you sure putting them through that again will give us anything new?"

"No, which is why I want you to hunt down as many people as you can who knew them. I'm talking about friends, family, employers. Hell, find the person who delivered their mail if you can," Renquest said.

"What do you want me to ask them?"

Renquest paused for a moment. He hadn't really thought about what he wanted. He leaned forward and scratched his head before answering. "I want you to ask anything you can think of. If they had a beef with someone, I want to know about it. I don't care how mundane the details seem—I want it tracked down."

Flaherty looked concerned. "We have only two days before the chief goes to the council. Do you think this is the right play? I mean…"

Renquest interrupted. "You get out there and start beating the bushes and see what scampers out. Let me worry about the council."

Flaherty smiled and said, "Okay, boss."

Renquest could see the worry on the detective's face. He didn't blame him or the others for their concern about his choices. After McNally fired him, they all might be next. The thought made him angry. He would not let that happen. If he went down, he'd go down alone.

As Flaherty stood and walked to the door, Renquest said, "Take Sanchez with you. Two of you can cover more ground than one."

Flaherty nodded and disappeared into the hall.

Renquest looked at the file sitting on the edge of his desk. His fingers flicked through the open edges like a deck of cards. As the photographs brushed over the tips of his fingers, he closed his eyes. The images flashed in his mind. He knew the leverage he now had over McNally and what that information meant to the county council if he used it. His mind wandered to his old partner, Paul Dodge, who was much more adept at leveraging people's weaknesses than he was. What would he do in this situation? He scoured his memory for any case they'd worked together where they had to leverage information to get the desired outcome. This was simply a more polite way to say… blackmail. Then, like an ear mic blasting in his head, he heard Dodge's voice. But the words weren't what he'd expected.

Over and over, he kept hearing: *Put it in a drawer and forget about it. It's a politician's move, and you're no politician.* The words sounded strange coming in Dodge's voice. He was not one to shy away from a fight. An end justifies the means type of cop. That's why their partnership had been so successful. Renquest was a by the book detective. There are reasons for rules. And just like that, the voice in his head changed back to his own.

As a cop, he understood that the case's success or failure depended on its merits. If you spent the time working the facts, following leads—you would either solve the case or it would go cold. Honest detectives didn't get down and wallow in the mud with the pigs. That was a politician's job. And McNally was a politician in a chief's uniform. He opened a desk drawer and dropped the file in. This time he locked it and placed the key in his pocket. It was time to get to work.

Chapter 24

The courthouse buzzed with excitement. Renquest could hear the metal detectors working as people passed through the entrance and made their way to the television screens mounted on a wall near the elevator banks. The monitors continuously cycled through cases, in alphabetical order by the defendant's name, with a courtroom assignment. Everyone seemed to know the drill. Find your name and take the elevators to the floor and courtroom assigned to you, then wait some more. The drill was the same everywhere. He truly enjoyed most of his job. Going to court was the one part he detested.

As he fought his way through the growing crowd, he hoped his plan wouldn't earn him more enemies. There were only so many battles he could fight at one time. The heavy wooden doors, which led to the county council hearing chamber, rattled as he knocked. After a minute, the handle turned, and the right-side door swung open. Councilman Ramone Diaz stared back at him. His politician's smile appeared when he saw Renquest.

"Detective, good to see you again. What can I do for you?"

Renquest held his hand out, in a *may I pass* gesture. Diaz stepped aside. Once his guest was inside, he closed the door behind them. A twist of a knob secured the lock.

As Renquest stood in the large room, he couldn't help but notice the layout was much the same as a courtroom. Rows of chairs for the public lined the room from left to right. To make public attendance look organized on the evening news, they evenly spaced each chair and row. A small wooden divider separated the citizens from the council. Carpet covered the floor between the council desks and the gallery. A virtual no-man's-land. Any attempt to reach the council members during a session, and the police would respond quickly to subdue the would-be assailant. And just in case someone made it to the council's perch before officers could get to them, a small rise in the floor placed the top of the council's platform above chest height for an average-sized man. It provided the council members with a few precious seconds to get away if something were to happen. It was an excellent design.

Renquest stepped through the gate and leaned against the rail of the wooden barrier. He faced the rest of the board members. Diaz followed closely behind him.

Renquest watched as the councilman opened a gate on the right side of the room—the hinges squeaked and the wood clapped as the spring-loaded door quickly shut behind him. The councilman, wearing a suit that likely cost more than Renquest made in a month, made his way up a set of stairs and sat in the empty seat. The council comprised four men and one woman.

Two other members flanked Diaz on either side. The power seat was his.

"What can we do for you, Detective?"

Ten eyes, all focused on the new guy in the room. Some were curious. Others showed a hint of uncertainty. But all carried serious stares. So, he waited silently for a moment. When he saw Diaz glance at the other members and open his mouth to ask a question, Renquest spoke.

"For those of you who haven't met me, I'm Detective William Renquest."

"We know who you are, Detective," a voice boomed from his right. "We hired you."

A gold placard listed his name as the Honorable Mr. Wilson.

"I imagined you knew, but I wanted to put a name to the face. This is the first time I've met you all in person," Renquest said. "Except for Mr. Diaz, with whom I had the pleasure of speaking a few days ago."

"Well, we are all here now and you have our attention, so what is it you want, Detective?"

Renquest looked to his left. The placard read The Honorable Mr. Chen.

"Well, as you all are aware, my team and I have been looking into the killings that happened over the past few months. Most of them took place before I arrived, but two have happened under my watch. I just want to reassure you we are doing everything we can to solve these heinous crimes and bring the person or persons responsible to justice."

"We have faith in your abilities, Detective," Diaz said. "That's why the vote was unanimous to bring you on board."

Renquest leaned back against the decorative wooden security barrier. "Technically, Chief McNally hired me."

"With our approval and recommendation," Councilman Wilson shouted from his right.

Renquest nodded.

"Understood. Any word from any of you about the future of Chief McNally?"

"That is a matter for the council and none of your concern. You just concentrate on stopping this lunatic who is terrorizing our city. We will handle Chief McNally," Councilman Chen said after sharing a quick glance with Diaz.

"Well, I have to say, the distraction of all of this is causing angst amongst the staff. Especially my team working on these homicides. This type of distraction can be counterproductive. I hope the council will find a remedy soon. For the sake of the department and morale."

Diaz spoke up. "If you have something you wish to share with the committee, Detective, please do. I assure you; we will maintain the strictest confidentiality regarding anything you say in here."

Renquest's eyes moved from one member to the next. He could sense them drooling over what he might have to reveal to them. Then he looked back at the only woman on the council. The placard in front of her read, The Honorable Ms. Reinert. He then came back to Diaz.

"As you said earlier, I will leave that matter to the honorable council."

And with that said, Renquest stepped back over the barrier. On his way out, he left the large wooden door to the meeting room open. He heard the door slam shut as he walked back toward the employee entrance to the police department. After badging in, he made for the reception area. As he stepped into the small, rectangular room, his eyes focused on the thin, frail woman sitting at the desk closest to the thick glass wall separating the office from the public waiting area. He stood silently and waited until she noticed him. When she did, he stepped closer, but not too close. If he were correct, he wouldn't want to be too imposing.

"Margaret, I need to speak with you for a moment," he said, motioning over his shoulder toward the hall behind him.

The young woman looked surprised. Her eyes opened wide, and before a word could slip through her lips, Renquest bent over at the waist and whispered, "I know it was you. We can talk about it here or somewhere else. The choice is yours. But we are going to talk about it."

Her expression turned to one of dread. She looked around the room at the other staff and then back to the Renquest. Without saying a word, she leaned over and grabbed her purse from under the desk. She stood and Renquest stepped to the side, extending an arm toward the hall and his office. Margaret smiled as she brushed past him, but in her eyes, he saw fear.

She peered into each office they passed. He assumed she was trying to avoid being seen going into his office. She was a front-line employee, and his title of Chief of Detectives provided him with supervisory duties that covered some of the clerical staff. He knew no one would question the two of them together. Which served to further raise his confidence that his theory was right.

He closed the door behind them and motioned for her to take a seat in the chair opposite his desk. He circled around behind and propped up on the corner of his desk, facing her. She gazed up at him. He said nothing. Just stared back at her. As far as he was concerned, this was the same as any of the victim interviews he'd done over his career. The only difference being, she would still need to work here when this was over. So, he had no intention of their conversation leaving the confines of his office.

When he finally spoke, his voice contained a hint of compassion.

"Margaret, do you want to tell me what is going on here?"

She gave him her best blank stare. "I'm sorry. I don't know what you're referring to?"

It sounded more like a question than a statement to Renquest. He slid over a bit on the desk. But he wanted her to feel like he had closed the gap between them, just a little.

"Margaret, I met with the city council today. During that meeting, I learned something interesting," he said. "Do you know what I found out?"

She shook her head without looking up at him.

"Well, I found out the council comprises mainly men. Except for one woman."

Her eyes stared at a fictional place on the floor between her and his desk.

He continued, "And her last name was Reinert. Now, unless I'm confused, and I'm sure I'm not, that's also your last name."

She continued to sit quietly. But he noticed she had busy hands. She was picking at her cuticles, a tell of sorts. A nervous reaction to being in a situation you'd rather not be a part of.

"So, I ask again, Margaret, do you want to tell me what is going on here?"

It was then that he noticed a single tear roll down her cheek. Leaning back, he reached across his desk and pulled a tissue from the box he kept for moments like this. He handed it to her, then waited for her to finish drying her cheeks and eyes. He was sure she was ready to spill everything. All he had to do was make sure he didn't push too hard. If she became too emotional, he wouldn't get any useful information. He also risked someone in the outer offices hearing her cry. Plus, he'd feel pretty shitty about it.

That's how it was being a detective. One minute you are going after people, threatening them with life in prison, and then flip a switch to become their protector and friend. Interrogation was a weird business. His old partner, Paul Dodge, was one of the best he had ever seen. He himself had learned the tissue trick from Dodge.

He once told Renquest, "Always have a small roll of tissues in your pocket, in your car, and on your desk. It'll keep the witness from having to go to the restroom to get cleaned up and break the moment. Don't give them time to think about what they are about to reveal to you." The advice had served him well.

"You want to tell me what happened? I have a pretty good idea, but I need to hear it from you," Renquest said.

She blew her nose and crumpled the used tissue up in her hand, and stuffed it into her purse. It was her way of maintaining some dignity. A show of feminism by not asking him to throw away the piece of paper that contained her emotional reaction to the situation.

"Do you have the photos?" she asked.

He nodded.

"Well, I guess it is all out in the open now."

"What. What's out in the open?"

She looked up at him with horrified eyes. "You have the pictures! Do I have to draw them out for you too?"

Renquest sat back. She was getting defensive, and he thought if he gave her more space, she might let her defenses down.

He placed his hands on the table, where she could see them. When he spoke, his tone was calm and non-threatening.

"You'll have to be more specific. I can help you, but I need to know everything. No matter how embarrassing it is."

She reached for the tissues and pulled a single white sheet from the box. He watched as she dabbed the moisture from her eyes, wadded the tissue up and placed it in her purse.

"I really need you to tell me everything. Just start from the beginning."

She took a deep breath and sighed. Then, she used the back of her hand to wipe her eyes once more. Once calmed, she told him what had happened all those years ago. Every sordid detail. Renquest knew Margaret had left nothing out, because she stopped several times to regain her composure. People can fake a lot of things, but the eyes always give them away. A deep look into the eyes can reveal a person's true intentions. In Margaret, he saw fear and rage. But by the time she finished talking, there was calm behind her eyes. The simple act of talking about her ordeal lifted a weight from her shoulders. The fear and shame she felt could now jump-start the healing process.

He reached across the desk to pull a tissue from the box one last time, but she waved the gesture off before he could get one out.

"I'm okay," she said.

Renquest slid off the corner of the desk and placed his hand on her shoulder to relay a sentiment of understanding.

"Do you have anyone you can talk to?"

Her eyes darted around the room before looking up at him.

"No, I'll be fine. I just need a few minutes." Her fingers rubbed the red spots under her eyes. "I must look atrocious," she said.

Renquest smiled. "Why don't you splash some cold water on your face? When you're done, you can walk across the street and get a cup of tea or coffee." He reached into his pocket and pulled out a five-dollar bill and handed it to her. "It's on me."

She hesitated.

"Go on, take it. The coffee here is low-grade toilet water."

Hesitantly, she pulled the bill from his hand, cupping it in hers as she stood to leave. She looked back at the man who had just been told about the most humiliating moment of her life and forced a smile.

Renquest smiled back. "Thank you for being honest with me. I know it was hard."

He watched as she disappeared down the hall. The information Margaret provided was solid, and he felt he was a small step closer to having what he needed to deal with McNally. Internal politics were a messy business. Definitely not the murky waters he enjoyed wading into, but it was necessary this time. He needed to create some breathing room so he could work the murders his way. The right way.

And just like that, his mind pivoted back to the open cases. Flaherty's interview with Kim Norman earlier had shed some light on a couple of glaring issues with Sullivan's murder. The one thing he now knew was that Sullivan wasn't the intended victim. As he ran through the timeline in his mind, everything pointed to Kim Norman being the target. Therefore, Sullivan's murder was connected to the others, but separate. One of those wrong place at the wrong time scenarios. But now the killer had made a mistake. He got emotional, and that the detective could use to his advantage.

Chapter 25

The lobby of the courthouse bustled as most of the courts broke for lunch around noon. People filed out of the elevators and poured into the courtyard, many of them lighting the cigarettes dangling from their lips the moment they cleared the revolving doors. Some were happy and hugging their loved ones as they made their way past the law enforcement memorial to the front doors of the jail on the other side of the square to meet the newly freed. Others were crying because they had no one to hug. Instead, they lined up at the jail, waiting their turn so they could look at their loved ones for a few minutes on a video teleprompter. As he made his way through the crowd, a somber feeling befell him. This was part of the job he hated. Crime ruined lives. And court day only served as a reminder of how one poor decision could affect so many people.

After finishing the sandwich he purchased from the deli across the street, Renquest sat at the conference table in his office, staring at the timeline on the whiteboard. There was something about the assaults and the murders that had bothered him from the beginning. The assaults appeared to happen on some sort of schedule. The first victim was Donald Deevers. Then, exactly one week later, Cynthia Lewis. Two weeks after Lewis, Robert Harrington was attacked. Finally, Mary Chao's assault one week later. One, two, and one.

The words kept repeating in his head. One-two-one. One-two-one. It had to mean something. Crime patterns always relate to some sort of event. Like phases of the moon or holidays. Sometimes it's personal to the assailant. The events could correspond to birthdays or anniversaries. Though he doubted that was the case this time. The odds were astronomical that the killer had enough important dates close enough to each other to fit the pattern of these attacks.

After finding nothing that easily fit the pattern, he switched his attention to the murder victims. Yoast was the first of the murder victims found, followed by Wallace less than a week later. Kemp only a day after, and Pratt three days after Kemp. And while he'd ruled out Sullivan as an intended victim, the killer had picked that time and place to go after Kim Norman. Which meant that Sullivan's name stayed on the murder board. As hard as he tried, he couldn't find a pattern in the murders. And what about Pratt? He couldn't figure out how he fit into all of this. In fact, he was sure Pratt's murder had no relation to the others. Now he wondered if he'd been looking at the murders all wrong. What if no connection existed? Just several random events with commonalities that made it look like they were all connected.

As he stood to get a better look at the board, his chair rolled back and bumped against his desk. He looked back at the chair resting against his desk, then back at the board. His mind went to work, deciphering what his subconscious picked up on. Three objects in his office, which had no relation to one another, but were all inexplicably joined through no fault of their own, by him. Or, to be more precise, an action by him.

And like a light bulb illuminating from the flick of a switch, the puzzle came together in his head. He reached into his pocket to get his phone, but it was empty. His hands patted his pants and chest while he looked around the room. Then he remembered he had placed his cell in his inside jacket pocket when he left the meeting with the county council. He grabbed the jacket off the back of his chair and texted the other members of his team.

Meet me at the coroner's office in thirty minutes.

He stuffed the phone into his front pants pocket and slipped on his jacket. He hurriedly walked past the reception area, where he saw Margaret working—her head up and eyes bright. She was laughing with some of the other office personnel. Hopefully, this was a sign that she was feeling better. He exited the door, walked through the first-floor mezzanine, and out the front exit into the courtyard. Lawyers filled the rectangular area. Some were smoking, while others talked to their clients and family members. Some smiled, happy with the outcome of the day. Others, not so much.

The air was hazy, and the smell of cigarette smoke seemed to linger at nose level. Renquest quickly wound his way through the crowds of people and pockets of smoke-filled air. He crossed Courthouse Road and headed directly toward the Courthouse Metro station. He stepped onto the escalator for the short ride into the tunnels of the subway station. Renquest had been in the passages before when he first arrived in town. One thing that caught his attention that day was that several buildings had direct entrances to the subway station, so patrons wouldn't have to step outside to catch a train. But he was interested in one such passage in particular.

By the time Renquest arrived at the coroner's office, Flaherty, Brooks, and Sanchez were waiting in the lobby. The three officers were whispering among themselves. All three turned and watched as he came through the door.

Brooks stepped forward. "Detective." She looked back at the others. "What are we doing here?"

The detective walked briskly past the three, his hand signaling for them to follow. He quickly made his way through the hall and pushed open the doors to the autopsy room. The sudden intrusion surprised Johansen, and she nearly dropped the tray she was holding.

"Detective," she sputtered. "What are you all doing here?" She looked past Renquest at the other three officers following him.

"We need to see the files on the five dead vics," Renquest said. The autopsy table in the middle of the room was empty, and he leaned against the cold steel side and watched as Johansen retrieved the reports he wanted. When he was sure she was out of sight, he turned back to the three officers.

Flaherty asked, "Sir, what are we doing here?"

Renquest stood straight. "I have an idea about what is happening here. But I need to see the reports to confirm my suspicions." He looked at Brooks and saw a flash of recognition in her eyes.

Sanchez noticed the look and spoke next. "What is it you two aren't telling us?"

Renquest checked the door before answering. "I realized we had been looking at this all wrong. When we all met the other night at my place, we mulled over the details of all the attacks and murders. We all came to the same conclusion—the last murder, Sullivan, was an outlier. His connection to the other victims was tenuous at best."

The three officers nodded in agreement.

"But what if we were wrong from the beginning? What if Sullivan was the *only* murder victim related to the assaults? What if the others were decoys? Copycats used to cover up the murder of someone else?"

Flaherty looked puzzled. "Ok. Say you're right. Let's say Sullivan was the target of the same person who attacked the four victims who survived. And let's suppose the other four victims are unrelated to Sullivan or the assaults, but related to each other. Then who was the actual target out of the unrelated four vics? Is there someone else out there we need to find who might be in danger?"

Sanchez's face lit up. "Pratt."

The other two officers stared at their comrade. Not in disbelief, but in admiration.

"The actual target was Pratt," Sanchez said. "He was the one victim who always stood out from the rest."

"What do you mean?" asked Brooks.

"Well, when the detective and I went to the basement he was renting on the north side, we were both taken aback by the cleanliness of the place. The dishes were done and put away. There were no dirty clothes lying around. The place was spotless."

"So, he kept a tidy house." Flaherty said. "How does that make him the target?"

"It wasn't just clean," Renquest chimed in. "Hell, the place was nicer than mine."

Brooks said, "Okay, I hate to ask again, but how does that all tie Pratt back to the other murders?"

"Sanchez and I also met the owner. He was a piece of work," Renquest said.

"He was an asshole," Sanchez retorted.

"Agreed," Renquest said. "But we found what we thought was a small hidden room in the basement, tucked along one of the outside walls of Pratt's apartment. I haven't been in the house's upstairs to see if the room is accessible, but I suspect the old man used to rent to young college students from the law school, probably females."

"Gross!" Brooks exclaimed. "A peeping room."

"Yeah. He probably used the room to spy on his tenants. But as the area around the law school grew and more housing options became available for students closer to campus, the rent pool dried up. He started renting to anyone who would pay regularly."

"And he found out something about Pratt? Something worth killing for?" Brooks asked.

The veteran detective rubbed the stubble on his face. "It's usually about money or jealousy."

The three officers looked at each other. None of them had uncovered any large bank deposits or unusual withdraws in Pratt's accounts. Brooks herself had gone over every inch of the victim's financials. Account by account. Page by page. And while Pratt seemed to get by, the ex-soldier was not rolling in money. In fact, Brooks had described him in her earlier reports as someone who qualified for public assistance but made ends meet without the government's help. Pratt was poor, but lived within his means.

Brooks seemed to take offense at the idea. "There was no way I missed anything. I pulled all his bank accounts and cross-referenced them with his three-bureau credit report. Every credit card. Every payday loan. Hell, I even had his PayPal account info. There was nothing there."

"That's correct. All the information you had showed Pratt was chugging along like the rest of us. He lived paycheck to paycheck like most of the people in this country," Renquest said.

"So, what did we miss?" Flaherty asked.

"Nothing. At least not as far as recorded financials are concerned. You hit them all."

"Recorded financials?" Sanchez asked.

"Not everyone keeps all their valuables in a bank," Renquest stated bluntly.

Sanchez laughed. "What, was the guy burying gold in the backyard, or something?"

Renquest winked at Brooks. "Well, kinda. Not exactly gold and not buried in the backyard. There was one thing in that apartment worth dying for." His eyes darted to Sanchez. "You almost ran over it with the car the first day we were at his basement apartment."

Brooks and Flaherty stared blankly at Renquest and then turned to Sanchez. He stared back at them and shrugged his shoulders. But before they could ask him a question, his head spun back to Renquest.

"The cat!" he shouted. A little embarrassed, he cleared his throat and said, "The cat."

"The cat," the veteran detective repeated.

"What cat?" the other two officers said in unison.

Sanchez spoke up before his boss could answer. "Pratt had a cat. We saw it."

"Smelled it," Renquest butted in.

"Yeah, you could smell the cat shit as soon as the door to the basement opened. It was noxious."

"Apparently, no one had been down to clean it since Pratt disappeared," Renquest said.

"What's so special about this cat?" Brooks asked.

"Nothing that I saw," Sanchez said.

"That's what I thought too," Renquest said. "Then I started thinking about the house. The secret room the old man had built so that he could spy on his tenants. He must have been down in the room one day and overheard Pratt say something about how he was going to have some money coming in."

"What does this have to do with the cat?" Flaherty asked. The tone of his voice relayed his growing impatience.

"If you stop interrupting me, I'll get to that," Renquest said tersely. "Since you all went over his financials with a fine-tooth comb, and there were no large deposits, the valuable thing had to still be in the apartment. Only

Sanchez and I had searched that place on two separate occasions, and we found nothing. So, I got to thinking about different things people had as valuables. Coins. Stamps. And pets. Specifically, cats and dogs are of rare breeds. Or show quality animals."

"Yeah," Brooks said. "I watched a documentary about dog shows. Boy, those people are weird. They treat those animals better than their children most times."

"And they spend a lot of money on them. They are an investment," Renquest added.

"How much can someone make from winning one of these contests?" Flaherty asked.

"Well, that's where I was before I came here. I paid a visit to the animal control office and spoke to the manager. She told me there wasn't a lot of money in shows at the local level. There were shows every couple of months with a grand prize of anywhere from a few hundred to a couple thousand. But smaller shows are often what she called feeder shows. Meaning if you place high enough in the early contests, that qualifies you for more prestigious events at the state and national levels. Prizes at those could be in the tens of thousands."

Brooks scratched her head. "So, was Pratt's cat a valuable one?"

Renquest nodded. "It was."

"Okay. But how would the old man have been able to collect money at shows? Surely, everyone in the circuit knew Pratt, and if someone else tried to enter that cat into a show, someone would've noticed. And I'm just guessing here, but I bet the cat has a locator chip under its skin. So, anyone who bought it would find out at the first veterinary visit that the rightful owner wasn't the seller. These show people, they trace the animal's lineage and the owners. They want to know everything about the animals' upbringing. So how would he have made money off this cat?" Brooks said.

"That was the same question I asked the animal control manager. She told me the real money isn't in the shows. It's in the breeding. People will pay thousands of dollars for a chance to breed their cat with a proven show cat."

"That's insane!" Sanchez said. "But I'm pretty sure the cat in that basement was male."

"I think you are right, Lieutenant. And that makes it more valuable." Renquest said.

"How?" Flaherty asked.

"By selling its semen," Renquest said.

"That's disgusting!" Brooks said.

"Disgusting or not, people pay good money to get a sample from a champion animal."

"What kind of money are we talking about?" Flaherty asked.

"Ten thousand a pop for a rare breed," Renquest said. "It's like having a home equity line of credit. As long as the cat can produce samples, there is no end to the amount of money to be made."

"Being killed over cat sperm," Sanchez said. "This is a messed-up world."

"With Pratt dead, and no other family to claim his possessions, the old man could keep everything left on his property," Renquest said.

"Even the cat," Brooks said.

"Especially the cat. Hell, he would look like a hero for not taking it to the shelter or turning it loose to rummage through trash cans for food," Renquest added.

"And that explains the cat still being in the basement. But why didn't he clean the litter boxes? I mean, that can't be good for the animal."

"My guess, he was just lazy, and he hadn't figured out a way to collect the goods yet. So, it was better he didn't go in there and risk letting the cat out of the bag, so to speak."

"That explains Pratt, but what about the other three murders?"

"Red herrings. All done to keep us thinking that the person responsible for the assaults was also killing people. Three murders to cover for one," Renquest said.

"Alright. But who killed those other vics?" Flaherty asked. "Cause it damn sure wasn't the old man you and Sanchez described."

"That I don't know," Renquest said. "Yet."

Chapter 26

Dr. Johansen returned with two files. She placed them on the stainless-steel table in the middle of the room.

Renquest looked at the files, then up at Johansen. "Where are the others?"

"I can't seem to locate them," she said. "Someone must have moved them out to the warehouse."

Renquest shook his head. "Why would they move them?"

She looked down at the table first, then back up. "Files get moved there all the time. We have only so much room here at the office. Procedure is to have the files transported to the storage facility as soon as the case is closed."

He turned to his three officers and tipped his head toward the exit. Brooks immediately understood and ushered Sanchez and Flaherty out. Once the doors closed and he was sure no one was within earshot, he turned back to Johansen.

"The cases were not closed."

"They were as far as this office is concerned," she said. Her voice cracked ever so slightly as she answered. "What is going on here?"

Renquest felt himself growing angry. He had been a detective for a long time. Never had a medical examiner closed a file and moved that file to another location where the investigating party would not have immediate access to it. Sure, he had copies of the preliminary findings, but he wanted to see the full reports. The ones completed and signed off by Johansen.

"Why did you move the files?" he asked. "I haven't finished my investigation, and until we catch this person, there could be more victims. I need the files to compare with any fresh cases that come our way."

"Cause of death was homicide. That's what I signed off on. If you have any reason to believe my findings were in error, please just come out and say so. I can have my assistant run over to the warehouse and retrieve them."

Renquest could tell she was not happy he questioned her professionalism. He was still the new guy in town and not fully trusted by anyone. He recognized his mistake and immediately tried to backtrack on his statement.

"I don't think there is an error in your findings. No one is speculating anything different from what you came up with. I just needed to see the original files to confirm a hunch I had."

"You could just ask me," she said. "I know those files inside and out. It's my goddamn job."

He glanced down at the two files on the table. Pointing, he asked, "To which two victims do those two files belong?"

"Pratt and Yoast. The first and fourth victims. Why?"

"May I?" he asked.

She picked up the files and handed them to him. His hand brushed hers as he took the files. She smiled. Which made him feel even worse for thinking she might have been trying to cover up the chief's ineptitude. Or worse, that she somehow got caught up in McNally's little blackmail scheme to make *him* look bad, to use dereliction of duty as an excuse to fire him.

Renquest fanned through the pages of Yoast's file. "Which page details the wound to the arm where the attacker drew his blood?"

Johansen pulled the file from the detective's hand and flipped to a spot roughly in the middle, then handed the folder back.

"About a quarter of the way down. Second paragraph." She pointed to the spot on the page.

He read and re-read every word on the page, trying to find that one detail. The thing that sets the murders apart from the assaults. On the fifth go-around, he saw what he was looking for.

Johansen must've noticed, because she slid over next to him and peered over his arm at the file.

"What is it?" she asked.

"Are you sure about this finding?"

"Yes, why?"

Renquest said nothing. He shuffled the files in his hand and opened the second one to the same page he had just been staring at in the other file. His finger traced the words from left to right until he found what he was searching for. Then he opened both files and tossed both onto the autopsy table.

Johansen followed his lead and leaned in to get a better view of what he saw. "What does it mean?"

"It means I need to look at the medical reports of the assault victims again."

"Why?" she asked. "What is it you think you see?"

"A right-handed pitcher," Renquest said. The exit doors cracked as the palms of his hands smacked the hard metal surface, forcing the doors open. Their hinges letting out a squeal as the tension released—the doors swung closed behind him.

The file room was in the basement of the police station. The department kept all physical copies, along with any evidence stored there indefinitely, unless a court ordered their removal and destruction. Around the clock staffing was policy. Anyone entering the room was required to sign in. Anyone taking information out of the room had to enter the file and case numbers in the logbook along with the time and signature. The process worked in reverse when the officer returned the files and property.

Renquest scribbled his signature in the logbook and headed toward the first row of shelves containing open case files. He spun the handle on the side of the shelving unit, causing it to slide effortlessly to the left, revealing several rows of files. As he walked down the aisle, he pulled a small piece of paper from his pocket containing the case numbers of the files he wanted to see. About a third of the way into the aisle, he reached up and pulled a box containing the file ending in 0322-22 from the shelf. He dropped the lid on the floor and opened the file to the page containing pictures of the victim's wounds. The room was dimly lit, so he held the photo up to the light to get a better view. He examined the right arm, paying close attention to the area around the inner fold of the elbow. The most common place for a needle puncture in his experience as a cop and a patient. He saw nothing.

Then he turned his attention to the victim's left arm. He quickly spotted the darker skin in the elbow's fold. Bruising was common in puncture wounds after death. He pulled the picture closer. Bringing the picture closer to his eyes was pointless. He had been in such a hurry that he forgot to put on his reading glasses. Once his glasses were in place, he recognized a puncture wound surrounded by bruised tissue.

He placed the file back in the box after picking the lid off the floor. Then he put the box back on the shelf. After sliding down another three feet, he saw box 0327-22 on the bottom shelf. His knees cracked as he knelt and set the box on the floor. It was harder to see as Cynthia Lewis had been an active user. Old needle marks covered her arms. But the attack left a bruise as the attacker had used a larger gauge needle. Renquest found the third and fourth victims' files. He spread them out on the floor. Both had new puncture wounds on their left arms. That was the pattern. That was the detail they'd been looking for between the murder victims and the attack survivors.

Once he had tucked the boxes back into their respective shelf spaces, Renquest found his way through the maze of cardboard-lined aisles to the exit. He signed the logbook. No need to give McNally any ammo as a *failure to follow procedure* disciplinary action. He pushed the up button on the elevator and waited as the numbers counted down from three to the basement. The doors opened, and he waited as another officer stepped out.

"Sir," the man said as he moved past.

Renquest acknowledged him with a nod.

Part of Renquest, the ego part, wanted to march straight into the chief's office and watch him squirm as he told him about his discovery. But being right was more important than his ego. Not to mention, he knew the new lead meant nothing if he couldn't make an arrest. The best way to save his job would be to hold a press conference in front of a lectern with the county logo plastered on the front. Cameras and microphones everywhere. All of this would please the council members, not that Renquest gave a shit about what they thought of him. But it would go a long way toward improving his status with the council. It might even give him some breathing room in the future. Making his job easier was something he cared about.

In the end, not giving in to his ego led him straight to his office. The door closed behind him, and he pulled his chair up to his desk. For the first time since starting this investigation, he felt satisfied with something he'd done. The whiteboard drew his attention. He hoped that in a few days the board sitting across the room would be blank. Wiped clean. Ready for the next case. The deadline McNally had set for him became arbitrary. Having a suspect bought him some valuable time. Even if McNally went to the council, they wouldn't approve of firing the detective who was mere moments away from solving such a public case. People were watching the council as well. Elected by the people of Arlington County. However, he needed to keep Councilman Diaz in the loop. But in a way that provided the least amount of information possible. The last thing he needed was the councilman jumping the gun and scheduling a politically motivated press conference before Renquest made an arrest. It was cynical, but he knew politicians placed their future before the well-being of the community. It was America. That's the way it's always been and always will be. His career got a little easier once he accepted that as fact. Something his old partner Dodge could never get past.

He pulled the phone from his pocket and dialed Brooks' number.

She answered on the first ring. "Brooks here."

"It's Renquest. Get Flaherty and Sanchez together and meet me at Pratt's apartment. Sanchez knows where it is." He grabbed his jacket and checked his belt for his badge. "And if any of you beat me there, park down the street. I don't want the old man getting nervous and trying something stupid. Besides, we know he had a partner. Physically, there was no way he could take anyone. He weighs all of a hundred pounds soaking wet. The accomplice could be in the house with him and killed four people that we know of."

"Roger that," she said, and then rang off.

Traffic was heavy. Cars lined up to get out of downtown. Highway 50 heading west was a steady stream of vehicles leaving the Pentagon and

Crystal City, an area ripe with government employees and contractors all trying to get home at the same time. He looked at the clock on his dashboard. It read a quarter past three. 15:15 on a Friday. He knew that if he stayed on the main roads, it might take him an hour to make it to the other side of town. So, he turned right on Glebe Road and drove until he hit North Carlin Springs Drive. Then he made a right onto North George Mason Drive. While George Mason was narrower with stop signs, it would take him right into the heart of the Yorktown Neighborhood and only a few blocks from Pratt's apartment. With any luck at all, he could make the trip in half an hour.

Chapter 27

Renquest received a text from Brooks with her location about halfway to the house. She had to park a couple of blocks away because so many residents' vehicles lined the streets, which didn't give her a direct line of sight of the house. Before she found a spot, she made a pass by the home and reported that there were no vehicles parked in front of the home or in the driveway.

The report from Brooks about her drive-by made Renquest nervous. The last time he and Sanchez were at the house, the little foreign car was still sitting in the driveway on two flat tires, piled full of trash. He didn't believe there was any way the old man could have repaired the tires and cleaned out the interior of the car by himself in such a short time. The work wasn't overly strenuous, but the guy couldn't step out onto his front stoop without breathing like he had just hiked Kilimanjaro. He needed help.

As he approached, Renquest slowed and scanned the parked vehicles for Brooks. He spotted her quickly. She was in the only parked car with someone sitting behind the wheel. Her driver-side window rolled down as he pulled up next to her unmarked cruiser. Renquest lowered his window.

"How's it going?"

She tipped her head toward the end of the block.

"All's quiet."

"There used to be a little foreign model parked in the drive," Renquest said.

"Well, it's not there now," Brooks said.

"That's what bothers me," Renquest said as he looked in his rearview toward the house. "It had a couple of flats with trash and old newspapers piled as high as the seats."

"Doesn't sound like a car that would be up for a long trip. Even if he fixed the wheels."

"I didn't even think it ran. But I guess I was wrong."

"Maybe," Brooks said. "Let me check and see if the county towed it for any reason. Normally, they don't allow abandoned cars to sit in view for more than a few weeks."

The detective smirked. "There is an ordinance against storing your own car on your property?"

"Yes. You must keep its tags up to date. If it doesn't run, the car needs to be placed in a garage or carport out of view from the street," Brooks said.

Renquest shook his head.

Brooks' fingers tapped the keyboard of her cruiser's computer. "The law has been on the books for quite a while, but not enforced. A neighbor needed to complain to the county for something to be done about it. Police could only ticket vehicles parked on the street, not on private property."

"So, why did it change? Why care about it now?" Renquest asked.

Brooks pointed out her window toward a couple of young Hispanic men doing lawn work at the house across the street. "Because of them."

"Who are they?"

Brooks snorted. "Not those two, per se. But the increase in Hispanic families over the last twenty years that now call Arlington home."

"So?"

"I don't know if you noticed, but old white men run this county. They want the Mexicans and Latinos to come cut their grass and paint their houses, but return to Fairfax or Alexandria before the sun sets each day," Brooks said.

She looked over at her boss, who was watching the two men take a break and laugh among themselves.

"What, you didn't have racists back where you're from?"

Renquest sighed. "We did. They were just more overt about it. Made them easier to spot."

"Welcome to Northern Virginia. The progressive stronghold of the wealthy," Brooks quipped.

After watching the men for a minute, Renquest returned his attention to the old man's house.

"Where are Sanchez and Flaherty?"

Brooks pointed to a line of cars parked about a hundred yards in front of hers. "Down there."

Renquest strained his eyes, trying to make out which vehicle the pair were in, but gave up quickly. He checked the time on the radio clock: 16:00. Four in the afternoon. *Now was as good a time as any,* he thought.

"Alright. Tell Flaherty and Sanchez to move in. Have Sanchez secure the back and the apartment entrance on the side. Flaherty can watch the front door. As soon as they are in place, we will head up."

"Roger that," Brooks said. Then she grabbed her radio and relayed the instructions to the other two. When she finished, she clicked off and looked back through the open window at Renquest. "Do you think he is in there?"

Renquest said nothing. He just stared up the street. He wished he could see what was happening, but there was a level of trust with his officers that you had to have when you sent someone into a potentially dangerous situation. Everyone in a tactical situation must trust the officers in front of and behind them. And the commander needs to trust his officers to do their jobs safely. One thing breaks down, people get hurt. And that would be on him.

A couple of minutes had ticked off the clock, and neither Sanchez nor Flaherty had checked in. The rule was not to break radio silence during an officer's approach, as a mic cue or voice over the radio could give away their position. Maybe one, or both, had to find cover to avoid detection because of something they noticed on the approach to the home. In that case, they would remain concealed until the threat had passed.

But knowing that didn't make Renquest any less nervous. It shouldn't have taken more than a minute for the two men to get into place. He gave a quick glance at Brooks. Her expression confirmed that she was thinking the same thing.

As he reached for the portable radio, a crackling noise popped from the unit's speaker. Then Flaherty's voice echoed through the car's cabin.

"Units one and two are in place."

Renquest, realizing he had been holding his breath for about thirty seconds, finally exhaled. He clicked the mic on the radio.

"Units three and four rolling."

He rolled his finger in the air, signaling to Brooks to switch on her emergency lights. Then he turned around at the next driveway. Dirt and debris sprayed the cars behind him, pinging off the metal fenders and hoods as the tires broke free of the pavement. The rear of the car squatted under the enormous amount of torque produced by the car's massive engine. The front of the car lurched forward, covering the distance to the driveway in front of the house in only a few seconds.

Renquest blocked the driveway with his car. Brooks swung the front of her vehicle toward the opposite side of the street, the lights in her grill and windows flashing red and blue, right behind Renquest's car. Creating an impassable roadblock for anyone who would try to pass through the scene.

The two jumped out of their cars and made their way up the drive toward the front of the house. Renquest drew his weapon from its holster. Brooks followed his lead. Flaherty positioned himself at the corner of the house closest to the drive. They couldn't see Sanchez's position near the entrance to the basement apartment Pratt had been renting. The blinds covering the windows were closed, preventing the team from seeing inside the home. As Renquest moved into position at the front door, Sanchez keyed the radio to let them know he was in place and ready.

Brooks had already made her move and was standing on the far side of the stoop, her back pressed against the wall and weapon in the ready position. Renquest nodded as he slid up next to the door. Brooks pulled on the handle of the screen door. The rusty hinges squeaked. The wooden frame appeared rotten from a lack of protective paint. Then, the screws holding the hinges to the frame released. The door fell out of the frame and caught his captain off guard. She recovered quickly, slinging the door across her chest and over the side of the stoop. It clunked and twisted; its glass broke as it smashed into the ground.

Renquest stepped back, ready to use his massive size twelve shoe to kick in the door, when he stopped. They lost the element of surprise when the screen door broke. If someone were inside the house, they'd be ready for him to charge in. He didn't like the idea of taking a load of buckshot to the face. He spun and placed his back against the wall. Reaching out with his right hand, he gripped and slowly turned the doorknob. It gave a little at first, then capitulated. The locking mechanism clicked. And with a little push, the door came free of the jamb.

Using the palm of his hand, the detective pushed the door the rest of the way open, then waited. He counted to five in his head. When no shots came through the open void, he tipped his head at Brooks. She nodded and then spun through the doorway. The inside of the house was dark. Only the light from the open door pierced the interior.

Renquest signaled to Flaherty to make entry through the back and Sanchez to clear the basement apartment. After Flaherty disappeared around the corner, he turned back to Brooks. She now held a flashlight in her left hand. Its beam cut through the darkness past the front door. She looked over at him and mouthed the word, *Go.*

Brooks didn't hesitate. She moved through the open door and quickly scanned the room for threats. The beam of her flashlight swept across the room. Only stopping when it illuminated something she couldn't immediately identify, but quickly moved on once she determined no threat existed.

Renquest followed closely behind his captain. Covering the pair's rear was his responsibility. As he moved deeper into the house, he noticed blackout drapes covering every window. The kind that people who work nights use to sleep more comfortably during the daytime hours. He jerked at the edge of the curtain closest to him. The curtain rod pulled away from the wall, and the thick black fabric tumbled to the floor. Beams of light tore through the darkness, forcing both officers to squint. He hadn't thought about the temporary blindness caused by the sudden introduction of light. It lasted only a few seconds, and once their eyes adjusted to the newly lit space, they quickly realized they were alone.

Renquest holstered his weapon and began looking through a pile of mail on a small corner table. Brooks still had her gun out as she checked the bathroom and a small bedroom just off the living room. Just as she was about to give the all-clear, a rattling noise caught their attention. It appeared to be coming from the back of the house. Renquest pointed toward the disturbance. Brooks nodded and moved cautiously through a doorway into what Renquest assumed was the kitchen. Renquest stayed behind near the front door. He didn't want anyone to sneak up behind them. He wasn't a fan of surprises. Especially ones that could get him killed.

While waiting to hear from Brooks, he took a mental inventory of the house's contents. The inside of the house differed from what he had imagined from his earlier visits. Though he never entered the home, he assumed the old man was a hoarder. The detective pictured every available space in the house, jammed from ceiling to floor with old newspapers and odd items he bought at estate sales and neighborhood yard sales. He couldn't have been more wrong.

He stood in a sparsely decorated living room. Near the front window sat a couch covered with a plastic slipcover, which had cracked and torn in several places. In its current state, the cover only actually covered about fifty percent of the couch's fabric. It seemed to be still on the couch out of habit.

Opposite the sofa was a brown recliner. One arm sagged, creating the appearance that the whole chair leaned to one side. The matted and discolored fabric covering the chair bore the signs of an overused piece of furniture. It was definitely the old man's favorite piece. Next to the recliner stood a small end table. An oversized lamp with a ratty shade perched on top. A television sat on a makeshift stand the old man made by stacking several boxes on top of each other. The whole setup appeared to be close to collapsing under its own weight.

Other than a small shelf with knick-knacks attached to the wall, nothing else stood out. The room was clean. It smelled of smoke and stale beer, but he kept the floors swept and free of clutter. He shook his head. *You never know someone until you get into their house*, he thought.

Brooks' voice cracked over the radio, giving the all-clear. A minute later she stepped back into the room, with Flaherty close behind.

"The back door had a chain, like the kind used in hotels. The noise we heard was from Flaherty trying to slip the chain from its base to get the door open," Brooks said.

Flaherty shrugged. "I should've brought bolt cutters." Then he glanced around the room they were in. "This is not what I expected."

"You and me both," Renquest responded. "But the smell of the place is on point."

Flaherty and Brooks both shook their heads in disgust.

The veteran detective smiled and let out a muffled laugh. Then he pointed to the door over his shoulder.

"Flaherty, head down to the basement and give Sanchez a hand."

"Yes, sir," the detective said as he stepped past his boss and out into the fresh air.

Renquest turned to Brooks.

"We need to check everything here."

She faced him. "There are two bedrooms and a bath at the end of the hall. One room is empty, while the other has a twin bed and a small nightstand. I cleared the kitchen when I unlocked the back door for Sanchez."

"Alright," Renquest said.

"What now?"

Renquest's eyes darted from corner to corner of the room. "There used to be a set of stairs in here that led down to the basement. He must have had them covered over at some point. We need to find the entrance to that room."

Brooks and Renquest began searching every inch of the living room. They pulled up the edges of the carpet near where the stairs should've been. Brooks even moved some rugs, hoping to reveal a trapdoor into the basement. They found nothing.

Then Renquest noticed a narrow door close to the front door. It appeared to be a coat closet or utility door of some kind. He hadn't noticed it before because someone had removed all the trim and painted the door the same color as the wall. Whoever did the work made sure the door fit tightly into the opening. So tight, the gap for the hinges was less than a quarter inch. Effectively concealing the edges of the opening.

The detective whistled at Brooks and pointed to the door. With her weapon ready, she moved to the right of the door. Renquest stepped up and counted down from three with his fingers. The door swung open into the room. Brooks shone her flashlight into the deep space. There were two jackets hanging on a wooden bar that stretched from left to right. That was it. Nothing else.

When Brooks switched off her light, she noticed something on the floor. A speck of light. She flipped the flashlight back on and focused on the spot. There was a tiny hole drilled in the floor just inside the threshold.

"Turn off your light," Renquest said.

Brooks clicked the switch on the back of the flashlight, extinguishing the beam. Renquest gave his eyes a moment to adjust, and then knelt. He could see a thin line of light tracing a square on the floor. His finger slipped into the hole, and he felt something give. He rotated his finger, and then something clicked.

"Shit," Renquest said as he fell backward.

Chapter 28

As Renquest lay with his back flat on the floor, Brooks looked puzzled. Renquest never shared with his team that an explosion almost killed him a few months prior while he was working on a case involving a serial killer. He and his partner, Paul Dodge, were searching for the suspect in an old warehouse. Just when they thought they had him cornered, a booby-trapped container exploded. The resulting blast killed one officer and damaged his hearing permanently. When he heard the clicking noise from the trapdoor, his brain went to just before the container blew up. Every muscle in his body worked at the same time to get him as far from the noise as possible.

He groaned a little as he pushed back up to his knees, choosing to ignore the look Brooks had on her face. The front edge of the trapdoor was now visible. It stuck up from the surrounding floor enough to get a finger under. When Renquest pushed the button, it must have released a latch, allowing some sort of spring-loaded hinge system to raise the lid. He slipped his finger under the edge of the door and pulled it up with relative ease.

The closet instantly lit up as light poured in from the room below. After the light came the smell. Next were the flies. Renquest backed away.

"It'll take a minute or two to clear the air."

"Is that what I think it is?" Brooks asked.

"Yeah."

"Does it always smell that bad?" she said, tucking her nose into the crease of her elbow.

"Sometimes worse," he said. "Remind me to tell you about this guy we found in a bathtub once."

"I think I'll pass," Brooks said through the fabric of her shirtsleeve. "You first."

Renquest took Brooks' flashlight and slowly approached the opening in the floor. That was the worst part about having to climb into a spider hole. It wasn't the idea of getting to the bottom and realizing your adversary is lying in wait, ready to cut you in half with a shotgun blast. It was peering over the edge into the hole. Knowing the same shotgun blast would remove your face. Anything above your shoulders, really. Not a good way to die. A closed-casket affair, to be sure.

He leaned over and took a quick glance into the hole. His weapon drawn in case he had to fire off a few rounds at anyone hiding below. As he peered over the edge, the square hole filled with light. It was bright down there, so he wouldn't need the flashlight and handed it back to Brooks.

"Alright," he said as he eased into the opening, placing one foot on the top rung of a metal ladder. "Cover me."

As he descended, Brooks moved into a position above him. She pointed her weapon toward the back of the closet. She couldn't see very far into the room from where she stood and knew any shots she got off stood a better chance of hitting her boss than somebody tucked away in the back of the room.

"I can't imagine anyone is just waiting down there. In that stench," she said.

Renquest continued to concentrate on making sure each footfall was hitting a solid rung before moving on to the next one. His hands slid along the sides of the ladder's metal frame as he descended. His grip on the ladder never loosened until he reached the bottom and his feet were on concrete.

As he spun to face the open end of the secret room, a waft of rancid air hit him in the face. It was like getting slapped in the face with a bag of rotten meat. The noxious odor hung heavily in the air. A mixture of decomposing flesh and ammonia. A smell he knew too well. It was cat piss, and lots of it, by the way it made his eyes burn.

He shook off the initial attack and scanned the narrow space. The room was only about twenty feet long and four feet wide. Enough room for a person to walk around in, but not enough to do anything constructive with. But it was the other end that caught his attention. It wasn't the small wooden chair pushed up against the cement basement wall, or the stack of what appeared to be raunchy porn magazines piled up next to the chair. What drew his attention was the source of the foul smell. A dead body.

The old man's body leaned against the back wall. His legs splayed out in front of him—his arms at his sides. A haunting expression on his face. His eyes were gray and sunken in their sockets. He looked like a mannequin, but an ancient and beaten mannequin. His skin had already faded and had the texture of the outside of a rotten apple. Renquest wasn't sure if it was the unhealthy lifestyle or the humidity in the basement room that had done the most damage. Based on the last time he'd spoken to the old man, he couldn't have been down there for longer than a couple of days. Yet the condition of his body gave the appearance of a week or more.

As he stepped closer, he noticed a small indentation on his forehead. Right above the bridge of the nose. The spot looked almost like an acne pot mark. But it wasn't a scar. It had a small red stain at the center and a black ring at the edges. The injury was a bullet wound. Based on the size, a .22 caliber. The black ring formed when the muzzle of the weapon pressed flat against the skin and the shooter pulled the trigger. The explosive gases burn the flesh and leave the unmistakable black circle of a contact wound.

He turned when he heard Brooks hop off the last rung of the ladder.

"He's been dead a few days."

"How?" she asked as she leaned over his shoulder for a closer look.

She had tied a piece of cloth around her face, like a handkerchief mask, but that wouldn't do much to combat the stench of death and cat piss.

"Looks like a single gunshot wound to the head," Renquest said, pointing at the wound. "Better glove up; we have another homicide."

His captain reached into her back pocket and pulled out two pairs of latex gloves. She handed one set to Renquest and donned the other pair. Once he had stretched the gloves over his oversized hands, he reached around the back of the old man's head and felt around. Starting at the base of the skull and working his way up to the top of his head. There was no exit wound.

"The bullet is still inside his skull. We'll have to get the doc to retrieve it for us."

"If it's not too damaged for ballistics," Brooks said.

Renquest was thinking the same thing. "It likely bounced around inside his skull, turning his brain into oatmeal and deforming the bullet beyond forensic use."

"That sucks," Brooks said.

"It does," Renquest replied, continuing to examine the body. "Get Sanchez and Flaherty on the radio. If they're done searching Pratt's apartment and have found nothing, tell them to call a bus and Johansen. Then, have them seal off the drive and doors with crime scene tape. And get forensics down here."

"Yes, sir."

Brooks turned and climbed back up the ladder. He could hear the boards in the floor above him squeak under her weight as she made her way out the front door. Then silence. Looking at the surrounding walls, he wondered why they could not hear any noises from Sanchez and Flaherty as they rummaged through Pratt's apartment. Drywall and insulation slow the travel of sound through walls, but they rarely stop it altogether.

He reached out and knocked on the plasterboard to his right. The sound returned solid. He imagined sound-deadening insulation filled the void between the sheets of drywall. Then he looked at the area directly in front of where the chair sat. About four feet off the floor, at eye level for an average person sitting down, there was a small hole in the wall. Renquest rose to his feet. He stepped closer to the wall and bent over to peer through it. As his eye neared the peephole, he realized the hole contained a fisheye camera lens. The lens itself was tiny. Maybe a quarter of an inch in diameter. The whole thing wasn't much larger than a pencil eraser. But using a cell phone's camera pressed up against the hole, the optics provided a wide-angle view of the living room and kitchen.

Renquest wondered if the previous renters, the college kids before Pratt, walked around in their undergarments. The peephole provided no view of the bathroom or bedroom. He found that a little strange. That's where the real action took place, so to speak. He thought back to his time on the Sex Crimes Task Force at his old job. The one thing you knew about a peeping tom was that you knew nothing about people's fetishes. There were as many fetishes as varieties of fish in the ocean.

As he studied the area around the peephole, he heard footsteps in the house above him. He could tell it was Brooks, back from managing the rest of the team. As he waited for the crime scene team to arrive, he took stock of the room. It was barren except for the chair and, of course, the dead guy. He looked back at the ladder as Brooks made her way back down. He watched as she carefully placed each hand on the rungs and lowered herself down, one step at a time. The scene made him wish they had gloved up before descending into the hidden room. Anyone who came down here had to leave something on that ladder. They now had to contend with extra prints and smears from both him and Brooks.

"The crime scene techs will be here in about five minutes," Brooks said.

"That was quick," Renquest said.

"We got lucky. They were in the area. You find anything else interesting?"

He pointed to the peephole. "Just that."

Brooks stepped around her boss and inched closer to the spot on the wall. She was a good foot shorter than Renquest and had to bend only slightly at the waist to see through the hole.

"Disgusting!" she said.

"At least I don't see any others in the bath or bedroom areas," he answered.

Brooks stepped back. They both glanced up at the sound of footsteps coming from the floor above. A voice powered down through the opening and echoed in the small room. It was Sanchez.

"The CSI team is here."

Renquest nodded to Brooks.

"Send them down," she shouted back up through the trapdoor.

A minute later, a man and a woman donning white cleaning suits scampered down the ladder and into the room. Four people. Five, if you included the dead guy, really crowded the compact space. So, Renquest and

Brooks stepped on the sticky pad the woman tech had placed at the bottom of the ladder to capture any trace evidence stuck to the soles of their shoes before exiting the pit. Renquest scaled the ladder first, and Brooks followed once he reached the top. The pair then made their way outside. Renquest took a deep breath of fresh air, holding it for a moment before exhaling through his nose. He'd learned over the years that doing this helped clean his nasal passages of any foul odors that lingered.

Sanchez and Flaherty stood next to Brooks' unmarked cruiser. Yellow caution tape stretched from the rear of the car to a county utility box in a yard across the street. The two officers were talking near the front of the cruiser. Renquest was still too far away to hear what the two men were talking about, but he noticed the group of people gathered along the perimeter of the area.

He never understood why crime scenes always attracted people. It was inevitable. Some people simply had a morbid curiosity about the macabre. They just couldn't pass up the chance to see a dead body. Though it didn't happen often, sometimes the killer came back to the crime scene as well. Renquest always made it a point to have one of his officers take pictures of the crowd surrounding a crime scene. He would do the same here. He signaled to the two officers.

Flaherty noticed him first and smacked Sanchez on the shoulder.

The three men watched the growing number of people gathered across the street. The spectators stretched across the yards of three houses and two to three deep the entire stretch. Renquest stopped counting at thirty.

"I want you," Renquest pointed at Sanchez, "to go over and make sure the group of people gathering across the street doesn't break the perimeter."

"What do you want me to do?" Flaherty asked, clearly satisfied that the crappy job of crowd control belonged to Sanchez.

"I want you to get a better look at the people in that crowd," Renquest said. "Use the county right-of-way between the backyard of our house. Make your way down about two blocks before you cross back over. I don't want anyone to know you're coming. Be just another curious face in the crowd." Flaherty turned, but Renquest stopped him. "Give Sanchez your jacket."

Flaherty slid the coat off his shoulders and tossed it to his partner.

"And un-tuck your shirt," Renquest said.

Flaherty followed the order and even ran his hands through his hair for a more unkempt look.

"Do you have a backup piece?"

Flaherty nodded and looked down at his right ankle. "Smith and Wesson. Three-eighty caliber Shield."

"Good, give Sanchez your duty weapon. I want you to seem as un-coply as possible," Renquest said.

Flaherty did as he was told and handed his duty weapon, still in its holster, over to Sanchez.

"How do I look?" he asked jokingly.

Sanchez smiled. "Too bad we can't do anything about that face."

"Ha-ha," Flaherty quipped. "Why don't you go over and start crowd control."

Normally, Renquest enjoyed banter; he just didn't have time for it right now. "Alright. Let's get to it."

Sanchez made his way over to the sidewalk where the crowd had gathered. Flaherty circled behind the house and out of sight. Renquest moved to a less conspicuous position. He didn't believe the suspect lingered long after the murder. To him, this seemed to be a greed killing. He wanted to take some pictures of the crowd, so he pretended to hold the phone out at arm's length. Hopefully, if anyone was paying attention to him, he'd look like he'd forgotten his reading glasses.

Brooks came out of the house just as the medical examiner's van arrived.

"Looks like the doc came herself for this one," she said.

The detective watched Johansen step from the cab and vanish behind the van. A few seconds later, she reappeared at the rear door of the county vehicle. She opened the door and pulled a small bag out with her left hand. Then, she closed the door and made her way to Renquest and Brooks.

"Good afternoon."

"The body is inside, Doc," Renquest said, pointing to the house. He also noticed she was wearing black heels. "The stiff is in the basement, and the only way down is a rickety ladder. So, I'd put on some other shoes if you brought them."

She smiled, then said to Brooks. "They think we can't navigate a ladder in heels." Johansen turned, flipped her hair over her shoulder, and walked away.

Perplexed, Renquest asked, "What was that about?"

The smile Brooks donned a second ago disappeared. "Men always want to come to the rescue of women. It must be some inherent primal desire to warn women of any perceived danger. As if we don't know the evil that lurks around the corner. We deal with it every day. Sexual assault. Rape. The unwanted ass slaps. Every damn day. Doctor Johansen is a capable professional in a field dominated by men. And you think her shoes are the thing she should worry about?"

The statement shook the old detective a little. He didn't intend to offend anyone, nor did he think he was trying to be a protector. Having been a cop for so long, he'd become accustomed to keeping others safe. It'd never crossed his mind that he might be unintentionally condescending towards the women in his life.

"I guess I still have a lot to learn," he said.

"Look, I know you meant nothing by what you said. And I do not think the doc did either. But ask yourself this: would you have made the same comment to a man wearing cowboy boots?"

He didn't like to admit it, but Brooks was right. If it had been Sanchez or Flaherty, he likely wouldn't have even noticed what shoes they were wearing. He wouldn't have commented if he had, and even if he had said something, the quip would have been in a joking manner.

"I guess I owe her an apology."

"I think that would be a good start," Brooks said.

The two stood in an uncomfortable silence that seemed to drag on forever to the humbled detective. Then he noticed Flaherty mingling among the gawkers across the street. Work once again saved him and broke the awkward tension.

"Flaherty is in place," he said to Brooks, tipping his head toward the crowd.

Brooks quickly spotted Flaherty and turned back to Renquest. Neither of them wanted to give away that they had someone watching the crowd from the inside.

"Give him five minutes over there, then signal him to come back. Make sure he comes back the same way he went. Just in case anyone is paying attention," Renquest said.

"What if someone remembers him from the crowd?" Brooks asked.

"Not likely. All eyes appear to be on us for the moment." Renquest looked over toward the house. "I'm going to head back to the station and get started on the reports. You three clean up things here and make sure the doc gets whatever she needs." He turned to walk to his car, but then stopped. "And see if you can find that damn cat."

Renquest crossed the yard to his car. He avoided the press corps that had gathered just outside the rope line. As he passed nearby, he could hear the reporters hurling questions in his direction. He ignored them all and climbed into his car. Then he signaled to a patrol officer to lift the yellow caution tape so he could pass. He watched the scene grow smaller and disappear in his rearview mirror.

Chapter 29

Completing the reports took longer than he'd planned. Before he could finish, he needed the notes Flaherty, Sanchez, and Brooks took at the scene. He also needed a list of any evidence the crime lab had gathered. By the time he returned home, the clock on the wall read half past ten. He slipped off his shoes and loosened his tie before slipping the loop over his head. There wasn't even an effort to put the items away. The tie fell on the back of the chair and his shoes by the sofa.

As he stood in the living room, a familiar smell penetrated his nose. He looked down to see one of Custus's old blankets wadded up on the floor next to his chair. The sight of the one item his old friend went nowhere without caused a rush of emotions that quickly consumed him. He reached down and picked up the blanket. Brown hair fell to the floor as he raised it to his face and took in the familiar scent he'd known for over a decade. His eyes scanned the room to the small urn sitting on the kitchen counter. A tear rolled down his cheek as he noticed the chew toys and the well-worn bed in the far corner of the room. Saddened again by the loss of his friend, he gathered up the bed, along with all the toys and other items scattered around the house, and gently placed them into an empty moving box he pulled out from the hall closet.

He hated the thought of tossing all those memories into the dumpster. The more he thought about it, the deeper grief sank its claws. He needed to decide whether to move on or remain in the past. For years, as a detective who had investigated hundreds of horrible crimes, the one thing he'd always done was encourage the victims' families to move past the tragedy. To hold on to the memories, but move on from the physical. It was much easier said than done when the loss was yours. The grief-stricken detective stood in front of a blue metal dumpster. A lifetime of happy memories stuffed into a cardboard box. The weight felt minimal in his arms, but crushed his soul like a load of bricks. He stood silently. Paralyzed with emotion. It took some time, but he soon regained his composure. He took one last look at the items that had become such a part of his life.

Then he said, "Love ya, buddy," and heaved the box over the side of the dumpster. The box made a thud as it contacted the bottom of the near-empty container. He wiped the moisture from his cheek and went back inside the building.

The next morning, rain pelted the windshield of his car during the short drive into work. Before he left, he placed a call to Chief McNally and told him they needed some results from the lab before they could provide another update in the Pratt landlord murder investigation. The chief was less than enthusiastic about another killing on his watch, and he promptly instructed Renquest to report to his office first thing in the morning. The seasoned detective knew from over twenty years of service as a police officer that a meeting with the boss first thing in the morning wasn't a good thing. Tired and overworked, and knowing he had an ass-chewing waiting for him at the station, he decided on a quick detour for a gourmet cup of freshly ground coffee. He wasn't sure how the meeting was going to go, but being late wouldn't be the deciding factor in whether he still had a job at the end of the day. Besides, he still had the county council on his side. A card he could play if necessary.

The lights in the reception area were off when he arrived at the station. The place was empty, though Margaret did work for four hours in the morning on Saturdays. For a second he thought he'd beat McNally there, giving himself a little time to prepare. But as he badged in and entered the hallway, the light beaming through the open door at the end of the hall extinguished any chance at even minimal preparation. Much like Lucy from the comic strip, the chief was in.

Renquest tightened his tie by pushing it into place against his collar. He fastened the two buttons on the front of his sports coat and flattened out any creases with his hands. Then he took a deep breath, ran his fingers through his hair, and stepped through the open door.

Chief McNally was sitting in a high-backed leather chair. This one was a little taller and a little wider than the one supplied to him by the county. A sign of who was in charge.

Renquest knocked on the jamb of the door as he entered.

"Chief."

McNally peered over the top of his reading glasses at his next in charge. The person hired to be his policy enforcer. The sullen look on his face beamed an expression of discomfort with his choice. He stared for a moment before pointing to the chair in front of a desk more fitting to that of a mayor. Or a mafia boss.

Renquest sat quietly and waited for his boss. The room was silent except for the ticking coming from the clock on the wall. The volume of which was proportionate to the silence of the two men. McNally broke first.

"I hear you think you know something about me?"

The statement caught Renquest off guard. He was sure he'd been called in about the murder at the Pratt house. He played dumb.

"I'm not sure what you are referring to, Chief," Renquest said.

McNally's eyes squinted, causing his brow to narrow. The squishing of his face caused an exaggeration in the size and number of wrinkles above his brow. A little vein popped out just below the peak on the right side of his military-style hairline. It pulsed when he spoke.

"Don't fuck with me. You know damn well what I am talking about," he said, his voice cracking as he tried to keep his tone low.

Renquest kept at it. "You'll have to be more specific, sir. I thought I was here to talk about the body we found at the Pratt house yesterday."

McNally's icy stare pierced the space between the two men.

"You think I care about that piece of shit?" he said. "Where the hell are the pictures?"

Renquest pulled himself up straight in the chair. He then leaned in a fraction and stared back at McNally before answering. The jig was up. No need to pretend he didn't know what was going on.

"They're safe. I've put them somewhere you won't ever be able to get to them."

McNally's eyes burned with rage. He was angry, but also scared about being backed into a corner. The most dangerous animal is one that feels trapped. Instinct takes over. Actions are driven by raw emotion and the need to escape. The best way to deal with a trapped animal is to show it an exit and see if it leaves.

Renquest leaned back in his chair with his palms on the armrests. A signal that he was open to negotiations. McNally's posture followed suit. Nothing too drastic, but Renquest noticed his balled fists relax and his white fingers turn flesh-colored again. The bulging vein in his forehead subsided. Message received. The trapped rat had one eye on him and the other focused on the newly opened door.

This is where things got dicey. He needed to be careful and not push too hard. McNally needed to believe that the idea of leaving and the manner in which that happened were his to make. When, in fact, the exact opposite was the case. Renquest would guide him in the direction he wanted his boss to go. The choice McNally makes has to appear to lead to the best and only acceptable outcome for him. The game was afoot, as Holmes used to say.

"First, I want to make sure the women in those pictures are safe and free from retaliation. If any of them decide to file a complaint, that complaint better make its way through without interference from you or anyone else in the department." He paused, ensuring the chief understood his demand before continuing. "Second, you destroy nothing you kept from the meetups. Any pictures, video recordings, or other spank material you will turn over to me. I'll keep it safe and make sure it never sees the light of day, unless you break the first condition."

Chief McNally tried to cut in, but Renquest talked over him. "Third, I want you to allow me to continue this investigation to its rightful conclusion. With no interference from you or the county council. No time constraints and no threats of taking my job. If I don't find out who's responsible in due time, you won't have to fire me. I'll resign."

McNally appeared to like what he was hearing. But he was still worried about his future. "What about the pictures? I can't have those out there hanging over my head forever."

There it was. He made his demand. "I'll continue to hang on to those. In case one day you decide to run for county council or state representative."

"How do I know I can trust you?"

"You don't. But this is all on you. If you keep your word, I'll destroy everything if all the victims agree to it."

The chief sat still in his chair. His hands cupped in front of his face. He was trying to visualize whether there was any way this could come back to haunt him. Finally, he looked up at his chief detective. He had decided.

"You won't go to the county council with what you have, as long as I do what you say?"

Renquest shook his head. "I won't go to the council if *you* keep your word. As far as the council is concerned, that's not my fight. Some members have a hard-on for you, and I would imagine you're going to have to defend yourself to them at some point. But it won't be because of me."

McNally had a look of defeat on his face. Then he pointed to the door and said, "Get out."

Renquest stood and turned. But he stopped.

"You want an update on the Pratt murder?"

McNally had already turned his attention to a stack of paperwork on his desk. He ignored the question, never even glancing up at his chief detective.

Then he said, "If you fuck me over, I'll take your friend, the coroner, down. Yeah, she was one of my first. I think I'll keep that as my insurance."

Renquest shook his head and exited the office. He then hurried down the hall, past the reception area, where Margaret sat at her desk. She watched him as he hustled out the door. He'd parked his car near the elevator on the first floor of the parking garage. Less than a minute later he was out of the garage and on his way to see Johansen.

Chapter 30

The rain had stopped, and his wipers squealed with each swipe of the windshield as he drove down North Courthouse Road. He switched the wipers off. The sun peeked through the gaps in the cloud cover; its rays burning through the morning mist caused a thin veil of fog to rise from the wet pavement.

It was the weekend, but he knew Johansen would be in her office. She would want to get the preliminary results out to him for the body they had discovered the previous day. The medical examiner was always on call. A 24/7 thankless job, much like his. But traffic was light, thanks to the weekend lull in government workers heading to the Pentagon. He pulled into the parking lot just five minutes after leaving his office.

That had to be a record, he thought as he opened his door and slid out of his car. It was so quiet downtown; he didn't even look for traffic as he crossed the street. The county offices were all closed. Only the cleaning staff would be in the office on a weekend. He and Johansen might be the only ones in the building.

He pulled the keycard from his pocket and tapped it on the receiver pad next to the door. The light changed from red to green, then the door clicked. Once inside, he continued to the coroner's office, where he found the main door to the office unlocked.

Why wouldn't it be, he asked himself. No one else is here, and anyone wanting to gain entrance must get past the locked main entrance. Still, as a cop, unlocked doors made him nervous. Instinctively, he tapped the grip on his duty weapon as he reached for the door with his off-hand.

The lobby was empty. The only noise was the hum of one fluorescent light above the door. As he approached the inner door leading to the autopsy room, he detected a faint reverberation. He could barely make out the beat. It reminded him of a song popular in the eighties. *Beach Boys*, he thought. The one from that movie where Tom Cruise was a bartender in the Caribbean. The music got louder as he approached the examining room. Through the observation window, he could see Johansen, her back turned to the door, her hips moving to the sway of the music as she flipped through paperwork. He didn't want to scare her, so he waited for a moment to see if she would turn and notice him through the glass. Even when she did finally turn to face him, she never looked up from the papers in her hand and continued working.

He would need to get her attention without startling her too badly. Using the knuckles on the back of his right hand, he rapped on the glass three times. She still didn't hear him. This time he knocked harder on the glass, turning his hand around. Blam. Blam. Blam.

There was no chance she wouldn't hear his attempt to get her attention this time. He had hit the glass in the middle of the pane. Its weakest point. A loud screech filled the air as the glass cracked from the top left corner to the bottom right. In less than a second, it shot across the entire pane. The fracture resembled a lightning bolt. Johansen leaped into the air and dropped the files she held, though she managed not to scream. Her expression as she spun around revealed that his unexpected presence had frightened her.

Johansen stared at him and then turned her attention to the broken window.

"Jesus Christ! You scared the hell out of me."

Renquest's head fell, embarrassed.

"I'm sorry about that," he said, looking over his shoulder at the cracked glass. "I didn't think I hit it that hard, but I was trying to get your attention without startling you by just appearing in the room behind you."

"So, your plan was to break my window?"

He shook his head. "Of course not. Like I said, that was an accident. I was trying not to scare you."

Johansen stared blankly at him. After a moment, a smile crept across her face. She started laughing.

"What's so funny?" he asked.

She covered her mouth with her right hand to hide her amusement. After a moment, she regained her composure and stepped closer to him. She placed a hand on his shoulder, leaned up and kissed him on the cheek.

"I'm sorry. But the look on your face."

"What's going on here?"

"That window had been loose for years. I have called maintenance at least ten times to get them to come up and fix it before it broke and cut someone. They just keep ignoring my requests. I was told it's not a priority, and to call them when it breaks."

"So, you knew this would happen," he said.

"A few of us had a pool going," she said. "I picked Steven, the FedEx delivery guy. So, I guess I'm out twenty bucks."

"Who had me?"

"I guess no one did. The pool started before you came here. Looks like I'll be getting my money back," Johansen said with a chuckle.

"I'm glad I could help," Renquest said with a smile.

But his smile soon faded. He extended his hand and touched her arm.

"We need to talk."

Johansen's expression also changed. To one of concern.

"Oh… okay," she said as she turned and led him to a couple of stools pushed in under a counter. She gestured to one of the metal seats and slid one out, then sat facing him on the other. Once seated, she said, "So serious. Are you alright?"

The detective towered over the much shorter Johansen. Her feet dangled a few inches off the ground. The soles of his size thirteen shoes rested flat on the cement floor. He paused for a moment to collect his thoughts. He liked her. But what he was about to do involved a very personal act. With the potential for embarrassment or perhaps even shame. He couldn't imagine someone prying into his personal life the way he was about to do. But he needed answers if he was going to protect her. He needed to know everything.

"I need to talk to you about something," he said. "I want to let you know up front that it's personal."

"Okay," she said, trying to sound calm, though her expression betrayed her.

The words he wanted to say swirled in his head. They just seemed to disappear before they crossed his lips. After decades of questioning hundreds of suspects, it finally happened. He didn't know how to start.

Johansen watched him intently. Her lips pursed and her brow narrowed. The concerned expression on her face disappeared. Replaced with a serious one. She rubbed the palms of her hands on her jeans, then folded them in her lap. Her back stiffened.

"Go ahead. Ask me what you need to ask me."

Renquest hesitated at first. But he knew he needed to do this. His personal feelings didn't matter. He needed to put all that to the side and do his job. Besides, in this case, McNally was the real threat. Not him.

"What I am about to ask will not be comfortable for you. But just know, I wouldn't be asking if it weren't important." He paused and waited for Johansen to object. When she said nothing, he continued. "There are some things happening at the police department. Some of it is politics. But not all of it is. A part of it is personal. And people are looking for ways to get the upper hand, and frankly, they don't care who they step on to get it."

"And you're caught up in all of this?" Johansen asked.

"I am," Renquest said. "In more ways than one."

"And your visit today — that's because you think I'm caught up in all of this as well?"

Renquest nodded. "I know you are. And so are a lot of other people."

"These other people, are they all women?" she asked.

"They are."

Johansen calmly brushed the hair away from her face. "Okay. I'm ready."

"Are you sure?"

"I've been waiting for this day to come for a long time. Let's get it over with," Johansen said.

Renquest nodded.

"I met with McNally this morning. I thought it was going to be about the new guy in your cooler over there, but that's not the direction the meeting went. Now, I'm going to be honest with you. I have some files in my possession. These files could be politically damaging to McNally and possibly embarrassing to others. The chief made it clear he wanted the files I have. Do you know what I'm talking about?"

Johansen dropped her head and let out a sigh. Her hands fidgeted with the seams of her pant legs.

"What is it, Rebecca?" Renquest asked.

Her eyes rose level with his. She stuttered slightly as she said, "You almost never call me Rebecca."

"Seemed appropriate."

"Even though I knew this day was coming, I still can't believe it's here," Johansen said.

Renquest reached out and placed a hand on her knee. "I need you to tell me everything."

Johansen's gaze shot around the room, trying to hide the tears in her eyes, but the detective noticed. He stood and grabbed a roll of paper towels from behind him, ripped off a sheet and handed it to his friend.

The normally resolute, headstrong doctor broke down. "This is about him and his perverted sexual fantasies, isn't it?"

"I'm afraid it is. I know most of what went on. Brooks came clean a few days ago, and she told me everything. I even know how I came into possession of the photos."

"She's a good cop. I imagined that one day she would do something with what she knew. I just hoped I'd be long gone by then," Johansen said.

"She told me she couldn't live with the secret anymore. It'd just weighed her down for too long. I guess I was as safe a bet as she could find," Renquest said. "Now, why don't you start from the beginning. Tell me what happened and leave nothing out. No matter how embarrassing it is, I need to know everything."

* * *

The rain must have started up while he was talking to Johansen, because the pavement was wet again. Though the sun had come back out and things were quickly drying off. He found it difficult to concentrate on driving after hearing what Johansen had told him. His mind wandered, meddling with details he didn't know how to process yet. He found it difficult to separate his personal feelings for Johansen from his professional ones. If there was anything positive in all of this, it's that some women moved past it. At least from outward appearances. Though he imagined all of them bore scars from the ordeal. Though some wounds ran deeper than others, and he might never know the true emotional damage McNally inflicted upon his victims.

As he turned right onto 14th Street North, he noticed lights at the top of the hill near the entrance to the public parking lot across the street from the courthouse and jail. A chill ran down his spine. The engine moaned as his foot pressed harder on the gas pedal. The car quickly sped up the hill, the top of which was cordoned off by emergency vehicles. As he reached the top, he rolled the window down and stuck his badge out the window at the officer manning the roadblock.

"What's going on here?"

The officer looked at the photo on the Arlington County Police ID and said, "Detective, they have been trying to reach you."

It was then he realized he had turned his phone off while at Johansen's office. He didn't want to be interrupted while he was meeting with her.

"Why are they trying to reach me? What's happened?"

The officer stepped aside and waved him past. "You'd better go on up, Detective."

Renquest maneuvered between the patrol cars, rolling up his window when he cleared the barricade. He parked the car along the fire trucks just past the intersection, then made his way past the troves of police cars, their lights flashing red and blue, and up to the steps leading to the plaza between the courthouse and the jail. Brooks was at the center of a group of officers. She was barking out orders, her hands gesturing to side streets and windows in the adjacent buildings. Each time she gave an order, the officers responsible for that task jumped into action. He couldn't help thinking that she looked like a genuine leader. He was extra proud anytime a woman made headway within the ranks. Misogyny and chauvinistic male bravado filled most police departments. He watched her for a second before moving in.

"Tell me what's happening, Brooks," the detective said as he approached her.

"Detective, we've been trying to reach you all morning!"

"Sorry, I was with a witness."

He could tell by the look in her eyes that they'd be revisiting this in the future.

"Well, an hour ago, a young man walked through the main entrance," Brooks pointed at the two glass doors about twenty-five feet straight ahead from their current position. "When he passed through the metal detectors, the alarm went off. There was only one deputy manning the station, being it's a weekend, not to mention the only offices open were code enforcement and us."

"Go on," Renquest said.

"After the deputy asked him to step back through, the man reached into his pants and pulled out a taser. Before he could get a hand on his weapon, the poor fucker went down like a sack of potatoes. The assailant hit the button one more time for good measure, cuffed the deputy, and locked him in the cleaning closet. He then made his way to our offices."

Renquest interrupted, "Is the deputy okay?"

"He is fine. A little shaken up. Mostly he's embarrassed, but he'll recover." She tipped her head toward the ambulance parked on 15th Street North, just a block over. "Once at the reception area, he rang the bell. Flaherty was getting a cup of coffee and opened the door to see who was there."

Renquest scratched his head. "Why did he open the door? Why wouldn't he check to see who's waiting by looking through the reception window?"

"A question that will come up once we get him out of there safely, I assure you," Brooks said. "Once inside, he used the weapon he had taken from the deputy to subdue Flaherty, and we don't know where he went after that."

Renquest nodded. "Is there anyone else in there? What about Margaret?"

"She never came in today. Called out sick before she was supposed to report for her shift," Brooks answered.

Renquest let out a sigh of relief. "What do we know about the perp?"

"Not much right now. He has been quiet and has made no demands. We are calling into the station to see if he will answer the phone, but we have had no luck yet."

Renquest held out his hand. "Let me see your phone."

Brooks placed the small cell phone in the detective's hand.

"Do you think he will talk to you?"

"We have cameras at the front of the building. He can watch everything we do safely from inside the station." He paused before dialing. "And the chief is in there."

"How do you know that?"

"I met with him in his office this morning."

"Well, that's good. Try calling him. See if he can tell us what's happening in there."

Renquest peered down at the phone in his hand. Something wasn't right. If McNally was in the building and not a hostage, he should've called for help by now.

"Has he tried to contact you?"

"No," Brooks said.

"Have you heard any shots from inside the building?"

"No," she said again.

"Then the chief is dead or a hostage. He is of no use to us."

Brooks and Renquest both went silent. Both chose not to speculate about the reality of the situation. After a moment, Renquest used the phone in his hand to dial the number to the office. The phone rang and rang, but no one answered. He then raised the phone above his head. Waved it in the air from side to side.

When he placed the phone back to his ear, the ringing had stopped. He could hear breathing on the other end. After a moment, a voice came through the speaker.

"Detective. I was wondering when you would show up."

"So, you know who I am," Renquest said. "I'm afraid you have me at a disadvantage. I don't believe we've ever met."

A low laugh echoed across the line.

Renquest asked, "What's so funny?"

The laughter ended as abruptly as it had begun. "I guess it isn't funny from your perspective. I know everything about you, and you know nothing about me. The show you put on for the media proved that."

"So, you were watching?"

"Of course, I was. It is always good for a hunter to know his prey."

"I agree. In fact, I was counting on it." Renquest said.

"What exactly is it you were counting on?" the voice asked.

Renquest picked up on a change in the man's voice. His condescending tone changed to one of anger. The veteran detective could use this to his advantage.

"The press conference. You see, it was all just a big show. A production scripted for one. Oh, and the way I told the world what you really were, I bet that pissed you off. You are a coward who preys on the weak to elevate your own self-esteem. Now, I'm no shrink, but I'd say it probably relates to some mommy issue you never dealt with as a child."

Renquest felt a tug on his shirtsleeve. He looked over to see Brooks staring at him, a look of concern on her face. While he understood her apprehension about his tone toward an armed man inside the police station with at least two hostages, he knew what he was doing. Or at least he hoped he did. It was a tactic he'd used before with hostage takers. The major difference this time being that he couldn't just kick in the front door after a few flashbang grenades exploded and take out the perpetrator. If he made one move toward the door, the chief and Flaherty would get a bullet in the head. He needed to keep up the ruse.

When he placed the phone back to his ear, he heard nothing but silence. Then the line clicked off. Had he pushed too hard? He turned to Brooks. She looked away. His chest tightened. Then he realized he hadn't taken a breath since the line went dead. He drew a deep breath in through his nose and exhaled. He needed to get into the building somehow.

Chapter 31

"What do you think he is doing in there?" Brooks asked. Renquest noticed her voice carried a hint of anger mixed with anxiety.

"Dunno," Renquest said.

"I think you pushed too hard."

"Maybe."

"Are you going to call him back?" she asked, her finger pointed at the phone in his hand.

But before Renquest could answer, he felt the phone vibrate, followed by an electronic ring. He placed the phone to his ear.

"Detective, I hope you enjoyed the moment of silence. I guess I felt you were being a tad disrespectful. I needed a little time to compose myself and work out some of the anxiety you caused me."

Renquest noticed immediately that the voice on the other side of the phone had calmed. So calm, in fact, it made Renquest nervous. The phrase "*work out some anxiety*" didn't ease his concerns any. As he thought about his next move, he decided it was time to try a different approach. Time to be the good cop.

"I apologize for my tone earlier. Let's start over, what do you say?"

The line was silent.

"What's your name?" Renquest asked.

After a moment, the voice on the other end of the line said, "Michael."

"I'm sorry we had to meet this way, Michael. But before we can move forward, I need to know that everyone inside is alive and well. As a gesture of good faith, I need you to have each of the hostages say their name. Can you do that for me?"

More silence. Then a voice shouted, "Flaherty." Then another voice, muffled and labored, said, "McNally."

Both Renquest and Brooks took a deep breath, then exhaled in relief.

Renquest followed up his question with, "Is everyone okay?"

Michael answered. "Now, Detective. You asked for names. You got what *you* wanted. Now it's my turn."

Renquest grimaced. He knew he wouldn't be able to keep the men inside alive forever. Not from the middle of the courtyard in front of the cameras. They needed to get inside. To be close enough to get off a clean shot if it came down to that. But with Michael's eyes on the security cameras, he was at a loss on how to make that happen without showing his hand.

He looked concernedly at Brooks, then faced the courthouse cameras and said, "Okay, Michael. What is it you want to say?"

The air was eerily quiet. Then everyone covered their ears in pain as the set of speakers mounted above the main entrance to the courthouse squelched to life with feedback.

"Now that I have your attention." Michael's voice echoed between the cement walls of the county jail and courthouse. "I want to tell you all a story."

"Don't do this," a voice mumbled in the background.

Renquest recognized the voice as Chief McNally.

"Shut up!" Michael screamed. "You don't get to talk anymore. For twenty-five years, you've been doing all the talking. Well, finally it's my time to talk."

Rustling sounds came from the speakers, as did continued pleas to stop. Then silence.

"Sorry about that. Your chief was being rude. It's not nice to talk when someone else has the floor," Michael said calmly. "But don't worry. I didn't hurt him. Nothing a little tape over his mouth couldn't fix."

Dodge looked around the courtyard. He spotted the big, black, military-looking vehicle belonging to the S.W.A.T. team on the street. It appeared that the men in the black pants and black shirts were getting restless. He grabbed the radio from Brooks and keyed up the mic.

"Delta-ten." Delta-ten was the call sign for the S.W.A.T. team leader. "Delta-ten, this is Renquest. Do you copy?"

The radio crackled. "Delta-ten here."

"Stand down. Do not approach the courthouse. Confirm."

Dodge's thumb pressed the mute button on his phone. He didn't want anyone inside the building to hear his next words, specifically Michael. Then, he turned away from the camera and faced Brooks. He raised his arms in the air and waved toward the armored vehicle blocking the street.

"Listen carefully," he said. "I need you to go to the S.W.A.T. commander and tell him to take his team a block away to the north. Set up on the other side of the jail. Tell him to tune to channel 29 on the radio and wait for my instructions."

"Sir," Brooks said, confusion in her voice.

"Do it now. We need Michael to think that we are giving him something. A gesture of good faith. But most of all, it could buy us a little more time," Renquest said.

Brooks nodded and double-timed to the armored vehicle. Renquest watched as she gave the commander his instructions. She turned back and gave a thumbs-up. The heavily armed men in fatigues slowly packed up and climbed inside the armored vehicle. Dodge watched the enormous truck until it disappeared behind the county jail. He then turned to the camera and lifted his phone; his thumb pushed the unmute button.

"Michael," he said. "I had the assault team move a block away. Consider it a gesture of goodwill for not hurting any of the hostages."

"If you're done, may I continue?" Michael asked.

Dodge nodded into the camera. It wasn't the response he'd hoped for, but as long as Michael kept talking, the hostages were safe.

"As I was saying, I want to tell you a story. It all started about twenty-five years ago. Right here in Arlington. You see, there was a young woman. She was smart. So smart, in fact, she graduated at the top of her class. Unfortunately, she didn't come from money, and her parents couldn't afford to send her to a big college. So, she enrolled at a local community college.

Like a lot of junior college kids, she took classes during the day and worked at a corner market, running the register at night. The owners trusted her so much that after a few months, they allowed her to close the store on her own. She was a happy young woman. Things were looking up for her. Then, one cold December night, a man came into the store and changed everything."

Everyone in the courtyard listened to Michael as he told the story of how a man entered the store, held his mother at gunpoint, and took the money from the register. But only after he kicked and beat her before running off. As she lay on the cold tile floor, terrified, bruised, and bloody, she wondered if the man would return to finish the job. Half an hour passed before a cop car rolled to a stop at the curb outside the store's entrance. She used the register counter to pull herself up and limped to the front door. A young patrolman, fresh out of the Marines, hopped out of his car and hurried to the door to help.

"She used to tell me the story at bedtime. Her face would light up as she described how her white knight, dressed in blue, came to her rescue." The speakers went silent as Michael paused. "But the smile soon faded. She tucked me into bed each night and told me I was the best thing that had ever happened to her. But I never believed her. Something inside me said she was lying. I was a burden she never wanted. It was always him she longed for. And it was my fault that he left her. Had I never been born, my mother and her rescuer would've lived happily ever after."

Renquest figured it out almost immediately after Michael began telling the story. Chief McNally was the cop who found Michael's mother. He was also Michael's father. Everything that had happened up to this point was because McNally had taken advantage of a victim. He used his position to gain her trust, and when the romance led to a pregnancy, he abandoned them. An unwed mother living in one of the most expensive places in the United States. He understood Michael's anger. But this had gone too far. Outing him would've been easier and safer for everyone involved. But there was something he was missing, and Michael was about to fill in the gaps.

Renquest tapped a message into his phone. Then he looked around the courtyard as he waited for a response from the S.W.A.T. commander. The crowd had grown as word got out there was a situation at the courthouse with the chief of police being a hostage. The street was now lined with news vans. They painted large numbers on the sides of the vans to show their affiliation. Tall antennas extended from the vehicle's roofs high into the air, broadcasting live. It wouldn't be long before the national news corps showed up. The last thing he needed was a couple of cops being shot on live television. He needed this to end before that happened.

His phone buzzed in his hand. Brooks leaned over and read the message with him. She nodded and then faced the growing crowd of people. Her voice deep and commanding, she pushed the onlookers back. Clearing an area around Renquest of about twenty feet. Camera operators shouted and cursed. Reporters blurted out freedom of the press claims as a line of officers formed between them and the courthouse entrance. Renquest wasn't concerned about violating the rights of a few reporters. He needed the show. The distraction. Michael could see what was happening with the security cameras mounted outside. Hopefully, it was the only thing he was watching. The distraction needed to allow enough time for S.W.A.T. to enter the tunnel under the courtyard that was used to escort prisoners from the jail to the courthouse for hearings.

Brooks relayed Renquest's hasty plan to the S.W.A.T. commander earlier, which was why Renquest wanted them to leave the area on camera. The veteran detective guessed Michael would think he was trying to trick him, or just buying some time for the S.W.A.T. team to organize and plan how to get into the courthouse. What Renquest hoped for was that Michael would think cops would use the building's elevators in the parking garage to make entry. While listening to Michael's story, Brooks was busy researching Michael and his dead mother. They needed to gather enough information to run a criminal record check on him. Michael had a clean record and had never set foot in the Arlington County Detention Center, as far as they could tell. Which eased Renquest's mind a little. Michael wouldn't know about the tunnel used to move inmates between the buildings. Once inside, the entry team could then take the special elevator used to get the inmates to the various holding cells while awaiting their case to be called. The plan didn't put them right outside McNally's office, where the S.W.A.T. team knew he had the hostages after using a thermal imaging drone to pinpoint Michael's spot in the building. But they were a hell of a lot closer than out here. The move also provided a slight element of surprise. At least for now.

Michael's voice reverberated over the speaker again. His tone changed. The words came more quickly. He'd rehearsed this part. It was the beginning of the end. An ominous feeling filled his chest. They needed to resolve this soon.

Careful not to be noticed, he sent a "911" text to the S.W.A.T. commander. "911" being the cue for the armed team to make their entry into the courthouse from the jail. The team had control of the cameras in the jail and the tunnel, as the sheriff's system was separate from the courthouse security system. But Michael could monitor the tunnel cameras from his location. To get around that, S.W.A.T. made a short recording of the empty hallway that connected the two buildings and played it on a 30-second loop. Michael wouldn't know they were coming until the team was already in the courthouse. There was nothing Renquest could do about that. Short of cutting the power to the entire courthouse. Even then, the emergency generators would kick in and restore power in a few minutes. But maybe a few minutes were all he needed?

Renquest unmuted his phone. "Michael."

"It's not polite to interrupt people," Michael responded.

Renquest raised his hands above his head. A gesture of apology. Then he said, "I'm sorry to interrupt, but I have something I need to tell you, and I didn't want it to happen without giving you a heads-up first." Renquest waited for Michael's response.

"Go on," Michael said.

"I was just informed by building services that the generators will cycle on for an hour as part of the building's maintenance routine. I was told this happens once a month to keep fresh diesel in the lines if an actual emergency happens."

The news didn't sit well with the man with a gun. "And you want me to believe that today, of all the days in the month, is the day this happens?"

"To be clear, you picked this day, not us. Building operations schedule the test for this time every month. They picked a weekend to minimize office interruptions. It's programmed into the computers that control the system, and there isn't anything they can do about it. I'm simply letting you know this is happening regardless of our feelings on the matter. I'm trying to be upfront and show some good faith, so you don't get nervous, then do something you can't take back." Renquest waited.

"How long?"

"How long, what?"

"How long will it take?" Michaels asked.

"The generators will be on for an hour. But the initial power interruption shouldn't last for more than a few minutes. What I need from you is to hold tight. I'll signal you right before the generators take over. Once they are running, the cameras will come back online. I'll be right here. I won't move from this spot. You have my word. Okay?"

"If you betray me, what happens to these two will be on your hands."

Renquest shook his head. "Nothing's gonna happen. You stay calm, and this will all be over in a few minutes."

Renquest turned to Brooks and nodded. She spun and double-timed it around the corner and out of view. Once off-camera, Captain Brooks took out her phone, dialed the S.W.A.T. commander's number and gave him the go-ahead.

Chapter 32

Renquest held his hand up to the camera and slowly counted down from five. When his last finger dropped, the lights inside the building flickered, then went dark. The cameras were dead, but they would reboot as soon as the operator engaged the generators. He told them to override the grid's automatic power transfer to the generators to provide the entry team time to get into position undetected. It was a hell of a risk, but he could see no other way to get the hostages out without being harmed.

The team had two minutes before the generators turned on and took over, and maybe another thirty seconds before the cameras rebooted and came back online. All he could do was wait for word that the team was in place. The seconds ticked by. Each felt like an eternity. As the first minute passed, Renquest checked his phone. Then, ninety seconds. Nothing from the team. Renquest got a bad feeling. He wondered whether something had gone wrong. But his bigger concern was whether Michael would hold off. At two minutes, the sound of the four large generators shattered the silence as they roared to life.

"Come on, damn it," the nervous detective muttered.

The lights inside the courthouse flickered on and off before switching on permanently. He looked back at his phone. Nothing. The entire plan was falling apart. If the team didn't get into place before those cameras came back online, the hostages were as good as dead. As he typed out a message to Brooks, his phone vibrated. The S.W.A.T. commander let him know the team was in place. The detective breathed a sigh of relief.

"Detective, I see the cameras are back."

"And as I promised, I'm still here." Renquest said. "So, now that it's over, why don't you tell me what's next?"

"What's next is I do what I came here to do," Michael said.

"It seems to me you've done that. I'm not a member of the county council or anything, but I'd say that your father's time as chief of police is likely over. Not a single officer here is going to respect him after this is over. And if the chief doesn't have the respect of his officers, he might as well move on. Hell, my guess is that the county commissioners are meeting as we speak to vote on a dismissal. It's over. You've won," Renquest said, and then paused for a response. None came. "Let the hostages go, and we can sit down and talk, just you and me. What do you say?"

Renquest knew he wouldn't be able to hold the entry team for much longer. The window to save Flaherty and McNally closed a little every second that passed. He needed to make a move. In a predetermined signal he'd worked out with the S.W.A.T. commander, he reached up, scratched his head, then covered his mouth with his right hand. The entry team was monitoring the camera feeds through a monitor that connected wirelessly to the courthouse security system. Waiting was all he could do now.

At that moment, the generator's silenced. The lights in the courthouse went dark. You could hear a pin drop outside. Renquest's heart pounded in his chest. He looked around to see if anyone could hear it, but all eyes were on the building towering in front of them. No one spoke. Then a bright light, followed by the crack of an explosion, rattled the windows. It was a flashbang grenade. A controlled explosive device to disorient anyone in a room before the team made entry. Renquest waited for gunshots. He hoped the team could take Michael alive, but that depended on Michael. Once the team entered the room, everything that happened would be to reduce the risk to the hostages. Anything that happened to the hostage-taker would be acceptable collateral damage.

But the air remained void of gunshots. After a minute, the radio crackled.

"The hostages are safe, and the suspect is in custody. No injuries to report. Please restore the power to the building."

A collective cheer rose from the officers in the courtyard. People were smiling, hands clapping. It was the best possible outcome. But Renquest knew his job had just begun. Michael had put the city of Arlington through hell for months. Residents were terrified to leave their houses for fear they might become the next victim of a ruthless killer. The residents of Arlington County wanted answers. He needed answers.

Three hours had passed since the S.W.A.T. team executed a flawless hostage rescue. Renquest met with the commander once the building was clear and Michael was safely in custody. The two men walked through the entire operation, looking for any mistakes that might have placed the team and hostages in jeopardy. Both men believed that the Virginia State Police and the Attorney General wouldn't have any issues with the operation. The men shook hands and congratulated the line officers on a job well done.

"Detective, I gotta say, your plan was good," the commander said. He pulled a pack of cigarettes from his pocket and offered the detective one.

"Don't smoke," Renquest said. "But I'll let you buy me a beer after he's convicted."

"Don't drink," the commander said.

Renquest simply smiled. "Two ships passing in the night."

"Longfellow fan?"

"It's one of the few lines of poetry that's stuck with me since high school."

"He had a way with words," the commander said.

"Strange man," Renquest followed.

The two men shook hands one more time and parted ways.

Renquest felt the charge in his bones. It was time to get back to work. Once inside and through security, Renquest made his way to the interview rooms on the jail's second floor. He gave the slip with the name of who he was there to see, along with his department ID, to the deputy manning the control pod. The jail was on lockdown after Michael's stunt at the courthouse, which made the place eerily quiet.

"Room 7, Detective," the deputy behind the safety glass said, his outstretched finger pointing to his right.

As he sat and stared at the walls, he noticed for the first time how small and stuffy the room was. He'd never had to sit and wait for an inmate before. It was he who made others wait. For a moment, he recognized how it felt. He'd requested a room without a clear safety divider separating the inmates from the interviewer; the sheriff refused and showed his displeasure about the interview taking place so soon after the incident. Renquest didn't argue. It was his jail and his rules. The safety glass didn't reach to the ceiling and had holes drilled in a circle in the middle so the interviewer and interviewee could converse normally. There was also a small space between the counter and the glass to slide paperwork between the two parties. Renquest leaned into the cheap plastic chair and waited for Michael to be escorted from his cell. He texted Brooks, Flaherty, and Sanchez while he waited to let them know where he was. He also requested to meet with the team briefly after medical cleared Flaherty.

Sanchez was also in the building when Michael took Flaherty and McNally hostage. He hid in Renquest's office when Michael overpowered Flaherty and took over Chief McNally's office. He and Flaherty had been in the breakroom and, unfortunately, he'd left his phone on a table in the room. When S.W.A.T. showed up, Sanchez came out of hiding and assisted in Michael's arrest.

There were several reasons for the meeting. First, he needed to see the members of his team involved in the hostage incident. It was important to let them know what happened wasn't their fault, but there were things that happened that everyone involved could learn from. The second reason was to let his team know he had no interest in taking the chief position if McNally ended up being removed by the county council. His long-term plan was to stay chief of detectives, but there was no desire on his part to sit in the chief's seat. The mess McNally put the department in was enormous. Whoever took that chair would be under tremendous pressure from the county council and the residents of Arlington County for years. In all honesty, he didn't expect the next chief to make it more than a couple of years. Smart money was on less than two.

He looked at the clock on his phone. It'd been over half an hour and still no Michael. Deputies always assumed the inmate was meeting with a defense attorney and found it funny to waste their time. A practice he found unprofessional, and he would be sure to have a talk with the sheriff. Although he wanted to leave and ask the deputy why it was taking so long, that would mean waiting to get buzzed out of the interview room, which normally required a few minutes' wait. After exiting the room, he was still in a secure area and forced to wait in the hallway until the control room deputy unlocked the door to the waiting room. Though he wasn't happy about sitting on his hands, it wouldn't kill him to wait a while longer.

Renquest looked up from the emails on his phone and saw the deputy coming his way. The young man appeared to be in a hurry and was making straight for the interview room door on the prisoner's side. He was all business. Something happened, and it wasn't good. The deputy flung his arm into the air, and the lock on the other side clicked. The door opened, and the young deputy stepped in.

"Detective," he said. His voice cracked with anxiety. "I need you to come to the infirmary."

"Infirmary," Renquest said. "Why don't you tell me what is going on?"

The deputy looked uncomfortable. His hands shook. He swayed from side to side on his heels. Now Renquest knew the news was bad.

"Sir..."

"Detective," Renquest interrupted.

"Sorry. Detective. I need you to come with me."

"Well, son. As you can see, you're on that side and I'm on this side," Renquest said.

The deputy pointed toward the end of the hall. "When you exit the room, turn to your right. You'll see a door at the end of the hall. I'll be there to let you through."

Renquest did as the deputy instructed. Within a few minutes, he and the deputy stepped off an elevator and pushed through the doors to the medical facility. People in all kinds of uniforms packed the room. The sheriff, county attorney, Dr. Johansen, state police, and a couple of line deputies surrounded a table in the middle of the room. Renquest stopped short of the crowd.

"Does anybody want to tell me what the hell is going on here?"

All eyes turned to him.

The sheriff said, "Detective, I've heard a lot about you."

Renquest looked over at the other people around the table and focused on Johansen. She appeared to be laser-focused on whatever lay on the table.

"Can someone please tell me what is going on? And where the hell is my prisoner?"

The sheriff looked at the others in the room and motioned for them to step back from the table. As they moved away, Renquest saw the outline of a young man appear. A white, blood-stained sheet covered him.

"Goddamn it," was all the detective could muster.

"It happened shortly after processing. His cell wasn't ready, so the deputy placed him in a holding cell. He must have pissed off one of the other inmates and got into a fight. When the deputy came back to check on him, he was face down in a pool of his own blood," the sheriff said. "Already dead."

Renquest moved closer to the table. He nodded at Johansen to pull the sheet down so he could see the wounds. Small puncture wounds littered his body. All smaller than a knife would make. All of them round, and each wound about the size of the tip of an ice pick.

"We haven't found the weapon," one deputy blurted out.

Renquest motioned for Johansen to re-cover the body. "Do we know who did it?"

The sheriff nodded. "He's being processed as we speak."

"I'm going to need to talk to him."

"He'll be in protective custody and on suicide watch until the trial," the sheriff added.

The detective felt his phone buzz in his pocket. The message was from Brooks, asking if he planned to make the meeting. He looked back at the bloody mess on the table, then shook his head.

"I need to tell my team what happened," Renquest said. "Do you think you can keep this suspect alive for more than a day?"

The sheriff nodded.

"Good," Renquest said. "Let's try to keep it that way."

As he made his way through the lobby of the jail and out into the now mostly empty courtyard, he wondered how Flaherty and Sanchez would take the news of Michael's death.

They had just spent hours as hostages of the man, and he imagined they wanted justice and maybe even some measure of revenge. Both feelings are perfectly normal after their ordeal. As long as they didn't act on the latter. And that thought reminded him of something he needed to do, but didn't want to do.

Renquest texted Brooks and told her to have Flaherty and Sanchez go to his office. He'd be there shortly to speak to them about Michael.

When he stepped through the doorway to his office, Sanchez and Flaherty were leaning against the conference table. Both held a cup of coffee in their hands.

"Did either of you have any contact with anyone at the jail after the sheriff took Michael into custody?"

The men looked at each other, then shook their heads collectively.

"I'm going to need to hear you say it," Renquest said.

"No," Sanchez said.

"Nope," Flaherty responded.

"Good. With that out of the way, let's get to work."

"Are we still working on the Pratt murder?" Brooks asked. "I mean, the old man is dead and was likely behind it, but clearly there were others involved."

"Yes, we are," Renquest said. "Sanchez and I will continue to dig into the old man and see if we can figure out who he got to kill Pratt. Once we know that, we'll have whoever did the old man too."

Brooks asked, "While you two are working on that, what are Flaherty and I going to be doing?"

Renquest leaned back against his desk. "There's been a murder at the jail. Michael won't see the inside of a courtroom."

"What do you mean?" Flaherty asked.

"Someone shivved him in his cell. It's a homicide, and it's our job to figure out who and why."

No one spoke.

"So, no one has questions?" Renquest waited, but received no response.

"Good. Let's get to work."

All three officers pulled out chairs from around the table and began strategizing how best to work the case. Renquest leaned back and watched his team. They were working together. It was a sight to behold. A sense of pride welled up inside him, and he didn't try to hide it. After a few minutes of admiring his team work the problem, his work phone buzzed on his desk. He pulled the receiver from the handle and held it to his ear. A voice on the other end told him that the county council had called an emergency meeting to discuss what to do about McNally. The details of his little side project were going to come out. Everything Michael said during the negotiations was recorded, and it wouldn't take the press long to file a freedom of information request for an audio copy and written transcripts. Someone's getting egg on their face, and Renquest guessed it wouldn't be Councilman Diaz. There was little doubt in his mind that one of two outcomes was about to happen. Chief McNally could resign and keep some dignity, or get fired publicly. Ultimately, the choice was his. He hadn't made good choices thus far, but maybe this time he would.

Chapter 33

The passing lights from the oncoming traffic hurt his eyes. He strained to block out the distractions and thought about the events of the day. Things could have gone very wrong. He'd been lucky no one got hurt, except Michael. Which he still fumed about, but was happy it hadn't been one of his own. Renquest knew it sounded awful, and not something he'd say out loud, but it's how he felt. Michael was a sociopath responsible for kidnapping and murder. As cops, they did their jobs. A hostage situation ended with no loss of life. A suspect is in custody. Overall, it'd been a good day.

The Charger came to rest in its assigned spot in the garage. As he sat quietly in his car, his thoughts turned to Custus. He missed that old dog. With all the events of the past few days, he hadn't had time to really grieve the loss of his loyal companion. He wiped a solitary tear that rolled down his cheek, then stepped out of the car. The elevator doors opened, and Renquest crossed the lobby and stopped at the bank of mailboxes. He inserted his key, turned the lock, and removed some flyers and a folded piece of paper.

He tossed the advertisements into the overflowing trash bin at the end of the row of mailboxes. Then, he looked at the sheet of paper in his hand, flipped it over, and unfolded it. Inside the words, *Welcome home. I heard you could use a friend, stated back at him*. No signature. No way of knowing who sent it or what it meant. Renquest then made his way to the concierge desk and rang the bell. A young woman stepped out from behind a door.

"Can I help you?" she asked.

Renquest held up the sheet of paper. "Did you see who left this in my box?"

The woman shook her head.

Renquest unclipped the badge from his belt and laid it on the counter. "I'm going to need to see the camera footage from today."

The young woman showed him into the room behind the counter. It had several monitors showing live video footage from around the property.

"Does this record?" he asked.

"Yes," the woman said. "We keep all footage for a month, then the system overwrites the old drives."

"Key up today." He started his search after the postal employee delivered the mail. The wait wasn't long. About an hour after the mailman delivered his haul, Renquest saw a familiar face slip something into his box. The man in the frame looked directly at the camera, smiled, then headed toward the elevators. In his arms, he carried a cardboard box.

"Dodge," he said, forcing a smile.

The detective stood at the door of his apartment. He wasn't sure what awaited him inside, but he hadn't seen his old partner, Paul Dodge, in quite a while. He knew the parole agent had been somewhere out west looking into a matter for a friend, but they had spoken little over the last few months. Dodge had made a stupid decision while chasing down a serial killer and almost gotten himself killed. Renquest had lost his temper over the cavalier agent's actions, and it was part of the reason he'd moved to Arlington for the chief detective job. He needed a change.

The door opened into a quiet room. He walked inside, shutting and locking the door behind him. After removing his badge and duty weapon, he placed them on the kitchen counter, then stepped into the living room. There, curled up on a chair, lay a small white dog. Upon seeing Renquest, the dog stood and wagged its tail. Renquest knelt in front of the animal and noticed a note wrapped around its collar with a rubber band. He patted the dog on the head before removing the piece of paper.

His name is Tobey. He followed me home from Dallas, and I thought you two would make a cute couple. Dodge.

Renquest simply smiled and stared at his new friend. Then he went to the kitchen, grabbed a beer from the refrigerator before sliding into the matching chair next to Tobey. It'd been a good day after all.

255